"Why do

"It's your turn to let Clyde try to take a bite out of you."

"He's your camel," Hassan said with a smile. "You're the one who named him, so you're the one who has to ride him."

"But I don't mind walking."

Hassan looked at her, and it seemed to him suddenly as though he couldn't breathe. This was the woman he had thought would be a burden, a female who would fall apart at the first sign of a crisis, who would complain of the heat and her complexion and drive him crazy with her demands.

But Christy wasn't like that; she hadn't panicked when the sandstorm hit them. She hadn't gone to pieces and wept when she knew that their situation was critical. She was a rare woman, a woman a man could depend on, and he vowed that he would do everything in his power to bring her safely through.

Dear Reader,

When two people fall in love, the world is suddenly new and exciting, and it's that same excitement we bring to you in Silhouette Intimate Moments. These are stories with scope, with grandeur. These characters lead the lives we all dream of, and everything they do reflects the wonder of being in love.

Longer and more sensuous than most romances, Silhouette Intimate Moments novels take you away from everyday life and let you share the magic of love. Adventure, glamour, drama, even suspense—these are the passwords that let you into a world where love has a power beyond the ordinary, where the best authors in the field today create stories of love and commitment that will stay with you always.

In coming months look for novels by your favorite authors: Maura Seger, Parris Afton Bonds, Elizabeth Lowell and Erin St. Claire, to name just a few. And whenever you buy books, look for all the Silhouette Intimate Moments, love stories *for* today's women *by* today's women.

Leslie J. Wainger
Senior Editor
Silhouette Books

IMRL-7/85

Barbara Faith
Desert Song

Silhouette Intimate Moments
Published by Silhouette Books New York
America's Publisher of Contemporary Romance

SILHOUETTE BOOKS
300 East 42nd St., New York, N.Y 10017

ISBN: 0-373-07173-6

First Silhouette Books printing January 1987

Printed in the U.S.A.

Books by Barbara Faith

Silhouette Intimate Moments

The Promise of Summer #16
Wind Whispers #47
Bedouin Bride #63
Awake to Splendor #101
Islands in Turquoise #124
Tomorrow Is Forever #140
Sing Me A Lovesong #146
Desert Song #173

Silhouette Special Edition

Return to Summer #335

BARBARA FAITH

is very happily married to an ex-matador, whom she met when she lived in Mexico. After a honeymoon spend climbing pyramids in the Yucatan, they settled down in California—but they're vagabonds at heart. They travel at every opportunity, but Barbara always finds the time to write.

Chapter 1

Below lay Marrakesh, red city of the *Arabian Nights*. As the plane began its descent and buildings and palm trees grew closer, Christy Chambers looked not at the city but at the mountains surrounding it. Beyond the mountains lay the Sahara, and the answer to her brother's disappearance.

Christy had started her quest for Matt in Casablanca. From there she'd gone to the United States Embassy in Rabat. After a three-day delay she succeeded in seeing the first assistant to the ambassador, an officious woman in her early fifties who told her that the ambassador had made inquiries about Matthew Chambers when he'd disappeared months ago even though—and here the ambassador's first assistant frowned at Christy—Mr. Chambers hadn't checked in with the embassy upon his arrival in Morocco. It had been five months since Mr. Chambers had taken a caravan into the Sahara, and it could only be presumed that he had perished there. The woman expressed her sympathy and shuffled the papers on her desk to show that the interview had ended.

Omar Fallah Haj, the man from the Department of the Interior of Morocco, had been more helpful but just as pessimistic. After he had seated Christy across from his desk he said, "As soon as your uncle notified our government that your brother was missing, we made inquiries. We discovered that he was last seen in Tafarout. That's a place just at the edge of the Sahara, Miss Chambers. Apparently he arranged there for a caravan to take him to Bir Lahlou."

"How do I get to Bir Lahlou?" Christy asked.

"You?" Fallah Haj looked surprised. "You can't go to Bir Lahlou. That's out of the question. It's almost three hundred miles across the Sahara."

Ignoring his comment, Christy said, "My uncle gave me the name of a man who might lead a caravan." She opened her purse and found a small red leather notebook, "Yes, here it is, Mustafa Ben Driss. Have you heard of him?"

"No, I haven't, Miss Chambers. But please believe me, it's madness for you to even think of going into the desert. I don't mean to be unkind, but I think you should accept the fact that your brother is dead." ·

Christy snapped her purse shut and started up out of her chair.

"I'm sorry I haven't been able to help you," Fallah Haj said. His dark eyes softened, and he stroked his short black beard. "I know how difficult this is for you, Miss Chambers. Why don't you allow me to make your stay here more pleasurable?" His gaze rested on her lips, then traveled leisurely down the white column of her throat to the rise of her breasts. "I have a summer place near Tan-

gier," he said in a softly insinuating voice. "It's lovely this
time of the year. Perhaps we—"

Christy was halfway to the door before he stopped her.
"I know someone who might help you," he said.

Her hand still on the doorknob, Christy turned and
looked at him.

The Moroccan's lips twitched with a smile. "Apparently what I have heard about red-haired women is true.
I'm sorry if I offended you, but a man must try, mustn't
he?" When Christy didn't answer he said, "There's a man
in Marrakesh by the name of Hassan Ben Kadiri. He
knows the desert better than any man in Morocco. Occasionally, if the price is right, he'll take a caravan into the
Sahara."

Fallah Haj opened a mosaic cigarette box, offered a
cigarette to Christy and, when she refused, took one for
himself and lighted it. After he had inhaled he leaned back
in his chair and said, "Kadiri was born in a Berber village in the desert. He's strong and he's tough. He's also a
troublemaker and an adventurer. If anyone can make it to
Bir Lahlou, he can."

Fallah Haj took one of his business cards from a brass
holder on his desk, scrawled a hasty note and handed it to
Christy. "Give this to Hassan," he said. "Perhaps it will
help."

"Thank you." Christy offered her hand.

"Don't thank me, Miss Chambers. I'm not doing you
a favor. The desert, especially now, at the beginning of
summer, is a dangerous place. But if you're determined to
go, then Hassan Ben Kadiri is the man you want." His lips
quirked in a mocking smile. "But be careful of him, Miss
Chambers. We Moroccans love women, especially women
as fair and lovely as you are. Hassan is no exception; you
may find him even more of a challenge than the Sahara."

* * *

Christy thought of Fallah Haj's words as she stepped out of the airport and tried to move away from the robed men and half-dozen boys that reached to take her luggage from the porter.

"*Balak!*" the porter shouted. "Get away! Watch out!" He put her bags into a waiting taxi and helped her in. When Christy handed him some money he smiled and said, "*Shukran*, thank you."

The noonday sun blazed down on the red ocher buildings of this most mysterious of all African cities as the cab turned onto the palm-lined highway. For the first time since she'd been in Morocco, Christy felt a thrill of excitement, for it seemed to her that she had stepped backward in time. Robed men led donkeys loaded with firewood across fields where camels grazed. Robed and veiled women followed behind.

Within the ramparts of the old city lay the Hotel de la Mamounia. Near the ancient walls, set in acres of secluded gardens, olive orchards and orange groves, it was classically Moorish in style. Again Christy felt as though she'd gone back in time.

As soon as she had registered she was taken to her room. After the bellboy left she went out to stand on the balcony overlooking the gardens and the pool. In the distance she could see the Atlas Mountains. Beyond them lay the Sahara—and Matt, because he was alive; if he weren't, she would have known.

Matt was all the family Christy had. Her mother had died when she was born, and two weeks later her father had taken her and six-year-old Matt to his brother's home in Montana. She'd lived there until she'd gone away to an eastern boarding school, when she was seven.

Being away from the only home she'd ever known and the brother she loved had been a strange and frightening experience for a little girl. For weeks she'd been silent and withdrawn. But in time she adjusted and became, in spite of her outward fragile appearance, strong and self-sufficient.

Thirteen-year-old Matt had phoned her every day for the first month she was away. Then their uncle had gotten the telephone bill and Matt had been grounded. Letters took the place of calls, and for all the time that Christy had been away from home he'd written her almost every week.

Christy saw little of her father during her growing-up years. A mining engineer who worked mines in South America, Mexico and Morocco, Harry Chambers had neither the time nor the desire to think about his daughter. When Christy was seventeen her father went into business with his brother Albert. Matt, who was in his final year at the Colorado School of Mines, urged Christy to come back to Montana to go to college. But the friends she'd made in boarding school were going to Bryn Mawr or Vassar or Smith, and she decided to stay in the East. She told herself that her father hadn't wanted her before, and she didn't want him now. But when he became ill a week before her graduation from Smith, she went back to Montana to take care of him.

When her father died, Matt took his place in the company. At his urging Christy went to work there, too, first as a secretary and then, with additional night school courses, as an assistant to the head of the geology department. She owned a town house and saw Matt frequently. She was surprised but not alarmed when he told her that he was going to Morocco, even when he said,

"Something funny's going on in Morocco, Christy. I want to find out what it is."

Their Uncle Albert had been furious, and when he demanded to know the reason for the proposed trip, Matt said, "I need a vacation. We have mining interests there, so I can combine business with pleasure."

The last card Christy received from him had been sent from Marrakesh, six months ago, which was why she was here now, why she had to see Hassan Ben Kadiri.

When she arrived at her hotel she sent Omar Fallah Haj's card by messenger. The following day a man phoned to say that Mr. Kadiri attended to certain business matters in his home and that he would send his car for her. Two days later, just as twilight settled over the city, Christy stepped into the chauffeur-driven black limousine that would take her up to Kadiri's office in the hills overlooking Marrakesh. As the car turned into Kadiri's long, palm-lined private drive, Christy wondered just what kind of a man he was and if he could help her.

When the chauffeur came around to help her out, Christy gazed at the two-story home in wonder. It looked, she thought, like a place right out of *The Arabian Nights*.

A robed and veiled woman greeted Christy. "*Marhaban*, welcome," she said. "Mr. Kadiri is expecting you. Follow me, please."

Christy glanced around as she followed the now silent woman. In the last rays of the sun the house looked beautifully mysterious. Sculptured Moorish arches lined the four sides of a patio. A center fountain held by four fierce-looking stone lions dominated the entrance. From somewhere Christy remembered a saying: "Algeria is a man, Tunisia a woman, Morocco a lion." Was Hassan Ben Kadiri also a lion?

"Mademoiselle?" The servant looked at Christy, her brown eyes between the narrow slit of headdress impatient. "Mr. Kadiri is waiting, *mademoiselle.*

"I'm sorry. I was looking at the fountain."

The woman didn't answer as she led Christy through a Moorish-arched entrance hall into the living room, where the walls were covered in red and gold mosaic. On the polished floor was the largest Persian rug Christy had ever seen. There were deep, low sofas, ornately carved tables and soft, overstuffed hassocks.

"Through here, please," the servant said as she led Christy along a cool corridor. Finally she paused before a seven-foot door and knocked. When a voice from within said, "Come," she held the door open for Christy to enter.

The man behind the large mahogany desk was tall, over six feet. Though he wore a silver-gray djellaba, a Moroccan robe, it was obvious that he was well built. His thick black hair had a slight curl.

His eyes...bedroom eyes, she thought, smoldering eyes. She took a deep breath. He was not a classically handsome man, but he was a man a woman would turn and look at and speculate about, because there was a strength about him, a masculinity that was almost overpowering.

"Miss Chambers?" He came around his desk to offer her his hand. "It was a pleasure to hear from my old friend Omar again. How long have you known him?"

His hand looked dark against her pale skin. She caught her breath and said, "I don't really know Mr. Haj. Someone from the United States Embassy suggested he might be able to help me. He thought you might be able to. He said you knew the desert better than any man in Morocco."

One black eyebrow raised in question as Kadiri led her to a black leather sofa. Then, instead of going back to his desk, he sat next to her. "Why don't you tell me what it is you want?" he said.

"It's about my brother," Christy began. "He came to Morocco six months ago, representing our company, Chambers Mining. The last we heard was a card from Marrakesh. From here he was going to Tafarout to take a caravan into the desert."

Hassan watched her as she talked. She was quite beautiful; her skin was like ivory touched by just the faintest hint of blush, her eyes were the color of the sea, and her hair... he couldn't keep his eyes off it. Her hair was the color of a sunset, red, but shot with the special shade of gold one sees just before the sun slips over the horizon.

She was a small woman, perhaps an inch over five feet, and she was finely made. Hassan looked at the pale hands folded in her lap and knew that he wanted to touch her. Suddenly and irrationally his muscles tensed with desire. Before he remembered that he'd quit smoking two months ago he reached for the silver cigarette box on the table in front of him. He opened it, looked longingly at the cigarettes inside and quickly closed it.

"Matt's destination was a place called Bir Lahlou," Christy said.

"Bir Lahlou? That's almost three hundred miles from Tafarout."

"I know." Christy clenched her hands together. "I want to put a caravan together, Mr. Kadiri. I want to go to Bir Lahlou and find my brother."

Hassan stared at her. "You want to go into the Sahara?"

Christy nodded. "My brother isn't dead, Mr. Kadiri. I know he isn't."

"How do you know that? What proof do you have?"

"I don't have any proof; it's something I feel."

"Something you feel!" He shook his head almost angrily. "You don't know anything about our desert. Very few people do. Even men who have lived on the Sahara all their lives lose their way and die. Your brother was a fool to make a trip like that, and you are a fool to think of going after him."

Christy stared at Hassan. She stood, her face frozen and stiff, and in a voice shaking with anger said, "Thank you for your time, Mr. Kadiri. I'm sorry I bothered you. Would you mind calling a taxi for me?"

"Yes, of course I'd mind. I am sorry if I offended you, but the idea of your going into the desert startled me." He stood, and, smiling down her, said, "But I am willing to talk about it over dinner."

Suddenly Christy remembered that Fallah Haj had told her that she might find Hassan Ben Kadiri even more of a challenge than the desert.

She looked into his dark eyes, took a deep breath and said, "Dinner would be fine."

Chapter 2

From the outside the restaurant was a plain, well-lighted building. The maitre d' who greeted them said, "What a pleasure it is to see you, Monsieur Kadiri." He led them through a foyer to an ornately carved door, then into a dimly lighted room that was a huge, opulently decorated Arab tent.

The knee-high table they were taken to was in a secluded corner. Two candles in tall brass candlesticks furnished the only light. Christy sat down on the low love seat and felt herself sink into the deep, soft pillows.

"A bottle of Dom Perignon," Hassan told the waiting sommelier. After the man had left he smiled at Christy and said, "The couscous is wonderful here, but we will order a bit later, if that's all right with you. I thought we would relax first."

Relax! His thigh felt warm against hers, and his face was so close that if she turned her head they'd be nose to nose. Christy took a deep breath and, smoothing the skirt of her green linen dress, said, "I don't think I'm properly dressed."

"Of course you are. You look lovely." Hassan's gaze rested on her face, then moved slowly down over her shoulders to the barely visible rise of her breasts. Again, as he had in his office, he felt an overwhelming awareness of her that surprised him, even as it amused him. For the past two or three years he'd rarely been excited by a woman. It wasn't that at thirty-six he felt any lessening of his sexual appetite; it was only that he hadn't been electrified by a woman in a long time. But this Miss Christine Chambers did strange things to his pulse and his breathing.

The champagne came. Hassan filled his and Christy's glasses, then raised his, saying, "Let us drink to your stay in Morocco."

Christy looked at him over the rim of her glass. "Will you help me find my brother?"

For a moment Hassan didn't speak. Then with a frown he said, "There are times when the temperature on the desert climbs to over one hundred and thirty degrees. It's so hot that it hurts to breathe. You feel the sun inside your skull setting your brain on fire. Heat waves rise on the sand, shimmering and blinding as you stumble toward an oasis that isn't there." His dark eyes were intense. "The desert kills even those who think they understand it, Miss Chambers. I do not even want to imagine what it would do to a woman of your fragility."

"I'm not as fragile as I look, Mr. Kadiri. I don't whine and I don't complain. When I was working on my degree in geology I made field trips into Death Valley and Anza Borrego. I know how hot the desert can be."

"I am talking about the Sahara," Hassan said. "Believe me, it is far different from your California deserts."

For a moment they glared at each other. Abruptly Hassan rose. "Come dance with me," he said. Before Christy could object he pulled her to her feet and, holding her hand, led her to where other couples were dancing.

When he put his arms around her Christy felt enfolded by him. He was big and broad and a foot taller than she was. Through the gabardine robe she felt his muscled shoulder and the strength of his arms. Her anger of a moment ago faded and for a moment she was overwhelmed by a *what-am-I-doing-here?* feeling that frightened her, even as it excited her.

I'm in Marrakesh, she thought, dancing in an Arabian tent with a robed man from a culture totally different from mine. He's not like anyone I've ever known.

She smelled incense and smoke and the sandalwood aroma of his skin as she rested her face against his shoulder and closed her eyes. The orchestra began to play "The Song from Moulin Rouge." Hassan urged her closer and Christy felt her breath quicken. She tried to move away, but he pressed his other hand firmly on the small of her back. She was a captive of the man and of the music, suspended in time as they moved slowly together.

Christy didn't know how long they danced. She was aware of snatches of remembered words.... "April in Paris, chestnuts in blossom...the autumn leaves drift by my window...you must remember this, a kiss is still..." She felt Hassan's body against hers and the strong, hard muscles of his shoulder under her hand. He was a powerful man, a sensual man. Hassan looked down at her. His eyes were dark, his nostrils flared with an awakening awareness. She was unable to look away. Everything but the here and the now faded. She felt wrapped in the drift of smoke and incense and sandalwood, stayed by this moment in time and by the arms that held her.

The music stopped. Hassan took her hand, brought it to his lips and for a fraction of a second Christy felt the warmth of his tongue against her skin. Then he let her go and led her toward their table.

"Hassan!" a voice called, and a hand touched the sleeve of his robe.

He stopped beside the table and with a smile said, "Rashid! I didn't know you and Katherine had returned from Paris." He took the woman's hand. "You are more beautiful every time I see you."

"Thank you, Hassan."

She smiled up at Christy as Hassan said, "Miss Chambers, I'd like you to meet two very good friends of mine, Katherine and Rashid Hasir." He put his arm around her waist. "Miss Christine Chambers from Montana."

Rashid stood up and took Christy's hand. "Please sit down for a moment." When they were seated he said, "Is this your first visit to Marrakesh, Miss Chambers?"

"Yes, it is."

"How long are you staying?" his wife asked. "I hope long enough for you and Hassan to come to dinner. Would Friday evening be convenient?"

"I...I don't know, Mrs. Hasir. I'm not sure how much longer I'll be in Marrakesh."

As they chatted Christy studied the other woman. Katherine Hasir was one of the loveliest women she'd ever seen. She wore little makeup. Her blond hair had been pulled back off her face into a classic chignon that would have made any other woman look plain but only enhanced her beauty. She sat close to her husband, and even though they didn't touch, it almost seemed that they did.

"How is your daughter?" Hassan asked.

"Jasmine's wonderful." Katherine reached for her husband's hand. "She's managed to twist Rashid around her two-year-old finger, though. You should have seen the two of them when we were in Paris. I think he bought her every kind of toy in the city."

Rashid smiled. "Why shouldn't I? She has her mother's looks, and that makes her the second most beautiful creature in the world." His eyes were full of love as he looked at his wife.

They were a spectacular-looking couple, Christy thought. From the streaks of gray in Rashid's hair it was evident that he was a few years older than Hassan. Dark and powerfully built, he seemed almost too overpowering to be married to such an elegant woman. The fact that she was an American surprised Christy, and she found herself wondering how someone like Katherine could have married a Moroccan.

"Miss Chambers has come to Marrakesh in search of her brother," Hassan said. "He disappeared on his way to Bir Lahlou five months ago."

"Five months ago?" Rashid frowned.

"I know that's a long time, Mr. Hasir," Christy said "but I believe my brother's alive. That's why I came to Mr. Kadiri. I want to take a caravan into the desert to—"

"You can't!" Katherine paled. "You don't know what you're saying. You don't know what it's like. You—"

"Easy, darling." Rashid put his arm around his wife and drew her closer. To Christy he said, "Katherine's had experience with the desert. I wouldn't want to see any other woman suffer the way she did." His eyes were concerned as he looked at Christy. "We can't tell you what to do. If Hassan agrees to take you, you will be in good hands. But think long and hard before you decide."

"She will," Hassan said as he stood up.

"Bring Miss Chambers for dinner sometime," Katherine said. As the two men said their goodbyes she turned to Christy. "If you find that you're free for tea tomorrow or any other day, please call me."

"I will, thank you." Christy smiled as she held out her hand. "It was lovely meeting you, Mrs. Hasir."

When Hassan led her back to their table, she said, "She's nice, isn't she?"

"Yes, she is. Rashid is a lucky man." Hassan filled her glass with champagne. "They've been married for three years, and they're still on their honeymoon."

"Why was she so upset when I said I wanted to go into the Sahara?"

"Katherine and Rashid were lost in the desert for several months. They almost died there."

Christy looked at him questioningly, but Hassan made no further comment. Very few people knew what had really happened between Rashid and Katherine in the desert; it wasn't his place to speak about it.

He and Rashid had been friends since their school days. He had known Rashid's younger brother, Jamal, too, but not as well. Several years before, Jamal had become engaged to an American, which surprised Hassan, because mixed marriages were uncommon in Morocco. He had meant to mention it to Rashid the next time they met, but before he got around to it word had come to him that Jamal's fiancée, Katherine Bishop, and Rashid had disappeared in the Sahara.

Jamal had come to Hassan and they had organized a search party. The two of them, along with three camel drivers, had searched for two weeks before they gave up and returned to Marrakesh. A few weeks after that, word had come to Hassan that Rashid and Katherine were safe at Rashid's desert home. When Rashid returned to Marrakesh, Hassan went to see him. He still remembered his shock and surprise when Rashid told him that he'd taken Katherine to his desert home by force.

"I knew that marriage was out of the question between a Muslim and a Christian," Rashid said. "I took her to my home in the desert to try to convince her that marriage to Jamal was impossible." Rashid had looked away before continuing. "That's what I tried to tell myself, Hassan, but it wasn't true. I took her there because I wanted her for myself."

Hassan had been appalled by his friend's confession. But he remembered now that a part of him had wondered what it would be like to be alone in the desert with a woman he desired.

He looked at Christine Chambers. What would it be like to be alone in the desert with her?

Hassan drained his glass and tried to tell himself that this beautiful woman with her soft white skin was no different from any other woman. But his hand shook when he set his glass down and his muscles tightened with the need to touch her.

When the table had been cleared after dinner and two glasses of mint tea placed in front of them, Hassan said, "Tell me about your brother. How old is he, and what does he do?"

"Matt's thirty-four, six years older than I am," Christy said. "He's a mining engineer and president of the company my father and uncle started ten years ago." She hesitated, reluctant to tell him too much about herself yet wanting him to understand the close relationship between her and her brother.

"I never knew my mother," she said. "My father was working in a mining camp in the Andes when I was born. They tried to get her to a doctor, but there was a storm and the company plane couldn't get in." Christy looked at Hassan and then away. "I was born and my mother died. My father never forgave me for that."

His dark eyes narrowed. "For being born?"

Christy's slim fingers tightened around the stem of her glass. "He and my mother had kept Matt with them, but after she died my father sent us back to live with his brother and his brother's wife." She sipped her tea and with a rueful smile said, "Poor Aunt Margaret. She did her best to cope with us, but it couldn't have been easy raising an infant and a six-year-old. Mostly I remember her bursting into tears every time I did something bad like spill a glass of milk or break a favorite dish."

"What about your uncle?"

"He was . . . I guess austere is the word."

"Did you see much of your father? Did he ever get back to Montana?"

"Once in a while. But I went away to a boarding school when I was seven, so I really didn't see much of him." Christy's eyes clouded with pain. "If it hadn't been for Matt, Mr. Kadiri, for his phone calls and his letters—for his love—I don't think I could have survived those years. He was my family; he never let me down. Now it's my turn. I won't let him down."

Hassan studied her face for a moment. In a gentle voice he asked, "Why did he come to Morocco?"

"The company has mining interests here. Matt thought something strange was going on. I asked him what it was, but he wouldn't discuss it with me. He said we'd talk about it when he came home." She looked down at her hands. "But he didn't come home, Mr. Kadiri. That's why I'm here. I've got to find him. I won't leave Morocco until I do."

"Putting a caravan together is an expensive proposition, Miss Chambers. Are you sure your company wants you to do this?"

"It isn't the company's money," Christy said. "It's mine. I'm the one who's going to pay for it. My uncle thinks Matt is dead. He didn't want me to come."

Her uncle was probably right, Hassan thought. But he didn't say that; instead he put some dirhams on the table and, motioning to the waiter, stood and helped Christy to her feet. "We can talk about this later," he told her as he led her out to his car. "Let's go back to your hotel for a drink."

He drove them to the hotel without speaking, but he was acutely aware of Christy beside him, in that enclosed place. Her perfume made him think of desert breezes touched by the barest hint of musk. He wanted to touch her again and knew that he shouldn't. Not yet.

When they were seated in the Churchill Bar and had drinks in front of them—a brandy for her, Perrier for him—Christy said, "Mr. Haj told me that you had lived in the desert."

Hassan nodded. "I was brought up there. My father was studying anthropology at the University of Casablanca. He was in his senior year when he and two other students went from Zagora into the Sahara to travel with a group of Berbers. That's when he met my mother."

"She was a Berber?"

Hassan nodded. "She was sixteen when they married. She had never known anything but the desert, and my father had rarely been out of Casablanca. Apparently it was easier for him to adjust to desert living than it was for her to get used to the city, so after they married they spent a lot of their time with her people. I was born in the desert."

"Then you understand it."

"Nobody understands the desert, Miss Chambers. I have seen men who thought they did go mad with thirst. It is difficult to survive in the Sahara. It—"

"But you survived," Christy said. Without thinking, she covered Hassan's hand with hers. "Please, Mr. Kadiri—"

"Hassan," he said. "My name is Hassan."

Christy took a deep breath. "Please take me to Bir Lahlou, Hassan. Please help me find my brother."

"What you want to do is madness," he said in a low voice. "You would not last a day in the heat. If anything happened to you, I would be responsible."

"Nothing will happen to me. I'm tougher than I look."

"Tough?" A slow smile crossed his face. He ran one finger down her cheek. "You are about as tough as a baby bird, and twice as soft," He stood, took her hand and said, "Let's take a look at the gardens."

A part of Christy wanted to say, I've already seen the gardens. But the other part of her, the part that made her heart beat fast and her legs go weak, allowed him to take her out to the tree-lined path leading to the pool and the gardens beyond.

A moon that was three-quarters full cast shadows of the swaying fronds of the tall palm trees. The air was soft and filled with the scent of orange blossoms. Within minutes Hassan and Christy were hidden from the hotel, surrounded by thick foliage.

"It's lovely here," Christy said.

"I'm glad you like the hotel."

"I like it, but that's not what I meant. I like Marrakesh, the way it feels and smells. I even like the way it sounds when I say it . . . Mar-ra-kesh." She smiled up at him. "Is the city very old?"

"It was built by the Almoravids in the eleventh century," Hassan said. "It was an important city even then, because it was the starting point for the trans-Saharan caravans. Goods came in here from all over the world: gold and silver, spices, jewels, fine cloth, even slaves to be bought and sold to the highest bidder."

"That's barbaric."

"A lot of things in life are, Miss . . ." He looked at her. "What is your Christian name?"

"Christine. Friends call me Christy."

Hassan stopped. With one finger under her chin he tilted her face up. "Then that is what I will call you."

It seemed that for a moment Christy's heart stilled. She gazed up at Hassan, knowing that he was going to kiss her, not sure whether to step away or... But it was too late. She looked up into his dark eyes, then slowly closed her own as he gently touched his lips to hers. His eyes were open, curious. He brushed her lips, sampled and retreated. Then with a sigh his mouth covered hers.

Never had a kiss been so sensuously demanding. For the barest fraction of a second Christy tried to resist, then her lips parted and her body softened against his. But when the kiss deepened and his arms tightened around her she broke away.

"No," Hassan murmured against her lips. He put his hands on either side of her head. "No, Christy." He kissed her eyelids, the tip of her nose, her cheeks, the corners of her mouth, so gently that her fear receded. Again his lips brushed hers, more insistently this time as he ran his tongue over her bottom lip and took it between his teeth to taste it before his tongue invaded the warmth of her mouth.

One small moan of protest escaped before Christy became lost in the kiss and the closeness. She was only half aware that his hands moved down her shoulders to cup her breasts. Only when she felt the heat of his fingers against her skin and the electric shock touch against the swollen peaks did she break away.

Holding his wrists, she said, "No, you mustn't."

"Why not?" Hassan's eyes were warm with passion. "I have wanted to touch you from the moment you walked into my office this afternoon." He took her into his arms again and with his lips against her ear whispered, "Where is your room, Christy?"

"My room?" Her body stiffened, and she stepped away from him.

"We cannot stop now, not when we both feel this way."

"You don't know how I feel." Christy took another step back. "You don't know anything about me."

"I know everything I want to know." Hassan gripped her shoulders. "Come make love with me," he said.

Once again Christy freed herself from his grasp. She turned and started up the path to the hotel, but before she'd taken three steps, Hassan stopped her. He stood looking down at her, this robed Moroccan whose eyes smoldered as they burned into hers. "I can help you find your brother," he said.

"What?" Christy's green eyes widened. "What did you say?"

"Fallah Haj was right. I *do* know the desert better than any man in Morocco. If your brother is alive I'll find him for you."

"I have the money," she said eagerly.

"I don't want your money." Hassan cupped her chin and forced her to look at him. "You know what I want."

Christy slapped his hand away. "Go to hell," she said in a low, venomous voice. "I don't need you. I'll find somebody else to take me into the desert, somebody who's willing to make a better bargain than you want to make. Somebody who's more of a man than you are.'' Before he could answer she turned and ran up the path to the hotel.

Hassan stood looking after her. He knew that he'd never been as ashamed as he was in that moment. Nor had he ever wanted a woman as badly as he wanted Christy Chambers. He'd wait a day or two, he decided. He'd call and apologize. He'd go slowly. But by Allah, he would have her.

In the meantime he'd make inquiries about her brother.

Chapter 3

A strange and haunting sound unlike anything Christy had ever heard before drifted across the early morning air. Still half asleep, she took her robe from the foot of the bed and went out to the balcony.

Marrakesh lay below, surrounded by red walls still shadowed by the night, as beautiful and mysterious in the mist as a fairy-tale city. Christy's hands tightened on the balcony railing as she looked around her and listened in wonder as the holy call to prayer floated out over the mosques and minarets to the city. It was wondrous, different from anything she'd ever heard before. Enchanted though she was, a chill of foreboding ran through her.

Christy closed her eyes, remembering how she had felt last night when Hassan Ben Kadiri kissed her. She shivered, assailed by the knowledge that for an instant she'd been tempted to yield to him.

As the call to worship faded into the dawn, she resolved that she must forget Hassan Ben Kadiri; her only

thoughts now must be of Matt and of how she could find
him.

Uncle Albert had given her someone's name, Mustafa
Ben Driss. Driss was a desert man, her uncle had said.
Perhaps he could help her.

There was no Mustafa Ben Driss in the telephone book,
so as soon as Christy dressed she went downstairs to speak
to the concierge.

"I know nothing of the desert or of the men who go
there," he told her. "But you might ask our grounds
keeper. Old Taoufik claims to know everything there is to
know about the Sahara."

Christy thanked the man and, following his directions,
soon found the grounds keeper, a skinny, toothless man
who said, "How can I help you?"

"I'm trying to find a man by the name of Mustafa Ben
Driss," Christy told him. "I want to put a caravan together to go to Bir Lahlou."

"Bir Lahlou?" Taoufik shook his head. "Impossible,
mademoiselle. Why would you want to go to such a
place?"

"My brother disappeared five months ago on his way
there. Before I left home my uncle gave me Driss's name.
But I don't know how to find him; I thought perhaps you
could help me."

Taoufik chewed thoughtfully on his bottom lip. "I
wouldn't feel right sending you to him. He's a shark, that
one. But there is a man. His name is Hassan Ben Kadiri.
Perhaps he—"

"No," Christy interrupted. "Mr. Kadiri isn't available. I want to see Driss."

"He has a shop in the Djemaa El Fna, on the Street of
the Tigers. But you mustn't go there alone. The Djemaa
is a dangerous place for a woman."

"I'll take a taxi," Christy said as she slipped a bill into the man's hand. "I'll be careful."

The giant square of the Djemaa El Fna, the world's largest souk, was a cacophony of sound, a whirl of brilliant sights and colors and heady smells. People gaped at the monkey trainers, trick cyclists, jugglers, flame throwers and acrobats. fascinated, Christy stared at all the sights surrounding her, spellbound when she saw the snake charmer seated cross-legged on the ground only a few feet from her, a wicker basket beside him. He plunged his hand into the basket and drew out a cobra. After placing the snake in front of him, he began to play a flute. The snake swayed to the music, its ugly flat head only inches from the turbaned man's face.

Suddenly a voice behind Christy said, "You like snakes, *mademoiselle*?" Before she could move, the man took a long black snake from around his neck and held it out to her. With a gasp of pure terror, hands in front of her to ward the serpent off, Christy turned and ran. People laughed; sellers blocked her way, shouting, "A silk robe, lady? Gold necklace, only forty dollar for you, lady. Hashish? Cannabis? Wallets, belts, slippers..."

Feeling as though her heart would burst from her chest, Christy pushed past the sellers, only to be confronted by a man dressed in a red suit. His wide hat was decorated with tassels and he had gold cups and bells strung around his neck and a goatskin bag draped over one shoulder. As Christy tried to edge around him, he said something, then squirted water from the goatskin bag into one of his gold cups and handed it to her.

It was the water seller, she realized. Shaking her head, she took out a dirham and gave it to him. "I'm looking for the Street of Tigers," she said. "Can you help me?"

The water seller hesitated, then pointed down a narrow alley to the left and said, "Bad. Very bad place. Go home."

Christy stared at the man with wide eyes. "I must find the stall of Mustafa Ben Driss," she insisted.

"Ben Driss?" The man shook his head. "Go home."

"I can't. *Shukran*." Before he said anything else she turned and ran toward the alley.

The stalls were smaller here, the things offered for sale shoddy and cheap. The sellers stared at Christy, and the few veiled women she passed stiffened against the stalls as though afraid to touch her. She wanted to turn and run, but the thought of Matt made her go on. She stopped in front of a fruit stall and said to the man in charge, "I'm looking for Mustafa Ben Driss."

"Ben Driss?" The man spat out of the side of his mouth, then pointed ahead and held up two fingers.

Christy stopped in front of the second stall down. It displayed herbs in plastic dishes. Next to each dish there was a drawing to indicate its use: a man holding his head, his jaw, his stomach; a woman far gone in pregnancy; a flaccid penis. Christy looked up. Black, suspicious eyes glared at her. That was all she could see of the woman, because everything else was covered. Her body—obviously fat—was hidden by her stained brown robe. Her hair was covered by a scarf that came down to her eyebrows; the veil covered half her nose.

"I'm looking for Mustafa Ben Driss," Christy said.

Still glaring at her, the woman jerked a thumb at the door behind her.

Christy stepped around the woman and knocked at the door. When a voice called out, "Yah?" she opened the door and stepped inside.

A man seated behind a paper-strewed desk looked up at her. His gaze started at her feet, moved up her legs, paused, studied her obviously expensive summer suit and stopped when he reached her eyes. Slowly he stood up.

"Mustafa Ben Driss?" Christy hoped he didn't hear the tremble in her voice. "My uncle, Albert Chambers, gave me your name. A man from the Mamounia Hotel told me how to find you."

"You're staying at the Mamounia?" He licked his too-full lips.

Christy nodded. "I want to put a caravan together to go to Bir Lahlou." Her hand tightened around her purse. "My brother disappeared on a trip there five months ago. I want to try to find him."

"Ah." He looked at her, then away. A sly smile quirked his lips, then as though suddenly remembering his manners, he came around the desk. He was of medium height, and his body was square and solidly built. His face was blunt, and there was a thin red scar that ran from his right eyebrow to his ear. He had a three-day growth of beard, and his gray djellaba was dirty.

Motioning Christy to a straight-back chair, he said, "What is your brother's name, *mademoiselle*?"

"Chambers," Christy said. "His name is Matthew Chambers."

"Ah." Driss took a deep breath. "I have heard the rumor that an American has disappeared into the desert. His interests were in mining, were they not?" When Christy nodded he said, "Caravans cost money, dear lady."

"I have money."

"How soon would you want to leave for Bir Lahlou?"

"Immediately, of course."

He laughed. "Immediately is more expensive." He ran a dirty finger down the side of his nose. "I suppose I could arrange to leave right away. But as I said, *mademoiselle*, it would be expensive. As much as . . ." He hesitated. "As much as six thousand dollars?"

Christy held her breath, then let it out. "When can we leave?"

"From Marrakesh? Tomorrow. We'll arrange for the caravan when we reach Tafarout."

"I'll give you three thousand when we reach Tafarout and three thousand when we get to Bir Lahlou. I'll have to go to the bank in the morning, but I can be ready to leave by early afternoon."

Driss stood up and held his hand out. "I'll call for you at the Mamounia at two. Do you have the appropriate clothes for such a journey?"

"I'll get them." Christy withdrew her hand. It felt damp from his.

Driss took her to the door. "I can accompany you to your hotel if you wish." He put one hand on her shoulder.

"No, thank you." Christy forced a smile. "I'll take a cab from the Djemaa."

When she went out the woman at the stall glared at her again. *"Shukran,"* Christy murmured, then turned and hurried back up the narrow alley to the relative safety of the square.

She didn't like Driss. He looked sly and even dangerous. She hated the thought of going into the desert with him, but she had no choice; she had to find Matt. As she got into the taxi to take her back to her hotel she tried to shrug her fears away. After all, it was Uncle Albert who had given her Driss's name; surely the man must be all right.

But I wish I were going with Hassan, she thought. Then she closed her eyes and tried not to think of him at all.

The night he left her Hassan told himself that what had happened between him and Christy was not important. She was only a woman, and Morocco was full of women. She was quite beautiful, but so were hundreds of others. Well, perhaps not hundreds, but many...a few who were just as beautiful as Christine Chambers. He had only to call one of them.

The night that Hassan left her he went directly back to his home in the hills above Marrakesh, for although his body was tense with desire, he knew that, at least for tonight, no other woman would do. Tomorrow, he told himself, tomorrow I will call Zolanda or Simone or Fatima.

But he didn't call them.

In the morning he attended to business outside of his home. He snapped at employees he'd never snapped at before. The next day was even worse. A dozen times he picked up the telephone to call Christy, and a dozen times he put it down. He called Fatima and asked her out to dinner. Thirty minutes later he called her back to say that something unexpected had come up and that he wouldn't be able to see her.

That night Hassan paced back and forth in his bedroom and faced the fact that he wasn't going to be able to forget Christine Chambers as easily as he had thought. He also knew that he was thoroughly ashamed of himself. What he had done, suggesting that perhaps he'd help her find her brother if she made love to him, had been the most ungentlemanly thing he'd ever done in his life. He started to call her to tell her how sorry he was, then decided it was too late and that he'd telephone her the first

thing in the morning. But that morning there was a business crisis and it was late in the afternoon before Hassan
was able to make the call.

"I'm sorry, sir," the telephone operator at the Mamounia said. "Miss Chambers checked out yesterday."

Hassan's hand tightened on the phone. "Did she say
where she was going? Did you make any other reserva-
tions for her?"

"Let me connect you with the concierge, sir."

Hassan asked the same question of the concierge, who
said, "Yes, I remember Miss Chambers. She asked about
the desert, and I suggested she talk to our grounds keeper.
I'm sorry, Mr. Kadiri, but I didn't make any other reser-
vations for her."

Hassan wanted to let it go, but he couldn't. He drove to
the hotel, and after a lot of questions he was directed to
Taoufik.

"Ah, yes, the beautiful foreigner with hair like fire,"
Taoufik said with a smile. "If I had been thirty years
younger I would have taken her into the desert myself."

"Into the desert?" Hassan's brows came together in a
frown. "Is that why she came to you?"

Taoufik nodded. "I told her you were the best if she
wanted to go into the Sahara, Mr. Kadiri. She told me you
were not available, and she wanted to know how to find
Mustafa Ben Driss."

"Driss?" Without thinking, Hassan fastened his hands
around the older man's collar. With an angry shake he
said, "You sent her to Mustafa Ben Driss?"

Taoufik struggled to be free, and when Hassan let him
go he straightened his robe and stepped back a pace. "I
tried to tell her not to go to the Djemaa, but she—"

"She went to the Djemaa alone?"

"She was determined, sir. No one could have stopped her."

Hassan looked at the other man. This was his own fault. He hadn't taken Christy seriously enough. He had paid no attention to her concern for her brother because his mind had been on *her*. If anything happened to her he would be responsible.

Hassan took a handful of dirhams out of his pocket and gave them to Taoufik. "I'm sorry," he said. "I am angry not with you but with myself."

From the Mamounia, Hassan went to the Street of the Tigers.

"Driss is gone," the fat woman told him after he gave her money. "He told me he was taking a caravan into the desert and that he would be back in a few days."

"A few days! That's impossible. A caravan to Bir Lahlou takes weeks."

"Who is to say he is going to Bir Lahlou?" The woman snorted. "Driss has a taste for money and for skinny women. He will have both, I think, before his caravan has finished."

Hassan stared at the woman, then turned and ran back down to the alley to the square. He thought of Christy, of her beauty and her fragility. And he thought of Driss.

Sellers saw the fury and the fear on his face and stepped out of his way as he ran past them. I must find her, Hassan thought. I must get to Tafarout.

Chapter 4

Driss was not a skillful driver, and several times on the trip over the snowcapped mountains to Tafarout, Christy clutched the dashboard and gasped in fear. Each time she did Driss laughed and said, "Be calm, *mademoiselle*. I have traveled this road many times. You're quite safe. Believe me."

Christy wasn't so sure. She neither liked nor trusted Driss; she was with him only because there was no one else she could turn to for help. She had the first three thousand dollars to give him before they left Tafarout. Yesterday she'd gone to the bank in Marrakesh and arranged to have the second half of Driss's payment waiting for them when they arrived at their destination.

That's my protection, Christy told herself as she glanced sideways at Driss. I don't trust him, but I think the promise of another three thousand dollars will guarantee my safety, at least to Bir Lahlou. Once I'm there and

I find out about Matt, I'll worry about getting back to Marrakesh.

Christy smoothed the skirt of her dress. Made of blue Egyptian cotton, it was of a bush design, with epaulets, two breast pockets and two skirt pockets. The rest of her desert wardrobe, bought at a safari store in Marrakesh, consisted of blue jeans, two cotton tank tops, a ventilated cotton T-shirt, a rolled-up desert hat and boots. She would leave her other clothes at the hotel in Tafarout.

She'd also bought a small revolver. She didn't like guns, but she knew how to use one. Matt had taught her how two summers ago, when there'd been a series of assaults in her neighborhood. "You'll probably never have to use it," he'd said, "but in case you do, I don't want you to blow your foot off."

Before she'd started the trip to Tafarout, Christy had wrapped the gun in a silk scarf and slipped it into her shoulder bag, feeling foolish but knowing somehow that Matt would have approved.

It was dark by the time they reached Tafarout, once a lonely military outpost, now a small city on the edge of the Sahara. Driss let Christy off at a hotel in the center of the town and said, "Tomorrow I'll begin making arrangements for a caravan, so I'll need money."

Christy nodded. "I'll give it to you in the morning."

"Why not now? You promised me three thousand American dollars when we got to Tafarout."

"I'll give it to you before we leave."

His mouth tightened, and his small eyes squinched almost shut. He seemed about to say something else, then shrugged and said, "As you wish, *mademoiselle.*"

The hotel was seedy but adequate. Christy slept little that night, but as soon as she knew the hotel restaurant was open, she dressed so that she'd be ready whenever

Driss arrived. She knew nothing at all about what it took
to put a caravan together, but she supposed it would be at
least three or four days by the time camels, men and provisions were arranged for. So she was surprised when
Driss arrived at the hotel a little before noon and said,
"Everything is in order, Mademoiselle Chambers. I have
hired two men and arranged for the camels. We leave in
the morning."

"So soon?" Christy stared at Driss in disbelief. "I
thought it would take several days to arrange for a caravan."

"I'm used to the desert. I know how to do these
things." Driss glanced at her shoulder bag. "But I must
pay the men and for the camels before we leave."

Christy hesitated. This was her last chance to back out,
and for a moment she was tempted to. She remembered
that the grounds keeper at the Mamounia had compared
Driss to a shark, and her hand tightened on her bag. But
she took a deep breath and told herself she was being
foolish. Uncle Albert had given her Driss's name; therefore the man must be all right. Besides, she had no choice.
She had to find Matt. Driss had said he'd take her to Bir
Lahlou; she wouldn't back out now.

They went to the bank, where Christy signed over three
thousand dollars in traveler's checks and handed the
money to Driss.

He smoothed the American dollars with his greasy fingers before he folded them and put them in his pocket. He
drove Christy back to her hotel, smiling and making
jokes, and when he let her off said, "I'll call for you at
five tomorrow morning, Mademoiselle Chambers."

Christy watched him drive away. It's not too late, a
frantic voice inside her head warned. Go back to Marrakesh while you can. Then she shook her head. She

couldn't leave, not after she'd come this far. Matt, or the answer to his disappearance, lay somewhere out in the Sahara—Matt, who had always been there for her, as she must now be there for him.

She thought of Hassan Ben Kadiri. In spite of what had passed between them, she sensed that he was a man she could trust. Chauvinistic he might be, but she knew somehow that he was a man of strength and character. He probably would have done his damndest to seduce her, but she was sure he'd also have done his damndest to see that no harm came to her.

Christy didn't feel that way about Driss. He was sly, sleazy and very likely dishonest. But if he was the only hope she had of getting to Bir Lahlou, then she had to take a chance. She had no choice.

The first few hours were harder than Christy had expected them to be. The two men Driss had hired seemed to be cut from the same cloth as he. He didn't introduce Christy; he only jerked a thumb in the direction of the men and said, "Ahmed, Saoul."

The man named Saoul led five camels over to where Christy waited. He took the canvas bag that held her clothes and slung it over the hump of the camel that would serve as a pack animal. Then he led another camel forward, struck the creature across the legs with a stick and when it kneeled he looked at Christy and said, *"Yala, yala."*

She eyed the camel cautiously. He was an ugly, motheaten beast with a drooping lip and watery eyes. She slung one leg over the saddle and grabbed the reins with both hands.

"Keep your legs back or he'll bite you," Driss warned.

I've got to sit on this creature's back for three hundred miles! Christy thought.

Thirty minutes later she was so nauseous from the constant rocking motion that she wanted to stop. Instead she took deep breaths and tried to think of something, anything, to get her mind off the awful pitching and rolling motion.

By the time they stopped at a small oasis to rest, Driss had to help her off the camel. She took a drink of the water he offered and went to sit in the shade of one of the palm trees. She'd known it would be hot, but she hadn't been prepared for this.

Christy rested her head on her knees. This is just the first day, she told herself. Anything takes getting used to. Tomorrow will be better. She looked over to where Driss stood talking to the drivers. He said something and one of them looked at her, snickered, then quickly turned away. She pressed her elbow close to the small revolver, snug against her waist now.

By late afternoon there was no sign of civilization, only mile after mile of endless rolling dunes. Whatever nausea she'd felt earlier had disappeared, to be replaced by a cold, hard knot of fear. Again and again Christy told herself that her uncle had given her Driss's name and that therefore the man had to be all right. But when, later that day, she asked him about Uncle Albert he said, "I don't know your uncle. Someone I do business with must have given him my name."

Who was that someone? Christy wondered. She looked around at the miles and miles of sand, then at the two men with Driss. She wanted to jerk the reins, turn her camel around and race back in the direction they'd come. But everything looked the same; she didn't know what direction they'd come from.

When the light began to change and the sky turned from blue to red, then softly faded to varying shades of gold and the shadows turned the dunes to magenta, Driss shouted something at Ahmed and Saoul and to Christy he said, "There is an oasis just ahead. We'll camp there to-night."

When they reached the oasis Ahmed fixed her tent while Saoud started a fire and heated coffee and rice. When it was ready he handed Christy a plate of rice and a piece of dried meat. She wasn't hungry, but she made herself eat, wondering as she did at the meagerness of the meal and if the provisions would last until they reached Bir Lahlou. She didn't think they'd covered more than fifteen miles today. Three hundred miles at the pace of fifteen miles a day. Twenty days!

As Ahmed went to tether the camels for the night Christy looked at the load the pack animal carried. She knew nothing about the Sahara, but she'd been on pack trips in Montana with Matt, and it seemed to her that for a week on the trail they'd been far more loaded down than was the pack camel now.

Christy sat in front of her tent for a long time that night, and when she finally went into it and tied it closed she sat cross-legged on the mat that served as her mattress, the gun on her lap, forcing herself to stay awake. But try as she might, Christy fell asleep, head forward on her chest, the gun loose in her hand.

She dreamed of a man in a gray djellaba and in her dream they were dancing again, but this time they weren't in the restaurant in Marrakesh; they were here on the desert, dancing on the sand. Hassan held her so close their bodies touched. She looked up at him and her breath quickened, then she frowned in surprise. He'd grasped her wrist and twisted something out of her hand. He ...

Abruptly, her heart beating with fear, Christy came awake. She felt for the gun and it was then that Driss said, "I took the liberty of confiscating your weapon, *mademoiselle*. It isn't fitting that one so lovely should carry a revolver." He grinned down at her. "And it certainly isn't very friendly." then the grin faded and Driss yanked Christy to her feet and pulled her out of the tent.

"Let me go!" Christy tried to get away from him. "Damn you, Driss, what do you think you're doing?"

"Ahh." He pretended to step back in fear. "Listen to this little pigeon. Come help me, Saoud. Defend me, Ahmed."

The other two men circled Christy. Sweat ran in dirty rivulets down Saoud's face. Ahmed reached out and yanked a strand of her hair. Christy swung her free hand, catching him on the side of his face, knocking him back a step.

He snarled. He grabbed her hand and, almost yanking her away from Driss, fastened the other hand on the front of her T-shirt and pulled her to him. "I get her first," he told Driss.

It was a nightmare; she'd wake up in a minute and be back at the Mamounia. Trying to fight her fear, Christy looked at the three men who surrounded her. The man Saoud was so close she could see the coarse pores on his face. For a moment she was too frightened, too filled with panic, to breathe.

The three of them drew closer. "Where is the rest of the money?" Driss asked.

"The money?"

"Three thousand dollars, Mademoiselle Chambers. It's an inconvenience that you have it in traveler's checks, but as soon as you sign them . . ."

"I don't have them with me." Christy managed to free herself from Saoud's grip and stepped away from him. "You don't think I'd be foolish enough to carry them with me, do you, Driss? The money is waiting for me in Bir Lahlou. You'll get it then—*if* I get there safely."

Driss glared at her. "You're lying." He jerked a thumb at Ahmed and snarled, "Check her things."

"It won't do you any good," Christy said when Ahmed pulled her canvas bag off the pack camel's back. But Ahmed ripped the bag open and began to throw her clothes out.

"Nothing," he growled. "Only clothes."

"Check her handbag."

"Leave my things alone," Christy cried. She started toward the tent, but Driss jerked her back, his hand cruelly tight on her wrist.

Ahmed brought her bag. He dumped everything out on the sand, and when he found her wallet he said, "Here it is!" He tore it open and gasped with pleasure when he saw the money. "American dollars," he said. "American—" His face darkened. "Two hundred dollars! She's telling the truth, Driss. She hasn't got the money."

"Perhaps it's on her." Saoud's dark eyes narrowed. "I think I will find out, yes?" He reached for her.

Christy struck out, but when she did Driss grabbed her other wrist. She kicked out, screaming in rage. Saoud muttered a curse as he dodged out of the way. "It will be a joy to tame you," he taunted her as he ran his dirty hands up and down her body.

When he was finished he said to Driss, "Nothing but a softness of skin and a roundness of curves."

"Then to hell with it." Ahmed stepped forward. "We have the three thousand. Let's head back to Tafarout before the sun gets any hotter."

"Not until I've had my bonus." Saoud moistened his lips.

"I'm first." Ahmed shouldered the other man aside.

"Then get on with it." Driss wiped the sweat off his face. "I want to get out of here."

"No! Please, don't. Please, I . . ." Christy tried to keep her sickening fear under control. "I'll get the money for you. Take me back to Tafarout. I'll have it sent there. I'll—"

"What you'll do is have the police down on our heads," Driss said.

"No, I swear I won't." Christy forced herself to speak calmly. "Six thousand is better than three, isn't it? I won't tell anyone what happened out here in the desert. I promise I won't."

"You won't tell because you're never going to make it back to Tafarout." Driss grabbed Christy's shoulders, thrust her at Ahmed and said, "Get on with it."

Christy thrust her fists against Ahmed's chest as hard as she could, then broke away and ran.

"After her!" Driss shouted.

Fear spurred Christy on. It didn't matter that there was nowhere to run except into the desert. Only one thought blazed through her mind—Get away!

A hand closed on her shoulder. She shrugged it away and kept running. She felt herself being grabbed again, her T-shirt ripping. Then she was on her knees as the three of them circled her.

"Now," Ahmed said as he began to pull his burnoose over his head.

"No, wait!" There was a note of alarm in Driss's voice.

"I wait for nothing." Ahmed's hands fastened in Christy's hair.

"Riders!" Saoud pointed out toward the desert. "Somebody is coming."

"Quick," Driss ordered. "Hide the woman in the tent until we get rid of them. Bind her and gag her."

Christy's hands tightened on the sand, resisting when Saoud tried to pull her to her feet. He swore and gave her a stunning blow on the side of her head. She closed her eyes against the pain and stiffened her body. He gripped her hair, closing his fist so tightly against her scalp that tears came to her eyes. She slammed back with her elbows when Saoud got her up. He let her go, and when he did Christy threw both handfuls of sand in his face. Turning away from him, she ran toward the desert. She knew she couldn't outrun them, but if she could make the riders see her . . .

Red-gold hair streaming out, Christy ran as she'd never run before. She heard the shouted curses behind her and the pounding of approaching hooves ahead of her before Ahmed grabbed her hair, spun her around and threw her over his shoulder.

A shot rang out. Ahmed dropped her. She broke her fall with splayed hands and rolled to a sitting position in time to see six riders gallop up to the oasis. More shots were fired. One of the riders fell. Ahmed screamed and grabbed his shoulder.

Christy looked around as robed men leaped off their horses. Words were shouted in Arabic. She saw Driss break and run. Someone slammed the butt of a rifle against his legs and he sprawled facedown in the sand.

Suddenly one of the robed men pulled Christy to her feet. "My God," he gasped. "Are you all right?"

Still too terrified to speak, Christy looked up at him. "You!" she gasped. "It's you!"

Hassan Ben Kadiri tightened his grip on her arms. "Of course, you little idiot," he said. And before Christy could speak, he pulled her into his arms.

Chapter 5

An hour later Hassan pulled his horse alongside of Christy's. "How could you have gone into the desert with a man like Driss?" he asked. "Couldn't you tell by looking at him that he was a bandit?"

"I knew he might be dangerous," Christy said, "but I had to take that chance. I had to get to Bir Lahlou." Her chin came up. "I still have to get there."

Damn! Hassan thought as he glared at her. This American woman was impossible. She had gone into the desert with Driss and his two cutthroats knowing they were dangerous, but determined to find her brother. She was either the most naive woman he had ever met or the bravest. If he hadn't come after her they would have killed her. But first they would have... Hassan's hands tightened on the reins. He'd seen the torn T-shirt and the bruise on her face. He knew what they would have done to her.

He'd arrived in Tafarout yesterday morning. It had taken only a few hours, a talk with the chief of police and one hell of a lot of money to organize a pursuit party. Even as he'd done it Hassan had told himself it was none of his affair. Christine Chambers was a headstrong woman who insisted on having her own way. He wasn't her protector. He had taken her to dinner once; he had kissed her once. Yet here he was, organizing men to go chasing into the desert after her.

It's because I feel guilty, he'd told himself. Because I tried to compromise her.

But it was more than that, Hassan thought now as he looked at Christy riding beside him. She'd almost been raped and murdered—she must have been paralyzed with fear—yet she sat straight in the saddle, not complaining about the heat or that she was tired.

Hassan remembered how he'd felt when he had seen her racing across the sand toward him, the blaze of her hair streaming out behind her, slender white arms raised in supplication. He had thought his heart would burst with fear for her, and he had dug his spurs deep, urging the huge Arabian on while his mind screamed, Christy!

Now she was here beside him. The men who had tormented her were bound and thrown like sacks of grain over the camel saddles, to be taken back to Tafarout and the justice that awaited them there. He and Christy would rest in Tafarout before they went back to Marrakesh.

He and Christy. Hassan glanced at her again, and as he had the first time he'd ever seen her, he felt his body tense with desire.

Hassan had known many women in his life, European as well as Moroccan women, but he'd never known anyone like Christine Chambers. He'd tried to tell himself as he'd raced toward Tafarout that he was going after her because he'd acted badly and that once he made sure she was safe he'd be able to forget her. Now he wasn't so sure.

He knew that before it was over between them he would have to lay her down in some quiet place and strip the clothes from her. He wanted to touch every inch of her pale ivory skin with his hands and his lips; he wanted to bury himself deep inside her and feel the softness of her surround him. If he didn't, the memory of her would haunt him forever.

Hassan looked at her again and saw that she was watching him. Because he was afraid that if he didn't get away from her he'd snatch her off her horse and disappear with her over the next sand dune, he said, "I'm going to check on things ahead," and spurred the Arabian forward.

Late that afternoon they arrived in Tafarout. Hassan took Christy to the hotel where she had stayed before and told her to rest while he turned Driss and his men over to the police.

"Meet me in the lobby at seven," he said. "We'll have dinner."

Christy's room was hot. She took her boots off and sank down on the bed, where she could feel the breeze from the overhead fan. She lay for a few minutes, almost too weary to move, but finally she made herself get up, shower and wash her hair. After she towel-dried her hair she got into bed and closed her eyes.

But as tired as she was, sleep was a long time coming. She'd begin to drift, then suddenly the memory of Driss and his men circling her as she lay helpless on the sand would snap her back to reality. She knew that she would have fought them as long as she had strength in her body, but in the end they would have overpowered her. And when they had taken her they would have killed her.

If it hadn't been for Hassan... She'd been wild with fear as she'd raced toward the approaching horses, not even

dreaming that one of the riders might be Hassan Ben Kadiri. Out of the confusion of shots and gunfire he'd
jumped from his horse. His white shirt had been open at
the throat, and there'd been a rifle in his hand as he'd
crushed her to him.

Hassan, Christy thought. Finally, with the memory of
his arms around her, she slept.

When Christy awoke she dressed in a short white
pleated skirt, a yellow and white polka-dot blouse and
high-heeled yellow sandals, all part of the wardrobe she'd
left behind at the hotel when she had started out with
Driss and his men. She brushed her red-gold hair back
from her face and let it fall in loose waves around her
shoulders. Because her face was sunburned, she touched
only a little shadow on her eyelids, mascara to her lashes
and a pale coral gloss to her lips.

Hassan took her to a small restaurant near the center of
town. He ordered *bastilla*, pigeon nestled beneath layers
and layers of tissue-thin pastry, and a bottle of red Spanish wine.

"We Muslims don't drink," he told Christy, "but I excuse my occasional lapses by telling myself that wine is
good for the digestion."

He gazed at her across the candle-lit table. "Your face
is burnt. Do you have anything to put on it?" When she
shook her head he frowned. "You didn't have a proper
covering for your head. With your complexion you need
something broad enough to shield your face. You didn't
wear the proper clothes, either. You should have worn a
long-sleeved shirt to protect your arms. You—"

"Please." Christy put her fork down. "Don't yell at
me. I'm not up to it tonight."

Hassan looked at her cross the table, then his face softened. "We'll rest here before I take you back to Marrakesh."

"I'm not going back to Marrakesh. I know I made a bad mistake with Driss, but now that I'm here in Tafarout I'll find someone else to take me. You've recovered most of my money, so I'll be able to organize another caravan." Christy hesitated. "I can't even begin to thank you for rescuing me, Hassan. I don't understand why you did, but I'll be grateful to you for the rest of my life. I'm almost a stranger to you, yet you came after me because you knew what kind of a man Driss was. If there's ever anything I can do to repay you, I will. But I'm here now. I mean to find my brother, and there's nothing you can say that will stop me."

Hassan was so angry he wanted to shake her. You almost died out there, he wanted to shout at her. Maybe you will die the next time. If you were my woman I would take you back to Marrakesh and lock you up if I had to. I would make you wear a robe and a veil and behave like a proper Moroccan wife. If you were my woman . . .

His anger faded and he felt his body tighten with need. That made him angry again, because he didn't want to feel this way about her. She was an American, and he didn't believe that a relationship—he used the word tentatively in his mind—with such a woman was possible, because she was of a different culture and a different religion. Christy was one of the most beautiful and appealing women he had ever known, but she belonged in her world and he belonged in his.

But, oh, how she made the blood stir in his veins, how she tightened his body with longing.

They walked back the few short blocks to the hotel. Outside, Hassan said, "Come up to my room. I'll get the ointment for your skin."

Christy hesitated. She didn't think she should, but after all he'd done for her, she felt foolish saying she preferred not to.

When they entered the room, Hassan opened his suitcase. He looked through it as he waved her toward the bed. He found the jar he'd been looking for and brought it over to the bed. "This should help the sunburn. Sit down and I'll put in on for you."

"No," Christy said hastily. "That's . . . that's all right. I can do it."

But Hassan gently pulled her down beside him. "Close your eyes," he said, and before she could object he began rubbing ointment on her face.

His hands were surprisingly gentle as they moved over her forehead to her temples. With his fingertips he smoothed the cream across her cheeks, down the length of her nose to her lips, and stopped.

Christy held her breath. She opened her eyes and saw Hassan's face close to hers, so close she could see the flecks of gold in his eyes.

Slowly his eyes never leaving hers, he rubbed a thumb back and forth across her lips.

A flame shot through Christy's body. She was caught, lost for a moment by the darkness of his eyes and the feel of the hand that cupped her face, unable to move when he opened the first two buttons of her blouse.

"Your skin is burnt here, too," he said as his hand moved down her throat.

"Hassan. . . . Please."

Easing her back against the pillows, he put more cream on his fingers and began applying it to her throat.

Christy closed her eyes. I shouldn't be here, she thought. I'll just stay a moment longer. A moment....

Hassan's hand moved lower, and when she opened her eyes he said, "You should have worn a shirt with a collar that you could have fastened at your throat." His voice was matter-of-fact, and she tried to tell herself that she was being foolish. But before she could stop him, he touched the rise of her breasts.

"No," Christy murmured, but her protest was smothered as Hassan's mouth covered hers. When she tried to sit up he took her in his arms, holding her close while he kissed her.

Christy had never been held like this or kissed with such hunger, such passion. As though with a will of their own her lips parted and her arms crept up around his shoulders.

"Christy," Hassan whispered against her lips. He held her away from him. His eyes were alight with an almost savage fire, and she felt a stab of fear because she was alone with him.

He curled a strand of her hair around his finger, then held it against his face to breathe in the scent of it. Slowly he unbuttoned her blouse.

"No, Hassan." Christy drew back. "No, I don't want this."

"Your skin is on fire," he said. "I'm only going to put cream on it. That's all, Christy." He slipped the blouse down over her shoulders. He looked at the delicate wisp of silk and lace that covered her breasts and let out a long sigh.

How pale her skin is, Hassan marveled, how soft. He kissed the space between her breasts, holding her so that he could taste her. He thought that if he tried he could take her. She would struggle, but he was stronger than she

was, and if he persisted he could make her yield. But that
wasn't the way Hassan wanted it to be. When Christy
came to him—and by Allah he would not rest until she
did—he wanted her to desire him as much as he desired
her. He wanted her to offer him the feast of her breasts,
to welcome him to the softness of her body.

Hassan kissed her again. He raised his head and said,
"Someday, Miss Christine Chambers, I will lie with you
and touch you and kiss you until it's too much for both of
us. When it is I'll do everything to you that I've ever
wanted to do to a woman." Christy started to speak, but
he put a finger against her lips. "You'll let me do these
things," he said, "because by then you'll want them as
much as I do."

His mouth covered hers again, hard and insistent, demanding a response. He ran his tongue across her lips,
and sighed with pleasure when at last she parted them. He
touched the corners of her mouth, then slowly edged between her parted lips to touch her tongue with his.

Christy was trembling when he let her go. He looked at
her for a moment, then rested his head against her breasts.
"You're so lovely," he said. "I've never known anyone
like you, Christy."

"Hassan . . ." She felt as though she'd never breathe
properly again. "Hassan, I—"

"No, Christy, don't say anything." He lay quietly for
a moment, then slowly rubbed his face against her breasts.
And when he felt the buds rise he took first one, then the
other, through the silken fabric, to gently tug with his
teeth until she moaned, "Oh, don't. Oh, Hassan,
please . . ."

He let her go. Then, taking her in his arms he kissed her
again, but chastely this time, to try to still the fire that
raged between them.

When he eased her back against the pillows he smoothed the hair back from her face. "My lovely American," he said, "what are you doing to me?"

"I think it's time I went to my own room," Christy whispered.

Hassan nodded. "In a moment," he said. "Now close your eyes and let me put more cream on."

Christy looked up at him, then with a sigh, trusting him, she closed her eyes.

He rubbed the cream on her burnt skin with gentle hands, caressing as he healed, her shoulders, her arms and the delicate skin at the rise of her breasts. Stirred and calmed, aroused but sleepy, Christy drifted. She was almost asleep when Hassan roused her. He helped her to a sitting position and buttoned her blouse.

With a sigh he helped her up off the bed and walked her down the hall to her room. When he opened her door and handed her the key he said, "Good night, my dear, sleep well."

Christy turned to thank him, and Hassan took her in his arms and kissed her. He let her go and, touching the side of her face, gave her a self-mocking smile. "Now go in and close the door," he said. "And when you sleep, dream of how it will be when I'm lying beside you."

Christy tried not to, but when she closed her eyes it seemed to her that she could still feel the warmth of his hands against her skin and the touch of his mouth on hers—Hassan Ben Kadiri, a strange and foreign man to whom she'd responded as she'd never responded to a man before.

With a sigh she opened her eyes and watched the fan rotate slowly above her. She wasn't sure what she'd have done tonight if Hassan had persisted. Would she have resisted, or would she have opened her arms to him?

She remembered the vibrant strength of his body close to hers and felt herself tremble. This was crazy, she told herself. She hardly knew Hassan. She mustn't allow herself to feel this way. Finally, still thinking about him, she buried her head in the pillow and went to sleep.

When she awoke the next morning there was a note under her door: "I am making inquiries about your brother this morning, and I will check with the police about Driss. I will see you when I return."

Christy bathed and dressed and then went down to breakfast. Afterward, to pass the time, she window-shopped in the streets close to the hotel. By one o'clock there was still no sign of Hassan. She had a club sandwich and went back to her room to wait for him. It was almost four before he knocked and said, "It's Hassan, Christy. I want to talk to you."

She was in a fever of impatience, but she tried not to show it as she led him out to her balcony and said, "Let's sit out here, where it's cooler."

Hassan loosened his tie and hung his jacket over the back of a chair. He looked good in Western clothes, Christy thought. His shoulders were broad, his waist and hips narrow, his legs long and powerfully built. He was a handsome and distinguished man, and dressed this way he could have been Italian or South American. Dressed in his robes, he became a different man, a little mysterious, a little dangerous.

"Your company has magnesium mines here in Morocco," Hassan said, breaking in on her thoughts. "Is that why your brother was here?"

"Yes," Christy said. "Were you able to find out anything?"

"Enough to make me want to find out a lot more." Hassan hesitated. "Tell me about your uncle," he said.

"You told me he was angry when your brother said he was coming to Morocco."

Christy nodded. "There was a lot of work to be done at home. I think Uncle Albert had the idea that Matt just wanted a vacation. He was furious when Matt insisted on making the trip."

"Who is the boss? I mean, who is actually the head of the company?"

"Matt's president, but Uncle Albert is chairman of the board. They run it together."

"Does each know what the other is doing?"

Christy looked puzzled, wondering at the direction the conversation was taking. "I don't suppose they know every detail. I mean, they probably don't check with each other on every phase of company operation."

"I see." For a long moment Hassan was silent. At last he said, "Your brother was here in Tafarout in December. He hired men, outfitted a caravan and set out the first of January."

Christy clenched her hands together. "What about the men he hired? Did the people you talked to know them? Were they reliable?"

"Yes, they were known in Tafarout—all but Driss."

"Driss?"

Hassan nodded. "He led the caravan, Christy. He came back; the other men did not." Hassan took her hand. "There's something else. I was told in strictest confidence by a man of questionable reputation that money had been offered to stop your brother from reaching Bir Lahlou." His hand tightened on hers. "How did you know to go to Driss, Christy? Who gave you his name?"

"Uncle Albert. But Driss said he didn't know my uncle." Her green eyes were wide with fear. "I don't understand, Hassan. What's going on?"

"I'm not sure, Christy, but I am going to find out. I will talk to Driss tonight. If he knows anything, I will get it out of him."

"You think my brother is dead, don't you?"

Hassan took his time answering. At last he said, "I don't know, Christy." He smoothed the back of her hand with his thumb. "But I promise you this: I am going to do my damnedest to find out."

Chapter 6

Dinner at the hotel that night was an almost silent affair. Hassan seemed so lost in his thoughts that Christy was almost afraid to speak. As soon as they finished dinner Hassan said, "I'm going over to the jail to talk to Driss now."

"I'd like to go with you."

"That is out of the question, Christy."

"But—"

"No buts. A woman doesn't go out on the streets here at night."

Christy raised her chin. "Perhaps a Moroccan woman doesn't, but I'm an American."

"I am painfully aware of that." Hassan slapped a handful of dirhams on the table, took Christy's arm and led her out of the dining room. "I am not going to stand here in the lobby and argue with you," he said. "If you want me to help you, then you will do what I say. I am

going to the jail, and you are going upstairs to your room.
Is that understood?''

Resisting an overwhelming urge to salute, Christy said,
"Yes, that's understood."

"I don't know how late I will be."

"I'll wait. I'd like to know what happens when you talk
to Driss."

"Very well." Hassan took her hand as though to kiss it,
and before Christy could pull away he turned it and ran
his tongue across her palm. In an almost inaudible voice
he said, "I love to taste you."

A shock of fire ran through Christy. She looked at
Hassan. His dark eyes were smoky with desire, but he
didn't speak. He squeezed her hand, and without a backward glance he hurried out of the hotel.

It was almost midnight before he returned. He knocked
at Christy's door and when he said, "It's Hassan,"
Christy put her robe on and opened the door.

Did you see Driss?'' she asked. Hassan stepped inside.
He looked down at Christy and put his hands on her
shoulders. "What is it?" she asked. "What did Driss tell
you?"

"Driss is dead." Hassan's hands tightened. "He was
murdered."

"Who...?"

"Nobody knows, Christy. Or if they do, they are not
talking. It happened just before I got there. One of the
guards went to get him and found him dead in his cell."

She stared up at him. "Do you...do you think his death
has anything to do with Matt's disappearance?"

"No," Hassan said too quickly. "Driss was a thief and
a cutthroat. He had enemies. Somebody finally caught up
with him." When Christy didn't answer he said, "Get
some sleep. We will talk about this in the morning." He

took her chin, lifted her face and kissed her. Before she could speak he went out and closed the door.

Hassan couldn't sleep. He lay naked in the middle of his bed and listened to the whir of the overhead fan. He thought about Christy Chambers and knew that he was going to help her, because he had begun to care for her and because there was something about her brother's disappearance that bothered him. When a man or, in this case, a caravan disappeared into the desert, eventually some trace would be found. No trace had been found of Matthew Chambers's caravan or of the men who had traveled with him. Only Driss, who'd come out of the desert at a different point than he'd entered, had survived. Now he was dead.

The day after he had taken Christy to dinner in Marrakesh, Hassan had telephoned his friend Fallah Haj to ask him more about Matt's disappearance.

"No trace of young Chambers has ever been found," Haj told him. "It is as though the Sahara swallowed him up. Why the interest, Hassan? You are not thinking of taking the Chambers woman to Bir Lahlou, are you?"

"No, of course not. But I was curious about her brother, and I—"

Haj's laugh cut him off. "Come, come, old friend. I know you too well. It is not the brother you are curious about; it is the sister. She is a remarkably pretty woman, isn't she? But I doubt you will get anywhere with her. When I tried, she turned those green eyes on me like a laser beam."

Hassan's hand tightened on the phone at the thought of Fallah Haj and Christy. But because he wanted more information, he tried not to let his anger show in his voice. "What is the government's position on the disappearance?"

"We are curious. There have been rumors that Chambers Mining has been selling magnesium to other countries through Morocco. Word has it that someone wanted young Chambers out of the way."

Hassan whistled softly. Christy had told him that it had been her uncle who had given her Driss's name. Driss had planned to kill her and now he was dead. If Christy persisted in her search, would she be in danger? How was her uncle involved in all of this?

Hassan tapped his fingers against the phone. When Haj asked if he was still there he answered "Yes." Then, making up his mind he asked, "Do you know who handled the investigation into Chambers's disappearance?"

"Several departments were concerned; Abdula Bouchaib was in charge."

"Bouchaib? Then it must have been top priority."

"It was indeed, my friend."

After Hassan had hung up, he thought about the conversation and the possibility that he might take a caravan into the desert to search for Matthew Chambers. He closed his eyes and felt the air from the overhead fan cool his body.

The desert. Hassan sighed, thinking of the terrible, consuming heat, the blinding sun and the sandstorms. He thought, too, of the coolness of the nights, of shadows cast on shifting dunes when the moon was full and of the silence. He had grown up in a Berber village and had enough knowledge to know that if a man was smart and careful, and if he had luck, he survived. It had been five years since he had made a trip like the one Christy wanted to make. The last time the desert had almost killed him. He didn't know if his luck would hold out again, but he knew that in spite of the dangers, there were times when the desert called out to him and that he longed for it, just as he longed for the woman.

The next morning he phoned the private number in Rabat that Haj had given him. When Bouchaib answered he said, "This is Hassan Ben Kadiri, Excellency. Omar Fallah Haj gave me your number."

"I know of your reputation, Mr. Kadiri. I also know of your interest in the matter of the disappearance of Matthew Chambers and that his sister wants to form a caravan to search for him. Have you agreed to do what she asks?"

"No, sir. In the first place, Miss Chambers insists on going along. In the second place, I doubt very much that her brother is alive."

"You are probably right about that," Bouchaib said, "but whether Chambers is dead or alive does not concern us as much as finding out if the rumors about his company selling magnesium to another country are true. If you should decide to go to Bir Lahlou, supposedly in search of Chambers, you would be in a position to find out if the magnesium is being shipped out of Morocco from there." Bouchaib hesitated. "Having the Chambers woman along would be a perfect cover for the trip—supposing, of course, you would be willing to help your government."

"Of course I am willing to help, Excellency, but I don't want Miss Chambers involved."

"She is already involved, Mr. Kadiri."

The two men discussed the details of the trip. Bouchaib said that in the morning someone from his office would leave Rabat for Tafarout to brief Hassan. The government would pay for the caravan. And yes, if Hassan insisted, the same man from Rabat would take Miss Chambers back to Marrakesh. It was further agreed that she would stay at Hassan's home under police protection until he returned from Bir Lahlou.

When Hassan replaced the phone, his dark eyes were serious. It was almost ten before he knocked on Christy's door. When she told him that she hadn't had breakfast, Hassan said, "Let's have it sent up. We can eat out on the balcony."

"Something's the matter, isn't it?"

Hassan looked at her, wondering how much he should tell her. She was fresh and beautiful this morning in a light yellow dress that made her eyes look like emeralds. Her red-gold hair had been brushed back from her face and fell softly to her shoulders. He wanted to touch her, but he made himself turn away. After he'd ordered breakfast he said, "Come, let's wait on the balcony."

Christy chose a chair; Hassan leaned back against the railing so that he could face her. "We need to talk about your brother," he said. He hesitated, wondering how much to tell her. "I think someone arranged his disappearance, Christy. Driss was involved, and he was probably murdered because somebody wanted him out of the way."

Christy's face went white. She shook her head as though to clear it. "What . . . what are you trying to say, Hassan? That Matt was mixed up in some kind of a conspiracy?"

"No, Christy, we think he might have been investigating a conspiracy."

"We?" Her green eyes widened.

"I called Rabat this morning and spoke to someone in the government about your brother. They think his disappearance has something to do with your magnesium being shipped out of Morocco illegally." Hassan's face was serious. "I am telling you this so you will know exactly what is going on and how my government is concerned." He took her hand. "I have been given the official go-ahead to initiate a search for your brother, Christy."

Tears sprang to Christy's eyes. "Thank you, Hassan. Oh, thank you."

"A government man is coming from Rabat tomorrow. He will take you back to Marrakesh."

"I'm not going to Marrakesh! I'm going to Bir Lahlou."

"No, you're not. It will be a long, hard, dangerous trip. I won't have time to worry about you."

"You won't have to worry about me. I'm quite capable—"

Hassan cut her off with an ungentlemanly snort. "Capable! You barely lasted a day when you were with Driss."

"That was different. Driss was different. I can trust you."

"Can you?" Hassan asked angrily. He stood up, glared down at her and said, "I am going to Bir Lahlou without you, Christy. And you are going back to Marrakesh, where you will wait until I send for you."

"No, I'm not! Matt's my brother. I'm going with you!"

Hassan had never before felt the need to throttle a woman. But Christy was the most obstinate, contrary woman he had ever known. If she had been a Moroccan he would have locked her in her room for a week and kept her on bread and water until she learned her place. But she wasn't a Moroccan, and he didn't know how to handle her. She looked as fragile as an angel, as delicate as an orchid. He towered over her and outweighed her by eighty pounds, but she stood toe to toe with him, her small fists clenched, green eyes ablaze, ready to do battle.

"If you were my woman," he said, "I would *make* you do what I say."

"But I'm not your woman."

"No, and thank Allah for that! You are—"

At that moment the waiter arrived with their breakfast. He brought it out to the balcony, poured their coffee, took one look at their silent faces and bowed himself out.

"You have had only a small sample of what the desert is like," Hassan said when the waiter had gone. "The trip to Bir Lahlou will take a least three weeks, possibly a month."

Christy buttered a croissant. "I'll need some long-sleeved shirts," she said.

Hassan spent the day taking care of all the things that went into putting a caravan together, the hiring of camel drivers, the selection of the animals, the purchase of supplies. He was hot and tired when he returned to the hotel that evening. Christy chatted all though dinner in spite of the fact that Hassan barely spoke.

He didn't phone her for breakfast the next morning. Christy dressed and went down to the dining room. There she saw Hassan dining with an elderly man who had a short gray beard. The man, like Hassan, was dressed in a dark djellaba.

Hassan frowned as she approached. He stood up, as did the other man, and said, "This is Miss Chambers, sir. Christine, I would like you to meet Rhourbi Ben Massad."

"Mr. Massad," Christy said as she offered her hand.

"Please." He held out a chair for her. "Won't you join us? I understand that you will be going to Marrakesh with me today."

"Why, no, Mr. Massad," Christy said with a smile. "I'm not going to Marrakesh; I'm going to Bir Lahlou."

"Are you? I am delighted to hear that, Miss Chambers. I appreciate your concern for your brother, and I can understand your desire to be a part of the caravan that will search for him. Mr. Kadiri tells me that you will be able to leave Tafarout by the end of the week."

"The sooner the better," Christy said.

Hassan scowled at her.

"It is settled, then," Rhourbi Ben Massad said. "We can now make the final arrangements."

Christy glanced at Hassan. "Then I'll leave the two of you alone, because I still have some shopping to do." She saw the anger and the threat in his dark eyes and looked quickly away. She'd won this round; she didn't think Hassan would let her win another.

At dawn on the day of their departure Christy stood on the balcony of her room, listening to the Imam call the people to prayer. She took a sip of strong black coffee as she gazed out over the city and felt a thrill of excitement course through her body. Today she would set out on a journey in search of her brother, a journey that could take two months. For the first time in a long while she had hope that somewhere out on that endless desert she'd find Matt.

One of the men that Hassan had hired was waiting in the lobby when she went downstairs. He took her canvas bag and motioned for her to follow him out to the waiting cab. When they reached the place from which the caravan would depart, Christy saw Hassan. The day he'd rescued her from Driss he'd been wearing riding pants. Today he wore a burnoose.

"Are you ready?" he asked.

Christy took a deep breath. Hassan had had little to say to her these past few days, and she knew he was still angry because she insisted on making the trip with him. Now she forced a smile and said, "Ready and raring to go." She looked at the camels. "Why can't we make the trip on horseback? You were on a horse when you rescued me."

"Only because I knew I would not be riding a long distance. For a trip like ours we must use camels." He glanced over to where his men were checking cinches on the two pack animals. "Camels know the desert," Hassan told Christy. "They can live without food for almost two weeks, without water for days. They have adapted to life in the desert because they can close their nostrils to the blowing sand. Their eyes are fringed with thick lashes to protect them, and their feet are padded and can spread like snowshoes to keep them from sinking in the sand." He looked at Christy and with a sigh said, "If you are ready, Raji will get you on your camel. Where is your hat?"

"Right here." Christy reached around and pulled the soft but broad-brimmed safari hat out of the back pocket of her jeans. "Do I have to put it on now?"

"Not for another hour or so."

Christy nodded, then turned and walked over to where her camel waited, well aware that Hassan's eyes were burning into her back.

He watched her, frowning at the way her jeans fit. A woman in pants! Allah help him! It wasn't that he hadn't seen women wearing pants before. While he didn't like the idea, it hadn't bothered him, because none of the women he'd seen wearing them had been his women. None of them had been Christy Chambers.

Hassan had been raised in a Muslim home. He had been taught that good women were obedient in the name of Allah, that their place was in the home, where they were properly dressed, which meant they wore a robe and a veil. They did not wear pants, especially pants that hugged their well-shaped bottoms and made a man want to reach out to cup that sweet roundness.

Damn! Hassan struck the side of his boot with his riding crop. They hadn't even begun the trip, and already his body was tightening with need. He thought of the weeks ahead, days and nights that he would spend with Christy. He knew deep in his soul that before their journey had ended he would possess her.

Chapter 7

By ten o'clock Christy's body was drenched with sweat. She opened the collar of her shirt and began to roll the sleeves up when Hassan said, "The sleeves protect you from the sun. Leave them as they are. Would you like a drink of water?"

"No, thank you."

Hassan studied her for a moment, then handed her one of the canteens. "We'll be stopping for lunch soon," he said.

"Don't stop on my account."

"I won't." He dug his heels into the camel and galloped ahead.

Christy glared at his retreating back and sat straighter in the saddle. She'd told Hassan that she wouldn't whine or complain, and by God she wouldn't. She'd forced him to take her along on this trip, and she was determined to show him that she was equal to it.

But it took almost a week for Christy's body to accustom itself to the heat and to Clyde's lurching roll. She'd named the camel Clyde on the second day, thinking that if she did and if she spoke to him in a friendly tone of voice, he'd stop trying to bite her ankles. But soon her mild-mannered "Now, Clyde, you really must stop that" changed to "Damn it, Clyde, if you try to bite me again I'll beat your scruffy ears off."

Mile after mile of endless sand dunes, broken only occasionally by an oasis or a sudden carpet of red and yellow flowers, became the pattern of their days. Without seeming to, Hassan kept watch over Christy. He stopped for a break whenever he saw that she was tired and insisted she eat when all she wanted to do was sleep. He was all desert man now. The blood of his ancestors, of sheiks and sultans and conquering warriors, came alive in his veins. This was the Sahara, the place where he had been born. He belonged to it as it belonged to him.

Sometimes they stopped for the night at oases, but other times they set up camp at the foot of a sand dune. Then the camel drivers would put up Christy's and Hassan's tents, start a fire for their meal and retreat to take care of the camels and to spread their own beds.

By the end of the first week Hassan had softened in his attitude toward Christy. A part of him had to admit that he was glad she was with him, even if he didn't approve of a woman in pants astride a camel. He admired her tenacity and the fact that she didn't complain. In spite of the hat and the sunscreen she used, her face and hands burned. He'd seen the weariness each night when she slipped off the camel and tried to suppress a wince of pain from her tired and aching muscles. She was a woman of strength and determination, completely different from anyone he'd ever known before.

But she wasn't the kind of woman Hassan was used to. Moroccan women did as they were told. They looked to a man for protection and rarely raised their voices above a whisper. Christy wasn't like that. She was a tiger. He'd heard her yell at Clyde the camel and use words that a Moroccan woman would not even dream of using as she tore her hat off and whacked the recalcitrant beast. She would be a difficult woman to tame but, oh, what joy there would be in the taming.

Hassan thought often during these days of his friend Rashid and of Rashid's marriage to the lovely Katherine. When he first heard of their marriage he'd been sure it would never work, because Rashid, like him, was a strong and dominant man. He'd been shocked when he learned that Rashid allowed Katherine complete freedom and that she was an equal partner in their marriage. This had puzzled Hassan, and when he found the opportunity he had asked Rashid about it.

"I have heard you let this American wife of yours do whatever she chooses to do and dress however she chooses to dress," Hassan had said disapprovingly. "Surely that is not true. Surely she is obedient to you."

"Obedient!" Rashid had thrown back his head and laughed until tears ran down his face. When he had stopped laughing he said, "My friend, there is no way I can explain our marriage to you. You will not understand unless you, too, fall in love with an American woman."

Hassan had vowed that would never happen to him. This attraction he felt for Christine Chambers was a transient thing. He was more attracted to her than he had been to any woman, and he meant to have her before this trip was over. But he wouldn't fall into the same trap his friend Rashid had, though the trap was a tender and lovely one. No, he would marry someone from his own world, someone who understood and accepted the wise words of Allah, who said that good women do what their husbands tell them to do.

But Hassan's attraction to Christy grew more intense as the days passed. He began to look forward to the time at the end of the day when they were alone across the campfire from each other.

So did Christy. The best part of the trip for her were the nights, when she and Hassen sipped their strong Arabian coffee and moved closer to the fire when the air grew cold.

Christy felt good, stronger than she ever had before, and proud that she'd been able to keep up. She fell asleep each night in the silence of the desert and awoke in the morning before the sun came up over the dunes. She was glad she'd insisted on coming, not just for Matt but for herself.

Tonight the camel drivers were out of sight, asleep behind one of the dunes. She and Hassan were alone. They'd spent every waking moment together for the past ten days, but he'd made no attempt to try to make love to her as he had done that night in Tafarout.

In many ways Hassan was still a stranger, as mysterious as the desert of which he was a part, more attractive than any man she'd ever known. Christy knew that it would be easy to fall in love with him and that she mustn't even allow herself to think of loving him. She was an American; she could never live the way a man like Hassan would expect her to live. She made herself a promise that if she felt herself falling in love with Hassan she'd conjure up a picture of herself in a robe and a veil.

Now Christy looked up and saw that Hassan had turned away to gaze out on the desert. The only light was from the fire and the millions of stars that shone down on the cool desert night. Again, as she had when she'd first arrived in Morocco, Christy felt as if she'd stepped back in time. She looked around her at the shadowed dunes and the camels outlined against the horizon. What had it been like long ago, when sheikdoms reigned, when men took what they wanted and women were possessions to be bought and sold?

Through half-closed eyes Christy studied Hassan's face. His skin looked bronzed by the light of the flickering, almost surrealistic flames. He hadn't shaved since they had begun this trip, and already he had the beginnings of a beard, which made him look even more as though he were a man from out of the past, a sheik or a caliph, reigning over a desert kingdom.

Christy gazed into the flames, and it seemed to her she could see what it had been like then, in another time, another century.

The man, taller than any man she had ever seen before, had come to their Bedouin camp surrounded by a dozen of his men. When he reined in his black stallion her father rushed out of his tent and fell prostrate before him.

"Rise, friend," the tall man said as he dismounted. "I mean you no harm. My men and I are tired. We need food and water."

"Everything I have is yours," her father said. He rose, clapped his hands and ordered a sheep be slaughtered and a meal prepared.

She, the daughter of the Bedouin leader, watched the scene before her with curious eyes. The sheik—for surely this tall stranger must be a sheik—threw back the hood of his black djellaba, and as he turned to speak to one of his men, she saw his face. His skin was bronzed, his hair was thick and black, his beard as dark as his eyes.

His gaze shifted; he saw her watching him. She froze, caught in his smoldering look, too frightened to move back into the shadows until he raised one hand to beckon her father. "The girl," he said. "Who is she?"

"My daughter, Excellency."

"Tell her to step out here, where I can get a better look at her."

"Yes, Excellency." Her father turned and shouted, "Girl, come here."

Feeling as though her heart would surely burst from fear, she stepped out into the sun and went slowly forward. The man's eyes followed her every movement, and when she hesitated he said, "Come closer."

She stood before him and a spark of anger replaced her fear. She raised her face defiantly and looked directly at him.

In a apologetic voice her father said, "She is a difficult girl, Excellency." He struck her shoulder with the flat of his hand and shouted, "Lower your head!"

"No." The stranger captured her chin and raised it. He looked into her eyes for a long moment, then his gaze dropped to her throat, her breasts, down the length of her. "I wonder," he said almost to himself, "how you would look in silk."

That night her father ordered her to serve him and his guest. She did so silently, aware that the stranger's eyes were on her. She tried not to tremble as she knelt with the bowl of pilaf.

"She's a stubborn girl," her father said, speaking of her as though she were not there. "I've had to take the stick to her more than once. She's my youngest. The other daughters belong to men of different tribes." He reached into the pilaf. "She is the most beautiful. Look how fair

*her skin is. See the shape of her breasts. I would not part
with her easily."*

"I would not expect you to," the other man said.

*She left the tent, and feeling faint with fear, went to her
mother and said, "I'm afraid. I think that father intends
to give me to the stranger."*

*"If he does it is the will of Allah," her mother told her.
"He looks to be a man of wealth, so at least you will not
starve."*

"But I don't know him," she cried.

*Her mother looked at her with compassion. "You
will," she said softly.*

*She left with him the next day. A few days later they had
stopped to rest with one of the nomadic tribes under his
domain. He had given orders to the women and they had
taken her into a tent, where they stripped her, bathed her
in sweet-smelling oils and dressed her in gossamer veils of
pale shades of pink and lavender and blue. Then they had
put a veil over her face and led her out of the tent to where
he waited.*

*He looked at her. His dark eyes widened, then nar-
rowed as his gaze lingered on her face, then traveled down
her body. Without a word he took the veil off. For a
breathless moment he looked at her. Then he led her to the
fire and motioned her to sit by it. "You will eat with me,"
he said.*

*She tried, but her hand trembled as she reached to-
ward the bowl of rice.*

*"It's all right." He took the bowl from her. "I will feed
you."*

*He dipped his fingers into the rice and brought them to
her lips. He found the choicest pieces of lamb and held a
silver cup of honeyed milk to her lips so that she could*

drink. Each time he did he gazed into her eyes, and it was as though they were alone in the starry universe.

One of the women brought a bowl of dates. He held one to her lips, where his fingers lingered. Without knowing that she was doing it, she touched the tips of his fingers with her tongue. She saw his eyes widen and heard the sharp intake of his breath.

Frightened now, she lowered her gaze and her heart began to beat so fast she thought she could not breathe. She knew that soon he would get to his feet. He would offer his hand and she would be forced to take it, forced to let him lead her into his tent.

The time had come; there was no escape.

She lifted her head and looked at him. "You are mine," he said. "Come with me now."

Her mouth was so dry she could not speak. She wanted to run away. And yet . . . she felt a warmth seep into her body and an excitement she didn't understand.

"Come," he said again.

"No, I'm afraid."

He picked her up and carried her into his tent. When she struggled he laughed, and, holding her closer, he kissed her.

She'd never known a man's kiss, and, panicking she tried to get away from him. "I won't hurt you, little bird," he said. Gently he placed her on a soft pile of pillows and knelt beside her.

"Please," she whispered, "let me go."

But he kissed her again, and this time she felt something she'd never felt before, something that frightened her even more than the hands that held her captive.

One by one he removed the gossamer veils. Soon she would be naked in his arms, helpless against his strength.

He leaned over her, and she was as pinioned by the passion in his hawk-dark eyes as she was by the arms that held her.

"Little bird," he whispered.

"No. I'm afraid. I..."

"Christy?"

"I can't," she said, still lost in the dream.

Hassan gazed at her from across the flames, wondering at the expression on her face as she stared at him across the fire.

"My dear..." He rose and came around to where she sat. She looked up at him, and in her green eyes he saw a look of such sensuous mystery that he felt as though his heart might leap from his body. He took her hands and drew her up beside him. Before she could speak he put his arms around her and kissed her.

Christy swayed against him, still lost in the dream as her arms crept up around his neck, yielding as he urged her closer. She could feel the strength of his thighs against hers, the hardness of his chest, his strong arms clasped around her. This is the dream, she thought. In a moment he'll take me into his tent. He'll lay me down. He'll...

Suddenly Christy pulled away from him. "No," she said in a voice trembling with emotion. "No."

"You want to," Hassan said. "Christy, you know that you want me just as much as I want you. I have waited for you to feel the same way I do. You do now, Christy. I know you do."

"I..." She tried to pull herself together, tried to control her voice. "We're different, Hassan. We come from different worlds. I...I don't want any emotional involvement."

"Emotional involvement? Christy, we are going to be together for two months. How do you expect me to keep my hands off you?" He cupped her chin and forced her to look at him. "Why can't we enjoy each other for the time we have, Christy? I agree with you. We *are* from different worlds. When this is over you will go back to your world. But in the meantime..."

Christy moved away from him. "I'm sorry, Hassan. I'm not casual about...about things like this. I never have been. I don't take love—*making* love—lightly." She looked up at him. "I'm sorry," she whispered, then turned away from him and hurried into her tent.

The heat became more intense every day, the occasional oasis farther and farther apart. There was no respite from the sun during the hot hours of the afternoon, no shelter but the stars at night.

Since the evening they had embraced by the fire, Christy had kept her distance, and Hassan, sensing her mood, had stayed away from her as much as he could. Now he spent the time around the campfire in the evenings with the drivers rather than with Christy.

"They're good men," he told her, "but they've been surly this last week. I don't like it; I think I'd better keep an eye on them."

"Is it because we haven't seen an oasis for a few days?" Christy felt a nudge of fear. "Do we have enough water, Hassan?"

"Of course we do. We'll be all right for a while yet."

How long was "a while yet"? Christy wondered. "How far do you think we are from Bir Lahlou?" she asked. "How many days away?"

"Eight or nine. But don't worry. We'll find an oasis anytime now. According to my map we'll reach one sometime tomorrow morning."

But they didn't reach the oasis the next morning.

It was barely light when Christy heard the roar. She lay for a moment, wondering what it was. Then she heard Hassan shouting for the men. Quickly she sat up, pulled her jeans on, then her boots. She stood up to put her shirt on, and she felt the force of the wind. *"Shergi, shergi!"* one of the men cried just as Hassan burst into her tent.

"Sandstorm," he snapped. "We must get your tent down. Do you have a scarf?"

"Yes, but—"

"Cover your nose and mouth. Get your gear together."

Quickly Christy threw her few toilet articles into the small canvas bag she carried with her. Before she could close it Hassan pulled her out of the tent, then quickly collapsed it.

Sand swirled around her. As she tied the scarf across her nose and mouth she saw that the men had pulled the camels closer, roped them together in an attempt to form a barricade and were stacking their supplies behind the animals.

The roar of the wind grew stronger, and now Christy could see the terrible whirling, swirling, moving cloud of sand that came closer and closer.

The drivers began to wail, *"Shergi, shergi!* We are all going to die."

Hassan barked an order. They glared at him and hunched down behind the makeshift shelter.

"How long will this last?" Christy asked as she crouched beside Hassan.

"A few hours, a day." He didn't add that a sandstorm like this could go on for days or that sands would drift and that the oasis he'd hoped to reach this morning might be buried in the sand before the storm was over.

Christy couldn't see; she could barely breathe. She nodded when Hassan shouted, "Keep your head down," and didn't resist when he pulled her closer to shield her with his body.

Hour after endless hour went by. Several times Hassan offered her the canteen he'd slung around his neck. His face and head were covered; all she could see were his dark eyes. But they steadied her. She nodded her thanks but drank only a little each time, because she didn't know how much water remained.

The sand piled up around them. They scooped it away and tried to make a trenchlike shelter. All the while the wind hit with explosive force. Christy stood up once, trying to look around her. She saw the camel drivers huddled together and the faint outlined humps of the camels. The sand stung her face and blinded her. Then Hassan pulled her down next to him. He put his arms around her, turned her face into his chest and drew his burnoose around her.

The storm raged all that day and night. They moved occasionally, to drink water from the canteen or to scoop away the sand that threatened to bury them. Sometime in the night, exhausted by the storm, still close in each other's arms, they slept.

The silence woke them. Slowly, moving as though they'd been ill, Hassan, Christy and the camel drivers began to stir. They looked around them. The shape of the desert had changed.

With anguished cries the camel drivers threw themselves to their knees and began to wail. Hassan shouted at them in Arabic, jerked them to their feet and shoved them toward the animals. One of the men pointed to the camels and began to wail anew. Two of the animals were missing.

"We're going to die!" one of the men cried. "We're lost. Allah has deserted us."

"We're not going to die," Hassan said between clenched teeth. But when he checked the supplies he knew the situation was serious. Some of the food had been lost; he would have to ration it and the water until they reached the oasis. There they would at least have enough water to get them to Bir Lahlou. They could get by for a few days without food if they had to. Christy could ride one camel; he and the men would take turns with the second. They would lead the pack animal, and with luck they would make it to the oasis.

While he worked he glanced at Christy and gave her a reassuring smile.

The drivers were angry and frightened when they started out in the afternoon. They huddled together, whispering among themselves. Hassan yelled at them and drove them on. He understood their fear but knew he had to control it and them. He insisted that one of them ride while he himself walked. The other two fought about that, arguing that one of them should have been riding.

Only Christy didn't complain, and if she was afraid, she didn't let it show. "I'm a part of this caravan," she said. "I should take my turn walking too."

"Don't be ridiculous," Hassan growled.

"The men are angry. I thought if I took my turn it would help."

"I will handle the men. You handle Clyde." He grinned up at her. "I think you have finally convinced the poor beast that you are the boss. He's not going for your ankles as often as he used to."

"He'd better not!" She grinned back at Hassan, then her face sobered. "We're going to make it, aren't we?"

"Of course we are," he said.

They found the oasis—what was left of it—at sunset. Half the date palms had disappeared. There was almost no water left in the pool. The drivers rushed to it while Hassan made the camel kneel and helped Christy dismount. He and Christy drank, then filled the canteens. By then there was almost no water remaining in the pool.

Hassan hesitated, debating whether to fill the casks or water the camels. Finally he compromised; he filled only one cask, then had the drivers lead the camels to the pool.

The remaining water didn't last long. When the pool was dry, the drivers dug deep, trying to find another source. When they didn't, they shook their heads and once again whispered to one another and cast angry looks at Hassan.

The dinner that night was half a cup of rice each, a few dates that Christy picked from the palms and a pot of coffee. After they had eaten, Hassan fixed Christy's tent, and when she said good-night and went inside he lay down in front of it.

Hassan stayed awake for a long time. The night was clear, the sky full of stars. He breathed in the smell of the desert and knew that in spite of everything he was glad to be here. He heard the movement of the camels and the low voices of the men. He turned his head toward the tent and wondered if Christy was asleep. He closed his eyes and thought of how she would look, curled up on the blanket only a few feet away from him. At last, with the thought of her so near, he slept.

Hassan didn't see the silent shadow slipping across the sand toward him. Only at the last moment, when the man raised his arm to strike, did he hear a movement. He opened his eyes and saw the figure. But it was too late. He felt a sickening thud behind his ear, then all the stars in the sky came crashing down upon him.

Chapter 8

Everything was quiet when Christy awoke. She sat up, rubbed a hand across her face and saw that it was already light. Usually by this time she would hear the drivers shouting as they prodded the camels to their feet and smell the coffee heating over the fire. But no drivers shouted; there was no aroma of coffee. She pulled her boots on, brushed the tangled hair back from her face and opened the flap of her tent just as Hassan groaned and tried to sit up.

"My God!" Christy knelt beside him. "What is it? What happened?" She saw the trickle of dried blood behind his ear. "You've been hurt!" she cried. "What happened?"

Hassan tried again to sit up, then, holding his head, said, "Water."

Christy ran back into the tent and grabbed the canteen. Lifting his head, trying to steady him, she held the canteen to his lips. After he drank his fill she poured some of the water on her scarf and held it against the lump on the back of his head.

After a moment he managed to pull himself to a sitting position. He took a couple of deep breaths, then said, "The men? Where are the men?"

"I . . . I don't know. They must be here with the animals." Christy stood up and looked around her. Only one camel was still tethered to the palm tree. She sank back on her heels and, almost afraid to look at Hassan, said, "Oh, my God, Hassan, they're not here. They've taken the other two camels, they—"

He swore. Staggering to his feet, holding on to Christy's arm for support he said, "We had better check the supplies."

Leaning heavily on her, Hassan managed to reach the camel. On the sand beside it was a sack of rice and another of dried fruit. The cask of water was gone. Christy's hand tightened on his arm. He took a deep breath and forced himself to think clearly.

"Can we go after them?" she asked in a shaky voice.

"They're long gone," Hassan said. "I think I had just fallen asleep when one of them snuck up behind me and hit me." He rubbed a hand across his beard. "I knew even before the sandstorm that they were getting restless. I should have watched them more closely. I should not have gone to sleep. I—"

"It isn't your fault, Hassan. You were exhausted from the storm; you had to sleep." Christy looked around her and with forced cheerfulness said, "It isn't so bad here. There's shade from the trees, a few dates . . . Maybe if we try digging down in the pond we'll find more water." She looked at him. "Someone will come along, Hassan. This is an oasis. Other travelers must surely come this way."

"How many other travelers have we passed since we set out from Tafarout?" he said.

"None, but..." Christy felt the panic that she'd tried to hold in check rise to the surface. "What..." She swallowed. "What are we going to do?"

"We shall rest here for the day. By tonight I will feel better; we shall start out then. It will be cooler, and I can chart our course by the stars."

"You said we were more than a week away from Bir Lahlou, Hassan. We can't make it, can we? Not with the little water that we have."

He hesitated, torn between telling her the truth, that their position was precarious and that only rain or a miracle would save them, and lying and telling her they weren't in any danger.

Hassan put his arm around her shoulder. "Our situation is serious, Christy," he said. "But with a lot of determination and a little luck we will make it. Now, let's see if there is still some coffee left in the pot from last night."

There was almost enough for two cups. Hassan built a fire to warm it, and when he finished his cup he felt better. They would rest today, he told himself. They would conserve their strength, drink as little water as possible and set out tonight. He didn't know how long they could last; he only knew they had to keep going.

Hassan kept Christy busy collecting dates. There were not many left on the trees after the storm, and when she had picked them clean he helped her dig through the sand. There was little hope of their finding any of the fruit, but he knew it would be better for her if she had something to do. As luck would have it, they found almost two dozen to add to the bag they already had. When they were ready for the one meal they would have that day he managed to get enough water from the diminished pond to boil a small handful of rice.

Later in the afternoon they rested in the shade of the palms. His head ached, but he felt better and knew that when evening came he would be able to travel. When Christy awoke he had her select only the things that were a necessity, the clothes she had on, to which she'd add her sweater tonight, a T-shirt and a few of her toilet articles. They each had two canteens of water, the rice—which would do them little good without water—the dried fruit and the dates.

When evening came Hassan said, "We're ready, Christy. It is time to mount up."

She tried to smile. "Wouldn't you know with my luck they'd leave Clyde?"

"I thought all camels looked alike. How do you know this is him?"

"He's got a chunk out of his left ear, probably bitten off by a snippy female." She climbed on the animal's back. "Well, here we go, Clyde old boy," she said. "You try to bite me tonight and I'll take a chunk out of your other ear." She didn't look back as they started away from the oasis.

A thin slice of moon shone in the sky. By its pale light and that of the stars they could see the rise and fall of the dunes. Hassan led the camel, and again Christy drifted back in time. She was somewhere in the Sahara desert, riding a camel led by a man in a burnoose. Except for the soft thud of the camel's feet, they were surrounded by silence.

A strange kind of peace settled over Christy. She didn't know what was going to happen to them, but it was enough for the moment to know that they were together.

They stopped when the first light of dawn touched the sky. Hassan helped Christy off, and when she had stretched her tired muscles they rested a moment, then ate a few of the dates. "Only a sip of water," Hassan cautioned her when he handed her the canteen. "We'll need it more as the day goes on."

Christy nodded, took one sip and handed the canteen to him. "Tired?" he asked.

"A little." She hesitated. "How will you be able to chart our course now?"

"I still have the compass, Christy." He put the canteen back over his shoulder. Then he whacked Clyde across the knees so that he would kneel and Christy could mount.

"Why don't I walk for a while?" she asked. "It's your turn to let Clyde try to take a bite out of you."

"He's your camel," he said with a smile. "You're the one who named him, so you're the one who has to ride him."

"But I don't mind walking," she insisted.

Hassan looked at her, and it seemed to him suddenly as though he couldn't breathe. This was the woman he had thought would be a burden, a female who would fall apart at the first sign of a crisis, who would complain of the heat and her complexion and drive him crazy with her demands.

But Christy wasn't like that; she hadn't panicked when the sandstorm hit them. She hadn't gone to pieces and wept when she knew that their situation was critical. She was a rare woman, a woman a man could depend on. He felt his muscles tighten as he looked at her. He vowed that he would do everything in his power to bring her safely through.

"Look," she said, "Oh, Hassan, look. Have you ever seen such a sunrise?"

He stopped and looked toward the distant horizon as the sun came up in a brilliant show of color—pink, vermilion, gold and red. It was beautiful now, but in another two hours its rays would blind them, its heat consume them. Hassan looked up at Christy. The reflection of the sun was on her face. He felt his breath catch; she was the most beautiful woman he had ever seen.

Hassan wanted to touch her then. He wanted to say, *You're brave and beautiful and I think I love you.* Instead he rested his hand on her foot for a brief moment and said, "All right, Christy, let's get going."

By three o'clock the temperature was well over 130 degrees. Christy had not asked for a rest, but several times in the past hour he had seen her sag, then quickly clutch the reins and straighten up. He had to get her out of the sun soon.

Finally, at the rise of a dune Hassan spotted a square of shade. "We will stop here," he told her. Christy didn't answer, but she managed a smile and a nod.

When she dismounted, her face was red and her legs trembled. "We will rest in the shade for a while," Hassan said as he took her hand led her to the dune. He gave her the canteen. She took only a sip, but he said, "No, take some more. You need it." Then took her scarf, dampened it and wiped her face off.

When he led her to the spot of shade, he said, "Lie down, Christy. We will rest here until the sun moves."

She looked up at Hassan through eyes almost blinded by the sun. The desert shimmered in undulating waves; she felt as though her body were on fire and tried to conjure up the vision of a California beach. The water had always been too cold for her in California, and she'd complained to Matt that she much preferred a pool. Now the idea of that cold water lapping at her feet made her sigh with longing. She'd never again say that it was too cold. She'd swim way out, so that every part of her body was covered. She'd put her face in it and swim down to where the water was even cooler.

Her mouth was dry; her lips were swollen. Think of strawberry ice cream, she told herself. Imagine the cold, sweet taste of it against your lips. Imagine . . . She felt the sun on her face and opened her eyes.

"We're losing the shade." Hassan said. "It is time to move on."

Hour after hour. Christy thought the day would never end. No one could live in this inferno. She couldn't bear it. She looked down at Hassan, walking in front of her, urging the surly Clyde on. Hassan's feet were deep in sand, so that he had to struggle with every step he took. His head was bent as he urged the beast forward, forward. Oh, God, Christy thought, when would the sun go down?

She didn't know how much longer she could sit in the saddle. She no longer thought about riding; she simply let her body go with Clyde's—sway, lurch, sway, lurch... She was barely conscious when Hassan said, "We will stop now, Christy. Hold on. I'm putting Clyde to his knees."

Only partly aware that the sun had lost its intensity, she half fell into Hassan's arms. He carried her to the foot of a dune, laid her down, then went back to take care of the camel. When he returned he put an arm under her shoulders, lifted her and said, "Here, drink this."

"Only a sip," Christy mumbled. "Have to save it for tomorrow. Tomorrow . . ."

"It's all right," he said. "Drink, Christy. Drink, love."

The water dribbled on her parched lips; it hurt to swallow. She took three sips, then closed her eyes. "I'll be all right...." She tried to smile. "Maybe it'll rain tomorrow."

Hassan smiled back at her. "Maybe," he said. He lay down beside her and took her hand. "We will rest for a few hours, then go on. I know you are exhausted, but it's best to cover all the ground we can at night."

She squeezed his hand. "I know," she said. Then she closed her eyes and slept.

Hassan didn't think they could last another day without more water. He was stronger than Christy; he would be able to keep going longer than she would. If he had to, if she lost consciousness, he would tie her on the camel's back.

He looked down at her, so still beside him. "Hold on, Christy," he whispered, knowing that she didn't hear. "Hold on, little love." Then he, too, slept, but only for a few hours. Then, although he hated to, he roused her and said, "Sorry, Christy. We must move on now."

As Hassan started to move away from her, Christy took his hand. "Tomorrow...today..." She swallowed. "If there comes a time when I can't go on, then I want you to take Clyde and continue without me."

"By Allah, what are you saying?"

"You're a desert man, Hassan. You'll make it to Bir Lahlou. I don't think I will."

For a long moment Hassan didn't speak. Then he took her arms and almost roughly he pulled her to him. "You will make it," he said. "You will make it if I have to carry both you and Clyde." Then he gently kissed her lips. "We have to hang on, Christy," he told her. "One minute at a time, one step at a time. There are still a few hours left before daylight. We had better take advantage of them."

When she was once more astride Clyde, Hassan rested his hand on her leg. "Today we will find an oasis," he said.

"Of course we will." Christy summoned a smile. But in her heart she knew they were both lying.

Chapter 9

Christy sucked on the date pit and tried to tell herself that it helped. She opened her eyes a fraction of an inch so that her world narrowed to the top of Clyde's head and the burnoose shape of Hassan. The world was on fire. Every tree, every sign of vegetation, had been burned. The sun seared through the canvas covering of her hat, through her hair and her skull; it burned into her brain. She was beyond conscious thought, beyond hope.

I'm sorry, Matt, a small part of her brain whispered. I wanted to find you, big brother. I tried. But I can't go on, Matt. I want to. I . . . She felt herself falling then, but it didn't matter. Nothing mattered except the heat. The heat. . . .

"Christy!" Water dribbled on her lips, but her lips were so dry, her tongue was so swollen, that it hurt to swallow. "Drink some water, Christy."

She tried again and this time managed to swallow. Then her hands closed around the canteen and she drank thirstily.

"All right," Hassan said. "That's enough for now." He took the canteen. "Did you hurt yourself when you fell?"

"I didn't fall," she whispered. "Clyde pushed me. Where is he?"

"You're under him. He was the only shade I could find." Hassan took the last date out of his pocket and handed it to her. He looked up at the sun. There were at least two more hours before sunset. The last canteen was almost empty. When that was gone... Hassan shaded his eyes with his hand as he looked out over the desert. For the past two hours he had been seeing mirages, wondrous pools of water springing to life at the base of the dunes. Once, he had been so sure that he had almost called out to Christy. Instead, he had hurried his pace, swearing in frustration when the pool disappeared.

He didn't think anything could save them now, but he was determined to go on. He looked at Christy. Her eyes were swollen almost shut, her lips caked and dry, her face and hands cruelly burned. He took her hat off and brushed the hair back from her hot face. "We must go on, Christy."

"I can't." She looked up at him. "Take Clyde and go on. Find Matt and tell him..." She leaned her face into Hassan's shoulder.

He held her. He rested his face against her hair. I wanted time for us, he silently told her. I wanted to make love to you, Christy. I wanted to feel your body under mine. I wanted to kiss every inch of your ivory skin and feel myself inside you. I wanted to hear you whisper my name and tell me that I pleased you. He sighed as he kissed her hot temple. Then he got up, pulled the blanket out of the saddle bag and draped it over their heads.

Hassan tried to rouse her when the sun began to go down. He held the canteen against her lips, but she didn't respond. He got up and lifted Christy. His own strength was fading, but with the last bit of effort he managed to place her over the saddle. Then he drank from the canteen, gathered up the reins and said. "All right, Clyde, let's get moving."

Keep moving. Think about Christy, about holding her in your arms. Think about how it will be. He glanced back at her jeans-clad legs dangling over the saddle. I won't let her wear those damn things, he told himself. She will wear a robe and a veil. But nothing under the robe. That will be our secret. To the world she will look proper; only I will know of the beauty hidden beneath her robe. I'm going to take her home with me, home to Marrakesh.

Hassan licked his dry and swollen lips. He thought of the green sloping lawn of the gardens and the trees and how when the evenings were warm he would take Christy down to the swimming pool that was hidden by willow trees. They would swim naked in the moonlight, and afterward he would lay her down on the sweet-smelling grass and with her body still wet from the water he'd make slow and wonderful love to her.

Water. Hassan staggered and almost fell.

"I'm going to make love to you, Christy," he mumbled. "Going to kiss every inch of your sweet body. Going..."

Hassan fell to his knees. When he stood, it seemed to him that he could see the pool, there, just ahead of him.

He rubbed his hand across his eyes. Fool, he thought, you are a dying fool, Hassan Ben Kadiri. That's not a pool you see; it is only a mirage. Save your energy. It's almost dark. Lift Christy down. Hold her. Face the fact that it's over. Lie with her; die with her.

The pool shimmered in the setting sun. "Oh, hell," he said aloud as he headed for it, "what difference does it make whether it's real or not?" Then he stopped. He had already been fooled too many times today. He started in the other direction, but Clyde planted his four big feet in the sand and yanked his head. With a snort he headed for the mirage.

Hassan jerked on the reins, trying to turn the animal in the other direction. But it didn't do any good; Clyde was going where he wanted to, and nothing was going to stop him. Christy could have handled him. She'd have boxed his ears with her hat. She'd have . . .

"This is some mirage, Clyde," Hassan told the camel. "There are even trees. It . . ." The scene swam before his eyes. It tipped and swayed as his hands tightened around Clyde's reins. Dry sobs cracked his throat. "It's all right, Christy," he told her, though he knew she was past hearing. "It's all right, my love."

She dreamed that she was submerged in water. It was a lovely dream, one she never wanted to awaken from. Then someone slapped her.

"Christy!" he said. "Come on, Christy!"

She opened her eyes and looked up at Hassan. He stood waist-deep in water; the part of him that she could see was naked. He scooped up water in one hand and held it to her lips. She'd never tasted anything so good. When she drank her fill Hassan said, "How do you feel?"

"Shaky." She shook her head, trying to clear it. "Where are we?" Her voice was hoarse. "How did we get here?"

"We found an oasis," Hassan told her. "I thought it was a mirage. I almost turned away, but Clyde got wind of the water. Even you couldn't have held him back once he made up his mind this was where he wanted to go."

Christy turned and looked to where the camel stood under one of the palm trees, grazing from a large patch of grass. "Good old Clyde," she said with a smile. And to Hassan she said, "I didn't think we'd make it. Thank you for saving my life, Hassan."

He smoothed the wet hair back from her face. "There are plenty of dates here. And we have enough rice for a meal or two. Are you hungry?"

"I'm starving." Christy stepped away from him, suddenly wondering if he was naked all over. She wasn't, not quite. He'd left her bra and panties on.

She dipped down under the water, almost glad for the sunburn, which hid her flush of embarrassment.

When they came out of the water—she was relieved to see that Hassan still wore his shorts—she realized how weak she was. Hassan led her to the shade of a tree. "You rest here," he said. "I will start a fire and fix the rice."

"Thanks, Hassan. I guess I'm more done in than I thought." He nodded, and she watched him move away from her. His skin was dark; his shoulders were muscular, his legs long and strong and well shaped. His beard seemed only to enhance his masculinity.

With a small sigh of contentment, Christy closed her eyes. She didn't know what miracle had brought them to this place, but she thanked God that they were safe. She must have dozed, because when she awoke Hassan was beside her. She sat up, then, remembering she wore only her bra and panties, looked around for her clothing.

"Here, put your T-shirt on." Hassan handed it to her. "You can dress when it's cooler." He gave her a small bowl of rice, then sat cross-legged on the sand beside her.

Christy pulled the shirt over her head. It came just to the tops of her thighs, but she was too hungry to argue with Hassan and demand her jeans. She was alive and she was hungry; modesty could wait.

They slept that night under the date palm trees. The blanket was spread upon the sand; Hassan's burnoose covered them. Christy fell asleep almost as soon as she closed her eyes. She knew that Hassan pulled her close so that her head rested on the hollow of his shoulder and that his bare skin felt smooth under her cheek. She spread her fingers through the patch of his chest hair. Hassan, she thought, Hassan. Then she closed her eyes and went peacefully to sleep.

Hassan knew that they could not stay here for more than a few days, for even though there was water, there was not enough food to sustain them for long. Tomorrow they would finish the last of the rice; then there would be only the dates. He kissed the top of Christy's head. We have made it this far, he thought. Perhaps that means our luck has changed. We will rest and refresh ourselves, then move on. If his calculations were right, they were still four or five days from Bir Lahlou. If they could make it that far... Hassan's arms tightened around her, then he, too, slept.

Christy was in the pool when he awoke. He rolled to his side and watched her, leaning on one elbow. Clad in the wisp of lace that was her bra and the panties that he couldn't see, she stood waist-deep in the water. Her back was toward him, lovely and lean, and her red-gold hair flowed loose over her shoulders.

How lovely she is, Hassan thought, how brave, how dear. He felt the passion rise, but mixed with it was an overwhelming tenderness. He knew that he wanted to make love to Christy more than he had ever wanted anything in his life but that he wouldn't unless it was something she wanted, too.

Hassan got up and went to the pool. Christy heard him, and she turned and said, "Good morning, Hassan. Isn't this wonderful?" With a smile she scooped water up with both her hands and splashed him. "Doesn't that feel good? Can we stay here forever?"

"Almost forever." His dark eyes searched her face. "You are better, aren't you?"

"Yes, I feel wonderful. Did you sleep well?"

How could I not with you in my arms? Hassan wanted to say. With the thought of how she had felt so close to him last night, of the way her hair had spread loose on his chest, he tensed with passion. He had to touch her; he had to.... He put his hand on her arm and, moving closer, said, "Christy, oh, Christy."

She took a deep breath and held it, afraid to move, afraid to breathe. His hand went up to her shoulder, then her throat. He cupped her face with his hands and drew her closer. She looked into his dark eyes and saw the passion there, and the question. She tried to speak his name and couldn't. Instead she put her hands on his shoulders.

Hassan looked down at her for a moment, then with a low cry he pulled her into his arms and kissed her.

Christy melted against him. Her lips parted. Hassan ran his tongue over them, then quickly found the warmth of her mouth. Her tongue answered his, and his arms tightened around her.

"I have wanted you since that first day you walked into my home," he said against her ear. "You were so businesslike, so proper. So unbelievably lovely." He reached around her back to unfasten the wisp of lace that covered her. When she put her hand on his wrist as though to stop him, he said, "No, Christy, I have to touch you."

He tossed the bra up on the bank, then his hands circled her waist. He held her a little away from him so that he could look at her. Her breasts were small but perfectly rounded, the small tips the color of a talisman rose. For a long moment Hassan only looked at her, then he bent and began to kiss first one breast, then the other.

Her eyes closed, Christy clung to him for support as wave after wave of pleasure swept through her. She had never felt like this before, hadn't known that a man's touch could excite her so. His hands, dark against the ivory of her skin, held her breasts poised and ready. With his thumb and first finger he caressed one while he gently caught a rosy tip between his teeth to lap and tease until Christy was weak with desire.

"Oh, stop," she whispered. "Hassan, please...."

Without taking his mouth from her breast, he reached behind her to caress her sleek wet length. Moving lower, he cupped her buttocks, his hands warm and strong as he slid them under the silken fabric to touch the coolness of her skin and urge her against him.

Their bodies melded together, one to the other. She could feel the beat of his heart and the whole long length of him against her. His lips found hers and she clung to him. Nothing else mattered, because there was nothing else, only the two of them, here in this desert oasis. Yesterday she had almost died; today she was more alive than she'd ever been in her life.

Christy's arms went around his back, urging him closer as she stood on tiptoe, opened her lips, welcoming him, her tongue dancing against his as he fit his body tightly to hers.

Suddenly Hassan let her go. He looked down into her eyes, then without a word he picked her up and carried her out of the water. When he laid her down on the soft grass beneath the palms he leaned over her. "Tell me," he said. "Tell me you want me as much as I want you."

"Oh, I do, Hassan. I do."

He kissed her again, gathering her into his arms, holding her close, reveling in the coolness of her body against his. He sat up and stripped off his shorts. He bent over her, feasting on the wonder of her body, knowing that soon he would possess her. With a sigh he kissed her eyes, her nose, the corners of her mouth, then slowly moved down her throat to her breasts and once again began to kiss and gently suckle, while his hand, big and dark against her skin, caressed her and slowly moved down to part her legs.

Christy tensed. He raised his head from her breast, kissed the side of her face and said, "It's all right, my love. I won't hurt you."

She turned her face into his shoulder, trying to hold back the small moan that escaped as his fingers caressed her through the thin silk. Without even knowing that she did, she turned to him, sighing with pleasure, her body on fire with need.

"Hassan," she whispered. "Oh, Hassan." She raised her hips so that he could slide the panties down her legs.

He touched her flesh and her body ached with need. "Oh, Christy," he said. "I want you. I want you."

Then he was over her, in her, and she cried his name and said, "Yes, darling. Please, yes."

His big body quivered with pleasure as he moved deeper within her. His mouth found hers, his arms tightened around her and he rocked her slender body close to his.

Wave after wave of ecstasy swept through Christy. There was no reality. She and Hassan were one, and it was good. It was so good. The sun shimmering down through the palm fronds made patterns of light and shadow on his back. Christy caressed his shoulders; she whispered his name and told him she loved what he was doing to her as she lifted her body to his to meet his thrusts with answering thrusts.

Suddenly it wasn't enough. Christy knew she couldn't bear it another second. Her hands tightened on Hassan's shoulders; her nails dug into his skin as she rubbed her face into the matted hair of his chest.

Hassan's arms tightened around her. "Christy?" he questioned against her lips. "Yes, Christy?"

But before she could answer, the world exploded into millions of glittering pieces, up into the golden sky, taking her higher and higher until it was past bearing. She sought his mouth; she cried out and felt him convulse with pleasure.

Slowly, holding each other close, they drifted back to earth. Hassan kissed her lips. He told her how lovely she was and knew in his heart that he would never let her go.

Chapter 10

If ever there had been a perfect day, Christy thought, this was it, a day so pefect that everything that had gone before paled in comparison. She and Hassan had known each other for over a month, and for all of that time this feeling had been simmering just beneath the surface of their emotions. They'd held back, for their own reasons, reasons that seemed so unimportant now. Yesterday they'd been close to death; today they were more alive than they'd ever been before.

When they breakfasted on dates, Hassan insisted on feeding Christy. He held each date to her lips, and every time she took one his fingers lingered. This is my dream, she thought as she gazed into his dark eyes. This is what I've longed for from the moment I met him. Soon he will lay me down beneath the trees and make love to me again. She kissed his fingers and with a shaking sigh said, "Now I'll feed you."

Hassan gazed at her in wonder as she held the fruit to his lips. He took the date the first time, but when she offered him the next one he took her fingers into his mouth and slowly caressed each one with his tongue. He saw the flush come to her cheeks as her lips parted. He knew that she was once again aroused. He had only to gather her in his arms and she would be willingly, meltingly his.

But Hassan waited, because there was an excitement in the waiting when he knew that soon he would lose himself in her embrace.

There has never been a woman like Christy, Hassan thought as he gazed at her. He knew he'd never understand her, because she was so many women rolled into one. She was strong willed, independent and determined to have her own way. He'd been sure he'd have the devil's own time trying to tame her. This morning when she started to pull the T-shirt on over her panties he'd said, "No, Christy, I want to be able to look at you." She'd hesitated. He'd seen the flush creep into her cheeks, and he waited for her to lift her chin and defy him. Instead her eyes had softened and without a word she had laid the T-shirt aside.

Hassan delighted in looking at her. She was so slender, so gently curved, her waist so slender he could span it with his two hands. Her small breasts were high and proud, the rose-pink tips erect and waiting. His eyes lingered on them, and he felt a fire in his loins because he knew that in a little while he would taste them.

Hassan had told himself in the beginning that he wouldn't fall in love with Christy, because they were from different worlds, but he *had* fallen in love with her. This was their Eden; he wouldn't think about tomorrow or all the tomorrows to come. Christy was his, for as long as they were in the desert. That was all that mattered.

Now Hassan looked at her and, leaning his back against one of the palms, he said, "Tell me about when you were a little girl."

"What do you want to know?"

"Everything."

Her lips curved in a smile. "I was too skinny," she said. "I didn't like chocolates."

"No? Then what did you like?"

"Olives. I used to spend all my allowance on olives. But when they sent me away I didn't have an allowance, and anyway, the teachers wouldn't let me go shopping alone."

"You said you were seven when your family sent you to school? Why couldn't you have gone to school in Montana?"

"Aunt Margaret was..." Christy hesitated. "She was a nervous woman, Hassan. She'd never had children of her own, and I guess she just didn't know what to do with me. It was different with Matt, because he was older. She and Uncle Albert kept him with them until he was twelve, then he went to military school."

"What about your father? Did you see much of him when you were younger?"

Christy shook her head. "He was in South America when I was with Aunt Margaret and Uncle Albert. When I was older—in school, I mean—he went with a mining company in Torreon; that's in Mexico. By the time I went to college he'd come back to Colorado and gone into business with Uncle Albert." There was no self-pity in her voice as she spoke of her past, no hint of recrimination for the father who'd been too busy for her.

Christy went on, telling him tales of her school days and of her vacations in Colorado with her brother, Matt. Hassan watched her as she talked, wondering how a child who had been raised without love could have grown into

a woman so filled with love. Only her brother had been
there for her in those lonely childhood years. No wonder
she had been devastated at his disappearance, no wonder
she was so determined to find him. Matthew Chambers
had been the only one who had cared about her; he was
all the family she'd ever had.

Hassan put his arms around her and held her without
speaking. Tomorrow they would have to think about
leaving this place, because they could not subsist for long
on a diet of dates and water. But he would not think about
that; today belonged to them.

He took Christy's hand and together they went to the
pool to bathe. When they stood waist-deep in the water,
Hassan ran his hands over her naked body, slowly, sensuously, memorizing every sweet curve and secret place,
reveling in the feel of her and the softness of her skin.
When he kissed her he said, "Will you touch me, Christy?
Will you touch me, love?"

She looked up at him, her lower lip caught between her
teeth, then with a shaking breath ran her hands down his
flat stomach, around the narrow hips, and lower, to the
apex of his legs with a touch as soft as a butterfly's wings.

"Christy, oh, Christy." He crushed her to him. He
murmured her name against her lips and spoke in a language Christy didn't understand. But the timbre and passion in his voice sent thrills of pleasure through her body.
She moved closer to him, loving the taste of his mouth and
the long, hard feel of him against her naked body. Hassan, she thought, my love, my love.

He picked her up and carried her out of the pool, laid
her down on his burnoose and knelt beside her.

"I wish you could see how you look," he said in a low
voice. "Your skin is the color of a Reubens painting." He

smiled. "But you are shapelier than his women were; your breasts are smaller."

Christy reached up to pull him closer. "Come make love to me," she whispered.

But Hassan shook his head. "Not yet, Christy." He touched the tip of one breast, then slowly rolled it between his fingers. "I love the way your eyes widen when you are aroused," he said. "I love the quick little breaths you take and the way you say my name." He kissed her breast. "You are so lovely, my Christy. I don't think I will ever get my fill of you."

She cupped his head and, drawing him down to her, whispered, "Kiss me, Hassan."

His eyes blazed with a slumbering passion. "I will kiss you, Christy. I will kiss every lovely inch of you before the day is over."

His lips met hers with a fierceness, a possessiveness, that almost frightened her. He ground his mouth against hers; he found her tongue and fought a silken duel. When Christy was breathless with desire he let her go. She looked up into his desert eyes as he stroked the hair back from her face. He kissed her again, more gently this time, and caught her lower lip between his teeth to taste and tease. He nibbled the corners of her mouth and nuzzled her ear.

Then Hassan looked at her, took both of her hands in one of his and raised them over her head. Christy's back arched; her breasts were poised and ready.

Trembling now, she closed her eyes, waiting for that first brush of his lips against her skin.

"My darling American," he said. He kissed her breasts tenderly, then caught one peak between his teeth to gently pull and scrape until Christy said, "No, please..." and tried to free her captured hands.

But Hassan held her as he moved to the other breast. This time Christy moaned aloud and when she did he said, "Ah, Christy, how I love to hear you do that."

He let her go, kissing the hands that he had held. He lay down beside her, turned her on her side, rested his head against her arm and began to gently suckle her breasts. All the while he caressed the other breast, rolling the tip between his thumb and first finger, then tugging gently until Christy was weak with pleasure.

"Hassan," she whispered. "Please, darling. . . ." She yearned her body to his. "Now, please. I can't wait. I can't . . ."

"I love the taste of you, Christy. I love to feel you tremble like this." He kissed her mouth.

When he raised his lips from hers he looked at her for a moment, then with a sigh he began a torturous journey down and across her rib cage to her stomach. His lips were warm, his touch was soft, as he made his way down to her thighs. Gently he turned them so that he could kiss the tender inner flesh.

"No, no more," Christy pleaded. "I can't bear it, Hassan. I—"

"Be still, my love," he said against her flesh. While she trembled under his touch he spread her thighs, and before Christy could stop him he found the secret core of her.

With a cry of protest Christy tried to move away, but he held her. His mouth was so warm, his tongue so silken.

Christy was lost, disoriented, unable to think. Her body was on fire with longing as she whispered his name in a litany of want and need.

When he reached to touch her breasts she couldn't hold back. Her body arched up and she cried his name. She was totally his now, past reason or conscious thought, carried higher and higher on a tide of passion she'd never known before.

"Hassan," she whispered. "Oh, Hassan." Her body quivered like a leaf in the wind and his hands left her breasts to sooth and calm her. But all the while his mouth, his warm, sweet mouth, continued the lovely torture.

Suddenly he let her go and came up over her. With a cry he raised her hips and drove himself into her.

Through eyes half blinded by ecstasy, Christy looked up at him. His head was thrown back, the cords of his neck were strained, his lips pulled back to show his strong white teeth as his hands tightened on her shoulders. For a moment a shock of fear ran through her. It was too wild, too primitive, too... Oh, God, she'd never known such ecstasy. She lifted her body to his, lost in him, flesh of his flesh now, in these final moments.

Suddenly, like a bolt of lightning streaking across the desert sky, their bodies exploded and shattered in a kaleidoscope of wondrous passion. They clung together, not wanting this moment to end, heart beating against heart as they kissed and whispered each other's names.

Slowly they floated back to earth. But Hassan didn't leave her. He kissed her lips, her throat and her shoulders, and in silence he stroked her until at last, love filled and drowsy, her head in the hollow of his shoulder, she fell asleep.

That night they ate the last of the rice. "You know that we can't stay here," Hassan said.

"I know." Christy looked out beyond the oasis to the endless stretch of sand. She would never forget this quiet place or this time when she had begun to fall in love with Hassan Ben Kadiri. She didn't know what would happen to them when they left the oasis; she knew only that her life was in his hands and that even if she perished in the desert she would not regret setting out on this trip. She loved Hassan, and she thanked God for giving them this time together.

She turned to him, took his hand and said, "Let's stay just one more day, Hassan."

"All right, Christy. If that's what you want we'll leave tomorrow evening. We'll fill all of the canteens and take as many dates as Clyde can carry."

Hassan kept his voice matter-of-fact. They had four canteens; he didn't think they could make it all the way to Bir Lahlou unless they were lucky enough to find another oasis or stumble on a village. But he wouldn't tell Christy that.

That night Hassan watered the camel, then he spread his burnoose under the palms. They lay down together, side by side. This is the last night we'll spend here, Christy thought as Hassan took her hand. She looked up through the fronds at the starlit sky and knew this was the closest to heaven she'd ever been. She raised herself on her elbow and, looking down at him, slowly traced the line of his eyebrows, then under his eyes and down the length of his nose.

"It's a nice nose," Christy said, almost to herself. "Not too straight and not too broad." She ran her fingers across his mustache, then moved down to smooth his beard. "You look like a desert warrior," she told him. "Fierce and wild, ready to ride into battle, to slay dragons and ravish women."

"Only the ones with green eyes," he said.

"That's nice to know." Christy kissed him, smiling against his lips. Then her smile faded and the kiss became more intense. Hassan pulled her up over him, holding her close as he ran his hands up and down the length of her back.

"I love the feel of your body, Hassan," she whispered against his lips. "I love the warmth and the scent of your skin. I love to feel your arms around me."

With a hoarse cry Hassan lifted her onto his flanks. Christy looked at him, her eyes widening, realizing that he wanted her to take the lead. Her white teeth clamped down on her lower lip; she hesitated, then lowered herself on him and began to move. In the clear light of the stars she could see his face. He closed his eyes for a moment, then he opened them and reached for her breasts.

With a cry of delight Christy quickened her pace, moving closer. Her hands on his shoulders, she gave her breasts shamelessly, joyously, delighting in the feel of his body under hers and the warmth of his hands against her skin. She was all his now, frantic with desire, wanting to please him as he had pleased her. Her red-gold hair splayed across his chest, and he took great handfuls of it to rub against his face.

When his body arched to hers and he groaned with need she slowed her pace, because she wanted this to last. But suddenly he gripped her waist, holding her close while he plunged against her.

It was too much; it was past bearing. Christy's hands tightened on his shoulders and she cried his name as he pulled her down to him, to cover her mouth with his, to cry his cry of passion against her lips and tell her that she belonged to him now and that nothing would ever be this good again.

Christy collapsed against him, quivering in the aftermath of love as he caressed her. When at last she made as though to move from him Hassan said, "No, love, stay with me. Cover me. I want to feel your body on mine." He kissed her shoulder, smoothed the long line of her back and held her until she slept.

* * *

They had just come out of the pool the next morning when Hassan saw the cloud of dust on the horizon. He stared at it for a moment, then with a glad cry shouted, "Riders! They're coming this way."

Christy looked at him, scarcely believing what he said until she saw the camels emerging from the cloud. "I...I can't believe it. This means..." She threw her arms around him and began to cry. "We're going to be all right now, aren't we? They'll have food; they'll take us to a village. Oh, Hassan, Hassan, we're going to be all right."

He grinned down at her. "They're going to be here in a very few minutes. If I were you I'd get dressed."

Christy looked down. She'd gotten so used to wearing only her panties that for a moment she'd forgotten how she looked. Now with a squeal of dismay she grabbed her jeans and T-shirt and quickly pulled them on.

Hassan put on his boots and his burnoose and strode to the edge of the oasis as the riders grew closer. As they drew near, a shout went up. He saw the men now, ten of them, and he saw the rifles they raised above their heads. With a feeling of unease he started to reach for the gun he kept in his boot, then he straightened. A handgun would do little good against ten rifles.

Their robes were black, their faces dark from the sun. When they reined in, one of them motioned the others back, and urging his mount closer, he looked down at Hassan and said, "This is my oasis. What are you doing here?"

Hassan glared up at him. "My wife and I were taking a caravan to Bir Lahlou," he said. "We were caught in a *shergi*, the wind of the desert. We lost two of our camels, then our drivers deserted. It was only by luck that we found this oasis." His voice was ironic. "We didn't know it belonged to you."

"Well, it does." The man whacked the camel across the knees and slid down to the sand. He looked around, and when he saw Christy standing by one of the trees he looked at her curiously. "She is your wife?" he asked Hassan.

Hassan nodded. He glanced over his shoulder and with a motion of his head said, "Come here, woman."

Christy stared at him, not understanding the tone of his voice. Slowly she came forward to stand beside him.

"She is English?" the man asked Hassan.

"No, she is an American."

"An infidel." The man's face hardened. "You allow her to wear pants?"

"They were more convenient for travel. In our home in Marrakesh she wears robes, of course." He offered his hand. "Hassan Ben Kadiri," he said. "My wife's name is Christine."

"I am Ameen al-Shaibi, and these are my men. Our camp is a two-day ride from here." He motioned for his men to dismount and shouted orders that the camels were to be watered and that a fire was to be started for their midday meal. "Do you have food?" he asked Hassan.

"We have had only the dates today. Yesterday we finished the last of our rice."

"Then it is a lucky thing for you I came along. You and your woman are welcome to eat with us."

Your woman! Christy glared at the man. He was tall and broad. He had dark, piercing eyes, heavy brows, a nose that had been broken at least twice and a long, drooping mustache. He looked tough and he looked mean.

While two of the dark-robed men prepared a meal, Ameen motioned Hassan to sit with him. Hassan glanced quickly at Christy. "Sit there, by the tree," he told her. "I will bring you something."

"But—"

"Do as you are told. This isn't the time to argue." He turned his back on her and went to sit cross-legged across from Ameen al-Shaibi.

Christy stared after him, hands on her hips, as angry and as hurt as she'd ever been in her life. This was the man she thought she'd fallen in love with, and he was behaving...he was behaving like a chauvinistic Arab! She sat down and glared at his back. When the meal—dried meat, rice, bread and coffee—was ready, Hassan brought it to her.

In a low voice he said, "These men are nomads, Christy. If I don't appear every bit as tough as they are, God only knows what will happen to us. Especially to you. I am thinking of your safety, my dear. Please trust me." He hesitated, then his voice grew firm. "For as long as we're with them I want you to try to act like a proper Arab wife. That means you will speak when you are spoken to and when I tell you do something you will do it. Is that clear?"

"Very clear."

Hassan looked down at her and his dark eyes softened. "It's only until we are safe, Christy. I promise you that." Before she could answer he turned away.

The other men stared at Christy, curious. She dropped her gaze and tried to look the way she thought an Arabian woman ought to look.

When the men finished their meal Hassan called to her. "Clean up this mess," he said. "Wash the plates in the pond."

Christy glared at him. She opened her mouth, then snapped it shut. She gathered the tin plates and with her back straight as a stick marched to the pond and washed them. When she came back Hassan was still huddled with Ameen al-Shaibi. He motioned her over and said, "Ameen has graciously decided that we will accompany him and his men tonight. See that you fill the canteens and are ready to leave in a few hours."

"Yes, O great one," she said in English. Tears stung her eyes as she turned away. Oh, damn it, she thought. Damn it anyway. For a little while she'd tried to pretend that Hassan was different, but she knew now that he wasn't. He was from a culture where men took it for granted that they were superior to women. It was inbred in him, a part of his heritage, and nothing would ever change the way he felt. He'd told her that he had to act this way for her own safety, but deep down in her bones Christy knew it wasn't an act. This was the real Hassan; the other man, the man who had held her in his arms had only been an illusion.

Chapter 11

Ameen al-Shaibi, with Hassan beside him, rode at the head of his men. Christy rode at the rear of the column with the pack animals. A little before sunrise they stopped, and when Hassan came back to her and said, "Are you all right?" Christy glared at him.

"What difference does it make how I am, you—you Arab you!"

Hassan took hold of her arm. "Take it easy," he warned. "I don't know these men, and they don't know me. They are suspicious of us. They didn't want Ameen to take us along."

"I wish he hadn't. I wish he'd left us at the oasis."

"We wouldn't have lasted long if he had, Christy." Hassan's face softened. "Please," he said, "go along with this. Do what I tell you, and for God's sake, try to be inconspicuous."

"Like a proper Moroccan woman?" Her voice was contemptuous.

"Yes." Hassan's hand tightened on her arm. "I have heard stories about Ameen al-Shaibi. He is a powerful and a dangerous man, a cutthroat and a bandit. He can be a good friend or a bad enemy. I have told him you are my wife."

"You had no right to do that." Christy tried to pull away from him.

"I told him you are my wife," Hassan went on as though he hadn't heard her, "and unless you want him to pass you around among his men, you will act like my wife for as long as we're with him."

Christy stared up at him, unable to believe his words.

"This isn't Montana," Hassan said. "Nor is it Casablanca or Marrakesh. This is the desert, Christy. Civilized rules don't apply here. So for as long as we're with Ameen, you are my wife. Do you understand?"

She swallowed. There was no mistaking the seriousness in his voice. If this was a game, it was a deadly one.

"What . . . what about Bir Lahlou?" she asked.

"I don't know. I haven't mentioned it yet. I will, after we have been in Ameen's camp for a while."

"A while? How long is a while?"

Before Hassan could answer one of the men yelled, "*Yallah, yallah,* it is time to move on." Quickly Hassan put his hand against the side of Christy's face. "Drink some water from your canteen," he said. "We will probably ride until early noon, then rest." He hesitated. "Try to hold on, Christy. We're all right now, and we will continue to be all right if you do what I say. Things will be better once we reach Ameen's camp."

Christy looked at Hassan's retreating back, then she climbed onto the saddle and, urging Clyde up, said, "Here we go again, sport."

In the late afternoon they reached another oasis. It was small and there were only a few trees, but there was water. Once again Christy sat apart from the men, waiting until Hassan brought her a plate of food. And once again she cleaned the plates when the men finished eating.

When Ameen and his men stretched out under the trees, Hassan motioned Christy to a tree at the side of the pond. "We will rest here for a few hours," he told her. He spread a blanket on the sand, and when she didn't move he said, "Well?"

Christy lay down and turned her back to him. For a moment Hassan didn't speak. At last he said, "You had better get used to this, because, for a while at least, this is the way it is going to be." When she didn't answer he put his hand on her waist. "The desert is a different world, Christy. Men like Ameen make their own laws. They have lived the same way for hundreds of years, and nothing will ever change them. A woman is a second-class citizen here. Her duty is to keep her husband's tent clean, to cook his food and take care of his children."

Hassan's hand tightened on her waist. "It will be different when we're alone, Christy. But when we are with the others, you must act as the other women act. When I tell you to do something you must do it."

Hassan waited, and when still Christy didn't speak, he said, "I know this is a strange and different world for you, my dear. I will make it as easy as I can. Sleep now. We're going to travel most of the night. Ameen says that we should reach the nomad camp by tomorrow afternoon."

A different world, Christy thought. Can I adjust? How can I pretend to be someone other than who I am? She almost turned to Hassan then. She wanted to say, I'm afraid. This is all so strange to me and I don't understand it. I don't understand the way you are when you're with these other men. I think I love you, and that frightens me too, because I don't want to be the kind of a woman you expect me to be.

But she heard his even breathing and knew that he was asleep. So she didn't give voice to all the fears that were in her heart.

It was almost evening of the next day before they reached the nomad camp of Ameen al-Shaibi. Shouts went up when the riders came into view; both men and women rushed out to greet them. Christy drew back on the reins to slow Clyde as she looked around her at this city of black tents in the middle of nowhere. Tall palms grew alongside two spring-fed pools. There were other trees, fig and date palms, desert juniper, a sprinkling of flowers and small shrubs where goats and sheep grazed. To one side of the pool, under a canopy of black canvas, horses grazed.

Suddenly the crowd that had rushed out to greet the travelers grew silent. They stared up at Christy, then began whispering among themselves. Silent big-eyed children gaped at her. The women, many of whom wore no veil, pointed to her jeans and laughed. One, with a tattoo on her forehead and cheeks, reached out and touched Christy's leg. She tugged at the material, then turned to shout something to her friends.

Christy muttered an oath and jerked her leg back. With that Hassan jumped off his camel and hurried to her. He forced Clyde to kneel so that Christy could dismount. "This is my woman," he said to the women who surrounded her. "She is not used to our ways, and it would be a great service to me if you could teach her."

One stepped forward. She was of medium height, and although she didn't wear a veil, her head and forehead were covered by a black cheesecloth type of material. She wore a dark blue robe, a blue stone in one nostril, and there were rings on every one of her fingers. She looked at Christy, then, pointing to herself, said, "I am Zohra, the wife of Ameen al-Shaibi. *Marhaban*, welcome."

"*Shukran*," Christy said, "thank you." She glanced at Hassan. "What did you say to her?"

"I said it would be a great service if she would teach you our ways." And to Zohra he said, "My wife is tired now, but tomorrow I would like to see her dressed properly."

"Of course, sir, I will see to it."

"*Shukran*." Hassan bowed, and to Christy he said, "Now follow me, and don't speak unless you are spoken to."

So angry she couldn't speak, Christy did as she was told. She waited silently while Hassan spoke to Ameen. The man nodded, then said something to one of the other women. The woman led them to a black tent. She indicated that they were to enter and that she would return with water and food.

The tent top was too low for her to stand erect. Scattered Persian rugs and an array of pillows covered the ground. To one side there was a chest on which there were a teakettle, several battered pots, one plate and two cups. Home sweet home, Christy thought as she gazed around her. With a sigh she sank down on one of the pillows. She was more tired than she'd ever been in her life; every bone in her body ached. She was bewildered; she didn't understand any of this, the people, this place. Now she truly felt as though she were in another century, a century that frightened her.

She was almost asleep when two women appeared with bowls of food. Hassan thanked them, and when they had gone he said, "Tomorrow Zohra will teach you to cook."

"I know how to cook," Christy said indignantly.

"Over a campfire? On a spit?" His lips curved in a mocking smile. "There are no microwaves here, Christy. You will have to learn to do things the way nomads do them."

She frowned at him, then began to eat without speaking. When they finished Hassan lowered the sides of the tent. It was dark inside now, and Christy could barely see him as he turned to her.

"We must sleep," he said in a gentle voice. When Christy didn't answer he put his arms on her shoulders. "I know there are many things you don't understand, Christy. I can only ask you to trust me and to believe that I want what is best for you." He knelt, pulling her down to the rug with him.

"I'm tired," she said in a cold voice.

"I know." Hassan lay down beside her and, putting his arms around her, said, "Sleep, then. We will talk about this in the morning."

Christy lay rigid in his arms. When she tried to move away his arms tightened. At last, exhausted, she slept.

But Hassan didn't. He lay for a long time, his face against hers, feeling her breath against his skin. He didn't know how long they were going to be here in this desert camp, whether it would be days or weeks or months, but he knew that for as long as they were here Christy would belong to him.

He had been born in a place like this, and for him it was like coming home. But it would be hard for Christy. He would do everything he could to make it easier for her, but he couldn't change the customs of his people. Christy had no choice; she had to adapt to life in this nomad camp.

When she awoke she was lying on her side, her back to Hassan. His arms were around her and when she stirred he covered her breasts with his hands. "No," she mur-

mured, still half asleep. But Hassan didn't answer. He
caressed her, cupping her breasts, then soothing with fingers that reached for the tender peaks. She tried to squirm
away from him, but when she did he held her closer, tight
against his thighs. His hands were warm, his fingers teas-
ingly persistent. Little by little, in spite of herself, Christy
felt a small tickle of flame flare within her. Then the flame
grew and she barely smothered a moan.

Hassan kissed her neck. He touched the soft skin behind her ear with his tongue, then gently nipped the lobe.
And all the while his fingers caressed and teased the
swollen peaks of her breasts.

I won't respond, Christy told herself even as she moved
closer. Then Hassan was inside her, moving slowly,
deeply, his body tight to hers. He whispered her name. He
told her how soft she was and how good it felt to join his
body to hers. He told her she belonged to him and that he
would never let her go. He moved faster, urging Christy
closer. The breath rasped in his throat and she grew excited, knowing that she excited him. Her hands tightened
on his; she matched his rhythm with her movements. Then
suddenly, in a low anguished whisper, he said, "Now,
Christy? Now?"

"Yes, oh yes, oh…" She covered her mouth so that she
wouldn't cry out. His arms tightened around her; he buried his face in her neck, and together they tumbled over
the precipice of passion.

Christy hated the long white robe and the scarf that hid
her hair. Covered from head to toe, only her face and her
bare feet showing, she felt swathed in cloth.

Zohra had come that morning and led Christy to a sec-
tion of the pool that was hidden from the camp by a stand
of trees. When Christy had bathed, Zohra had handed her

a clean white robe. Christy had shaken her head and demanded her blue jeans and T-shirt. Zohra had shaken her own head and shoved the robe at Christy.

"Damn!" Christy had exploded, but when Zohra took a step forward Christy said, "Okay, okay," and put the robe on. Then Zohra covered her hair with a piece of blue silk. She stood back, looking Christy up and down, and gave a grunt of approval. "Now we cook," she said.

Even with a microwave Christy had never been able to prepare a decent meal. While most girls were learning culinary skills from their mothers, Christy had been in boarding school. In college she'd lived in a dormitory, and it wasn't until she moved back to Montana and got her own apartment that she had tried her hand at cooking. She'd been all thumbs at first, burning everything she cooked and making a mess of the kitchen. She'd finally learned to cook two things—meatloaf and spaghetti—but most of the time she ate out.

Now she was confronted with a charcoal brazier and a cooking teacher who shouted at her in a language she didn't understand. She burned the lamb, dropped the shish kebab into the burning coals and the rice into the sand.

"I can't cook!" she wailed to Hassan. "I'll never learn. If we ever get out of here I'll never set foot in a kitchen as long as I live. I'll eat cereal and tuna fish sandwiches. I'll—"

He stopped her words with a kiss. "You are getting better," he said. "The lamb wasn't half bad last night. Zohra says you are a good pupil."

"Zohra!" Christy groaned. "She hovers over me like a great, dark vulture. She shouts at me in a language I can't understand."

"Then it is time you did understand. From now on you are going to learn twenty words a day. You must be able to communicate with these people, Christy."

"But why? We're not going to be here forever, Hassan. We . . ." She took a deep breath. "How much longer do we have to stay here?"

Hassan shook his head. "I don't know, Christy. I talked to Ameen yesterday. I asked him if I could have a couple of men and enough supplies to get us to Bir Lahlou. He said it was out of the question, that perhaps later . . ." He hesitated. "I am sorry, Christy. I know how anxious you are to get to Bir Lahlou, and I think that eventually Ameen will let us go."

"Eventually!" Christy faced him. "My God, Hassan, what does that mean? Next week? Next month? Next year?"

"It means whenever Ameen decides the time is right," Hassan said. Then without a word he turned and left the tent.

The pattern of their days was much the same. Christy cooked Hassan's meals and washed his clothes. She began to learn Arabic and often sat around a campfire in the early evening, talking with the women. The women were curious about her, but it was the children who pressed close, looking up at Christy with inquisitive eyes. One night when she took the scarf off to adjust it one of the little girls touched her hair. She rubbed a strand of it as though trying to get the color out, then said, "Red! Your hair is red!" She turned her hennaed hands palm up. "Like my hands. Is your hair red to keep away the *jinn*?"

"The what?" Christy asked.

"The *jinn*," Zohra said, "the evil spirits. They don't like the smell of henna."

Christy said as best she could with her limited Arabic that no, her hair was not red to keep away the evil spirits, that she had been born with it and that it would always be that way. And she shook her head in wonder of the strange ways of these desert people.

That night when Christy left the women she sat in front of the tent she shared with Hassan. This was the time she liked best, this quiet time when the voices of children hushed and the women lowered the flaps of their tents and waited for their men. As she waited for Hassan.

Finally Christy went into their tent, and when she lowered the sides she bathed in the water she'd carried from the pond and then lay down to wait for Hassan. I'm changing, she thought. I'm becoming a part of this desert world. I cook, I wash clothes. I do things I've never dreamed of doing with a man who is different from any other man I've known. I don't belong here, yet in a strange way I feel myself becoming a part of it and of him.

When Hassan lifted the flap of the tent, he said, "Are you asleep?"

Christy raised herself on her elbow and looked at him through the half darkness. "No," she said, "I was waiting for you."

He pulled the robe over his head, then came to kneel beside her. "I saw you talking with the women tonight. Are they friendly toward you?"

Christy nodded. With a smile she said, "A little girl asked me if I put henna on my hair to keep away the *jinn*."

"Or to cast a spell on me," Hassan said. He leaned down, took a handful of her hair and rubbed it across his face. "You have cast a spell on me, Miss Christine Chambers," he whispered. "I love the scent of your hair, the silken feel of it against my skin." He pulled her into his arms. "Christy," he said, "oh, Christy."

They made love that night, as they did every night. And Christy could forget for a while that she was in a different place in a different time. She only knew that she was with Hassan, and for this night at least, that was all that mattered.

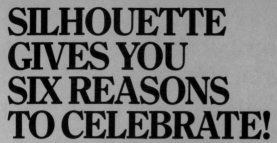

Yes, become a Silhouette subscriber and the celebration goes on forever.

To begin with, we'll send you:

- 4 new Silhouette Intimate Moments novels—FREE
- an elegant, purse-size manicure set—FREE
- and an exciting mystery bonus—FREE

And that's not all! Special extras— Three more reasons to celebrate.

4. Money-Saving Home Delivery. That's right! When you subscribe to Silhouette Intimate Moments, the excitement, romance and faraway adventures of these novels can be yours for previewing in the convenience of your own home. Here's how it works. Every month, we'll deliver four new books right to your door. If you decide to keep them, they'll be yours for only $2.25 each. That's 25¢ less per book than what you pay in stores. And there's **no charge for shipping and handling.**

5. Free Monthly Newsletter. It's the indispensable insider's look at our most popular writers and their up-coming novels. Now you can have a behind-the-scenes look at the fascinating world of Silhouette! It's an added bonus you'll look forward to every month!

6. More Surprise Gifts. Because our home subscribers are our most valued readers, we'll be sending you additional free gifts from time to time—as a token of our appreciation.

This beautiful manicure set will be a useful and elegant item to carry in your handbag. Its rich burgundy case is a perfect expression of your style and good taste. And it's yours free in this amazing Silhouette celebration!

SILHOUETTE INTIMATE MOMENTS®

FREE OFFER CARD

4 FREE BOOKS

ELEGANT MANICURE SET —FREE

FREE MYSTERY BONUS

PLACE YOUR BALLOON STICKER HERE!

MONEY-SAVING HOME DELIVERY

FREE FACT-FILLED NEWSLETTER

MORE SURPRISE GIFTS THROUGHOUT THE YEAR—FREE

Yes! Please send me my four Silhouette Intimate Moments novels **FREE**, along with my manicure set and my **free mystery gift.** Then send me four new Silhouette Intimate Moments novels every month and bill me just $2.25 per book (25¢ less than retial), with no extra charges for shipping and handling. If I am not completely satisfied, I may return a shipment and cancel at any time. **The free books, manicure set and mystery gift remain mine to keep.**

CBM017

NAME
_____
(PLEASE PRINT)

ADDRESS _____ APT. _____

CITY _____ STATE _____

ZIP _____

Terms and prices subject to change.
Your enrollment is subject to acceptance
by Silhouette Books.

SILHOUETTE "NO RISK GUARANTEE"
• There is no obligation to buy—the free books and gifts remain yours to keep.
• You pay the lowest price possible—and you receive books before they're available in stores.
• You may end your subscription anytime—just let us know.

PRINTED IN U.S.A.

FILL OUT THIS POSTPAID CARD AND MAIL TODAY!

Postage will be paid by addressee

BUSINESS REPLY MAIL
FIRST CLASS   PERMIT NO. 194   CLIFTON, N.J.

SILHOUETTE BOOKS
120 Brighton Road
P.O. Box 5084
Clifton, NJ 07015-9956

NO POSTAGE
NECESSARY
IF MAILED
IN THE
UNITED STATES

Chapter 12

Every morning Christy went to the pond to get water for coffee, then returned to make wheat cakes for the morning meal. When breakfast was finished she washed her and Hassan's clothes and spread them on the bushes to dry.

Without even being aware of it, she'd begun to settle into life in the nomad camp. Her command of the language grew so that now she understood almost everything that was said to her, and she enjoyed being a part of the nomad community. She'd even grown used to wearing a robe and having her hair bound.

But Christy would never get used to the subservient attitude of the women in the camp. Once she tried to speak to Zohra and the others, to tell them that they had rights, the same as their men had, and that they should demand to be treated as equals.

The horrified women looked at her as though she'd just landed from another planet. "Allah has stated that men are superior to women," they said. "What you are suggesting is wrong. You must never speak of it again."

It was hopeless, Christy thought. *I want to change them, but every day I'm becoming more like they are!*

One night Ameen al-Shaibi summoned Hassan to his tent. "I have been observing your woman. It seems to me that she is more obedient to you. How did this come about? Did you beat her?"

Barely repressing a smile, Hassan said, "No, but I spoke sternly to her and I threatened to beat her if she did not conform to our ways."

"Good," Ameen said with a nod. "But remember, spare the stick and spoil the wife."

"As it is written," Hassan said with a nod.

Ameen reached into his pocket for a cigarette and after he had lighted it he said, "I still don't understand why you would bring an American woman into the desert. You must have known that it would be a long and difficult trip to Bir Lahlou." He eyed Hassan suspiciously. "What is your real reason for this trip? Are you working for the government? Did they send you to rout me out?"

"If they had, al-Shaibi, I would not have dragged a woman with me."

Ameen's black eyes narrowed. "Ah, but maybe the government knew that having an American along would be a perfect cover for you. They have been trying to catch me for years, you know. They say the old ways are no more, that we of the desert should live like civilized men. How do I know that your story about taking the woman to Bir Lahlou is true? How do I know that in some way I don't understand you will lead the army to my camp?"

Ameen leaned closer. His lips tightened. In a low and ominous voice he said, "I have been biding my time, Hassan Ben Kadiri. Perhaps I should wait no longer.

Perhaps I should dispose of you and add the woman to my household. I have many enemies, rival tribes that are always ready to cut my throat. Now you are here, probably as a representative of your government, and I am suspicious that your motives are bad ones."

Hassan met the other man's gaze. He knew that from the moment Ameen and his men had picked them up he and Christy had been living on the thin edge. There had been times when he knew that all that had saved them was the nomad tradition that hospitality, even to an enemy, was a sacred duty. But Ameen al-Shaibi lived by his own laws. Any day now he might take it into his head to do away with him, Hassan, and keep Christy for himself. It was time to tell the nomad leader the truth.

"I am here representing my government," Hassan said. "But it is not you I have come to find."

"No?" Ameen reached inside his robe for the jeweled dagger he always carried. "Then suppose you tell me who it is you are looking for."

"I have told you that I was taking my woman to Bir Lahlou to search for her brother. That is true, but there is more."

Ameen's hand closed around the dagger. Hew drew it out and in a dangerous voice said, "Pray continue with your . . . story."

"Her brother is Matthew Chambers. He and his uncle, Albert Chambers, operate Chambers Mining. They have magnesium mines in Morocco. Matthew came here over six months ago because he became suspicious that Chambers Mining, without his knowledge, was doing business with Komali."

"Komali! That son of a camel!" Ameen stared at Hassan in disbelief. In a suspicious voice he asked, "If this is so, it still does not explain why you brought the woman along."

"For cover, just as you said. But it is not you that I am after. It is the men responsible for the kidnapping or murder of young Chambers."

Ameen sat back on his heels. He reached for another cigarette. "This is quite a story you have told me," he said at last. "I will have to think about it." He waved his hand imperiously. "You may go now, Hassan Ben Kadiri. We will speak again tomorrow."

Hassan nodded as he got to his feet. "As you wish," he said. His brows grew together in a frown as he turned away from the desert chieftain and made his way to the tent he shared with Christy. He had told Ameen al-Shaibi the truth, but he didn't think the man believed him. He and Christy had been there for almost a month, but to Ameen and his men they were still strangers and not to be trusted. Hassan was not afraid for himself, but the thought of what might happen to Christy if Ameen disposed of him made his stomach muscles tighten with dread.

She was asleep when he entered the tent. Silently he pulled the burnoose over his head and lay down beside her. She sighed and moved closer to him, then her breathing grew even. Hassan rolled onto his side. He put his arm around her waist and drew her closer. He touched her breasts through the cotton fabric of her gown. She murmured and turned her face into his shoulder as his hand traveled down her body. When his hand hesitated, then cupped her, he heard her breath quicken.

Hassan didn't speak. He lay still, feeling the warmth of her through her gown before he began to caress her. He knew that Christy was awake. He felt her tense, then relax, waiting, just as he waited, for that moment when she would turn to him and whisper, "Hassan, oh, Hassan."

At last Hassan raised the gown over her hips. He touched her flesh then, but still she did not speak, not until he turned her to him and began to kiss her breasts.

Christy put her hands on his shoulders, feeling the smoothness of his skin, the firmness of muscle. This was the moment she had waited for all day, this time alone with Hassan. The night belonged to them. She was completely his now as her mouth sought his and she murmured, "Oh, Hassan... oh, darling."

She didn't know how each time could be better than the time before. Every time they made love she thought, this is so perfect, this is the best. It will never be this good again. But it always was. Now as Hassan joined his body to hers, Christy couldn't hold back her cry of joy. They were once again united by a bond of passion that left her breathless with longing as they climbed higher and higher to that indescribable moment when they cried each other's names and whispered their love.

When at last Christy lay asleep in his arms, her hair spread across his naked chest, Hassan thought of his conversation with Ameen. Perhaps he and Christy should try to escape. They could fill the canteens, take enough food to last for several days and steal two of the Arabian horses. They could... Then he thought of the endless stretches of hot desert sand. He didn't know where they were, how far from Bir Lahlou or any other town. He couldn't risk taking her into the desert again.

Hassan rested his chin against the top of Christy's head. My love, he thought, how am I going to get you out of here?

* * *

The first shot was fired a little before dawn. Then came a volley of shots, startled cries and the screeching wail of attacking marauders.

Hassan rolled to his knees. When Christy tried to sit up and cried, "What is it? What's happening?" he shoved her back.

"Stay down," he ordered. He pulled the burnoose over his head, grabbed the revolver out of his boot and ran out of the tent.

Keeping low, Hassan looked around him, trying to make sense of the scene taking place before his eyes. Black-robed men urged their horses forward into the nomad camp, shooting as they rode. From somewhere behind Hassan two of Ameen's men appeared. One of them brought his rifle up to his shoulder, but before he could fire he screamed and fell. The other man hit the ground, rolled and came up firing. Hassan grabbed the fallen man's rifle. He took aim, fired and saw one of the mounted men fall.

Then there was no time for thought; there was only action and the terrible cries of fallen men. When Hassan ran out of bullets, one of Ameen's men threw him a bandolier. Hassan loaded the rifle, then slung it around his shoulder.

"Who in the hell are they?" he yelled to the man beside him.

"The tribe of Ahmed Ben Ismail," the man yelled back. "He and Ameen have been fighting for years. It is an old feud; their fathers and grandfathers fought before them."

Amid the cries of the men, the burst of gunfire, bright flashes of flame and the panicked whinnying of the horses, the wailing of the women could be heard. Hassan clenched his jaws and prayed, Stay down, Christy. Stay down.

Riders screamed curses, fired, then jerked their horses around to fire from the other side. Ameen's men returned the fire. Men fell on both sides. A woman darted out of one of the tents. She stood as though frozen, looking at the scene around her. Then with a scream she grabbed her breast and fell.

Hassan felt a sharp zzzing close to his face. He rolled, fired, then got to his feet and began a zigzag run to find another vantage point. Suddenly he saw Ameen rush forward, then, almost in front of him, Hassan saw one of the riders rise in his saddle and lift his rifle to his shoulder. "Ameen al-Shaibi," the rider shouted, "know that it is Amed Ben Ismail who kills you."

Ameen brought his rifle up as he turned, but his enemy had already taken aim. There was no time. Hassan leaped forward and swung his rifle, knocking Amed Ben Ismail off his horse. The man fell and hit the ground with a whomp. He rolled fast, reaching for a side holster. But before he could fire, the crack of a bullet split the air. The man grabbed his throat, then fell back, his eyes wide and staring.

"Thank you, Hassan Ben Kadiri," Ameen said, then dropped to the ground beside Hassan and began firing.

The fighting didn't last long after that. The leader of Ameen's enemies was dead. One day soon another would take his place, but for now the heart had gone out of the fight. They went almost as quickly as they had come, leaving a devastated camp behind them. Fallen horses lay with fallen men. Four of Ameen's nomads were dead; five were wounded. The woman who had been shot earlier had died instantly. All of the men looked stunned, their faces covered with sweaty dirt, their burnooses ragged and torn. There were three captives.

Women ran from the tents now, wringing their hands and crying when they saw the fallen men. Hassan saw Christy, white-faced and frozen as she searched for him. He held up his arm, made a circle with his thumb and first finger so that she would know he was all right, then turned to help with the wounded men.

The women began to restore order. They picked up rifles and overturned braziers, and when the wounded were brought into one of the tents they began to boil water and to attend to the men.

Christy found Hassan. Because he was in a circle of men she only touched his arm as though to reassure herself that he was safe. He smiled down at her and nodded.

"I'm going to help the women with the wounded," she told him. She glanced down at the three bound prisoners within the circle of men. She wanted to ask what would happen to them but knew that she shouldn't, so she turned away. Later, while she bandaged a leg wound, she heard three shots.

That evening as dusk settled over the desert and the sky turned to unbelievable shades of red, bright orange, bronze and gold, Christy sat in front of the tent she shared with Hassan. In her mind's eye she could see the battle that had raged earlier in the day. She closed her eyes, but still it seemed she could hear the screams of dying and wounded men.

It had been unreal, a scene from a movie or from a page of *The Arabian Nights*. There'd been dozens of black-robed men, long Berber rifles raised to fire at the men in white robes who rushed out to defend their camp. It had been wild and uncivilized, as uncivilized as the shooting of the three prisoners after the battle.

Christy leaned her head on her knees. She had tried to tell herself that Hassan wasn't really a part of this world. He was a civilized man, he lived in Marrakesh, he sometimes wore Western clothes, he traveled to Paris and Vienna and New York. He wasn't like these desert men.

Today, from the relative safety of the tent, Christy had looked out, trying to find Hassan. When she found him a terrible feeling of fear had clutched at her heart. He had looked like the others, just as wild and savage and primitive.

Christy remembered then that Hassan had been born to a Berber woman, that Berber blood ran in his veins. He'd been raised in a camp, perhaps one like this. She felt the rush of tears. She'd fallen in love with Hassan. This past month with him, in spite of the hardships, had been wonderful. She had begun to think that perhaps, after all, they had a future together. They'd leave here. They'd find Matt and they'd go back to Marrakesh. It would be all right.

She'd met Hassan's friends Katherine and Rashid, and she was sure, from the little she'd seen of them, that they had a good marriage and were deeply in love. For a while Christy had let herself believe that the same thing could happen to her and Hassan. She had told herself that Hassan loved her and that when they returned to Marrakesh he would ask her to marry him. And she would have said yes.

Would have. But not now, not after today. Hassan Ben Kadiri belonged in one world; she belonged in another. When they returned to Marrakesh it would be over between them. She would go back to where she belonged.

The next morning Zohra came to their tent. "Excuse me, Hassan Ben Kadiri," she said. "Ameen wishes to speak to you in his tent."

"Thank you, Zohra. I'll go immediately." With a nod to Christy, Hassan followed the other woman out of the tent.

Ameen sat cross-legged on a pile of pillows when Hassan entered. "Welcome," he said. "Will you take some mint tea?"

"Yes, thank you."

Ameen's face was inscrutable as he poured the tea. "You were a great help to us yesterday," he said as he handed Hassan a glass. "I owe you a debt of gratitude for saving my life. If you had not acted as fast as you did, Ahmed Ben Ismail would have killed me." He smiled, but it was not a pleasant smile. "Even dying I would have gotten a shot off. However, I prefer to live, my friend Hassan, so I thank you for my life."

Hassan nodded. "Anytime, my friend Ameen."

"Now perhaps I can do something for you and your woman." He looked at Hassan over his glass of tea. "I have heard rumors of an American being held in the town of Al Mahbas. I do not know why he is held, because that is of no interest to me, nor do I know if he is young Chambers. But tomorrow I will send a man to Al Mahbas to make inquiries."

Hassan touched his fingertips to his head and bowed. "That is kind of you, Ameen. I am surprised. I agreed to take my wife to Bir Lahlou because I know how much her brother means to her. But I had no hope that he was alive. Now you tell me there is a possibility that he is, and I am amazed."

"Just so." Ameen hesitated. "Perhaps you should not mention this to your woman until my man returns. It would do no good to build up her hopes, then have them dashed if the rumor is not true or if the American held in Al Mahbas is not her brother."

"If the rumor is true, Ameen, will you let me buy camels and supplies so that I can go Al Mahbas?"

Ameen laughed. "And what would you do in Al Mahbas alone, my friend? Storm the prison if that is where young Chambers is held?" The Arab chieftain shook his head, then, pointing a finger to his own chest, said, "No, Hassan Ben Kadiri, you are my brother in battle now. If there is to be a rescue, then I and my men will go with you. I, Ameen al-Shaibi, will lead the rescue."

Hassan stared at the man across from him. "I cannot let you do this for me. It is too much. It—"

"Let? No one *lets* me do what I want to do. The matter is settled. By this time next week we will know whether your woman's brother is alive in Al Mahbas."

Hassan didn't tell Christy. He wanted to, but he knew that Ameen was right; it would do no good to build up her hopes, then find out that the American being held was not her brother.

One week. In one week he would know whether or not Matthew Chambers was alive.

Chapter 13

Christy had changed. Hassan didn't know what had changed her; he knew only that there was a difference. During the day she seemed withdrawn and preoccupied. At night when he returned to their tent she pretended to be asleep. For several nights he lay silently beside her, not knowing why she had turned away from him. Whenever he asked, "What is it, Christy?" she said, "Nothing. I'm tired, that's all."

After three nights of lying beside her while she pretended to be asleep, Hassan put his arms around her and drew her to him. Christy didn't resist. She came into his arms; she even responded to him. But there was no joy in her response; a part of her had turned away from him. And it was that part of her, Hassan discovered, that he most wanted.

Hassan had always thought of himself as a totally physical man where women were concerned. There had been many women in his life, but they had been apart from his life and from the things that concerned him. He made love to them, and that was all he wanted from them.

But Hassan wanted more from Christy. When he took her in his arms and raised his body over hers, she became a part of him. He loved watching her green eyes grow smoky and her delicate nostrils narrow. When their bodies joined he was transported, because making love to Christy was unlike anything he had ever known before. He wanted to please her; he wanted to hear her whisper his name, to plead in incoherent words as she raised her body to his and cried out in joy against his lips.

That's the way it had been, but it wasn't that way now.

"What is it?" Hassan asked one evening when they sat together in front of their tent. "Please tell me, Christy. Have I done something to hurt you?"

Christy looked at him, then away. "No," she said. "No, of course not."

"I know you are worried about your brother, but we will leave here soon." He forced a grin. "Since the raid, Ameen has been more friendly; we are practically blood brothers."

"I'm sure you are," she said caustically.

Hassan looked at her, surprised. "I know you don't like it here, Christy, but at least we are not in danger. Ameen has accepted us, and so have the others." He took her hand. "I wish you would tell me what is troubling you."

"It's nothing." Christy stood up. "I'm tired," she said. "I'm going to rest now."

Hassan sat there for a long time, watching the rise of the full moon against the desert sky. At last he went into their tent. Christy lay with her back to him, pretending to be asleep. He took off his robe and, fitting his body close to hers, began to caress her breasts. Christy neither spoke nor moved as his arms tightened around her. He kissed the back of her neck and whispered her name as he entered her.

Hassan moved against her. He told her how soft she was and how good it felt to be inside her this way. When she didn't answer he buried himself deeper. "You are mine," he whispered in a hoarse voice. "You belong to me. You..." He buried his face in the softness of her hair. "Oh, God, Christy," he cried. "Oh, God."

When it was over, Hassan lay on his back looking up at the black canvas top, hating himself and hating her. For a moment he was tempted to make her face him, to demand that she tell him why she had changed. He wanted to say, I love you, Christy, and I want you to love me. But her back was still to him. He hesitated, then, rolling away from her, he closed his eyes and he, too, pretended to sleep.

Tears streaked Christy's face. She'd never felt so desolate. With all her heart she wanted to reach out to Hassan. She wanted to say, I love you, but I'm afraid of the kind of man you are. I don't understand you or your people. I can never be a part of them or of you, because you're foreign to everything I know, everything I believe in.

They lay there through the long night, together, yet alone, both of them wanting to reach out, both of them afraid.

Ten days after he had sent a messenger to Al Mahbas, Ameen called Hassan into his tent. "My man returned last night," he said. "It took him longer than he thought, because the people there are suspicious. He had to be careful, but he was able to find out that an American is being held."

"Was he able to learn the man's name?"

Ameen shook his head. "No, but he did learn that the prisoner speaks Arabic and that when he was taken he was in Morocco on some kind of mining business."

"Then it is Matthew Chambers," Hassan said emphatically. "He was born in Morocco, and his company has a mine here. Did your man find out why Chambers is being held and whether or not he is all right?"

"He found out that he is as well as a man can be who has been in prison for six months." Ameen lighted a cigarette. "When do we leave for Al Mahbas?"

"The day after tomorrow?" Hassan's brows raised in question. "Can you and your men be ready by then?"

"My men are always ready, Hassan Ben Kadiri." Ameen looked at Hassan through the smoke from his cigarette. "Will you take your woman with you?"

"I will have to, because I don't think she will stay behind."

With a laugh Ameen shook his head. "You have much to learn about women," he said. "You don't *ask* a woman what she is going to do. You *tell* her. Have you been married long, my friend?"

"We were married just before we started out from Marrakesh," Hassan lied. "That was almost two months ago."

"Then perhaps it is not too late. Before another day goes by, you must let this American wife of yours know that you are her lord and master, that you will tell her what to do and she will do it. This is the way it has always been; this is the way it will always be."

"Times are changing, Ameen. Even here, in our own country, women are coming into their own. They have more say in the marriage now. They expect to be treated as equal partners."

"Equal partners! Ha!" Ameen puffed angrily on his cigarette as he glared at Hassan. "If that is the way it is in our cities, then I will stay in the desert forever." For a long moment he didn't speak, then he said, "Very well, tell your woman she can accompany us. But she will have to keep up. I will not endanger my men because of her."

"Christy will keep up," Hassan promised as he got to his feet. "I thank you for helping us, Ameen."

Ameen waved away Hassan's thanks. "The next two weeks will be a test of our courage, my friend. The desert is not kind, even to men like us. I don't know how successful we will be in freeing young Chambers. If I see that it is impossible, I will not risk my men. I want you to understand that before we leave."

"I understand, Ameen."

"Good. Now, go and tell your woman that we leave the day after tomorrow."

"You know where Matt is?" Christy gripped Hassan's hands in hers. "He's alive! He's all right? Are you sure it's him?"

"Ameen's man said that the man being held spoke Arabic and that he was an American with mining interests in Morocco. Does your brother speak Arabic?"

Christy nodded. "He spoke it before he spoke English, because his nursemaid was Moroccan." She began to weep. "Oh, Hassan, Hassan," she cried. "Matt's alive."

Hassan put his arms around her. Her defenses were down as she clung to him. At least for the moment, Hassan thought, she is mine again.

She came into his arms that night, but there was still a part of herself she would not give. He determined then

that before this trip had finished Christy would belong to
him again, as completely as she had before.

Two days later they left at dawn. There were eleven men
and three women—Christy, Zohra and a woman named
Zahira, the wife of Ameen's most trusted man.

"I can't ride in this robe," Christy protested the morning they made ready to leave.

"I am afraid you will have to," Hassan told her. "The
other women—"

"But I'm not the other women, and I'll be damned if
I'm going to wear a robe."

"And I'll be damned if you are not!" Hassan glared
down at her. Maybe Ameen was right. Maybe it was time
he let Christy know that when he told her to do something he meant it. Her chin was thrust belligerently forward; her green eyes flashed with anger. It was all he could
do to keep from shaking her.

In a tone of voice he'd never used with her before,
spacing his words carefully, Hassan said, "You will wear
your robe or I will—"

"You'll what?" Christy yanked the robe off over her
head and reached for her jeans.

But before she could put them on, Hassan grabbed
them away from her and spun her around. "Damn it," he
said, "you will do as I say."

Christy stood on her tiptoes so she could look him
square in the eye. "I'm going to wear my jeans," she said.

Hassan looked at her for a moment. Then his hands
tightened on her shoulders and he shook her. He had
never been this angry with a woman before and he wanted
to be sure she knew that. He wanted to bend her to his
will. He wanted to... Oh, God, he wanted to...

His mouth crushed hers in an angry kiss. His lips
ground against her and his tongue probed, trying to force

her lips apart. When she gasped, his tongue invaded her mouth.

Christy tried to pull away, but his arms were like bands of steel around her. When she tried to turn her head, one hand fastened on her scalp as strong fingers spread through her hair. Hassan's kiss was fierce; he held her so tightly she could barely catch her breath. She swayed toward him as a traitorous heat crept through her body. She answered his kiss, and her tongue darted to meet his as her arms crept up around his shoulders.

He let her go for a moment, then his lips only a millimeter from hers, he said, "You *will* wear your robe." Before Christy could answer he swatted her once, smartly on the bottom, picked up the robe and handed it to her.

She sighed as she took the robe from him and said smiling sweetly, "All right, Hassan, whatever you say."

It was only later, when they were well away from the nomad camp, that he realized she'd worn her jeans under the robe.

The first two days were the hardest. Without realizing it, Christy had become accustomed to life in the camp. Although it was more difficult than the life she was used to, it had been relatively easy compared with desert travel. But she'd done it before, she told herself; she could do it again. And this time she was going to find Matt. That made all the difference. That gave her the strength she needed to go on.

When they camped for the night, most of the men rolled themselves up in their blankets and went to sleep. Only Hassan, Ameen and Rahma, Zahira's husband, had tents. While the men tended to the camels, the women prepared the evening meal. They didn't eat with the men but sat off to one side. Nor did the women take part in the men's conversation. Instead, with voices lowered they spoke of what they would prepare for the next day's breakfast.

That frustrated Christy, because she wanted to listen to what the men were saying and be a part of the discussion. It was her brother they were talking about. Why couldn't she put her two cents' worth in?

While the men continued talking, the women retired to their tents. Christy lay fuming, waiting for Hassan to come to bed so that he could tell her everything that had been said. But the talk went on, and finally, exhausted from the day's ride, Christy went to sleep. The next morning there was no time for questions; breakfast had to be prepared and the camels readied.

Christy had insisted on riding Clyde. He was as recalcitrant as ever, and she still had to whip the hat off her head—she had refused to bind her hair with a scarf on this trip—and box his ears. But Clyde was her camel, and in spite of his rotten disposition and his attempts to bite her ankles, she preferred him to any other animal.

The caravan traveled only during the early hours of the morning. When the sun grew too hot in the afternoon, they stopped and, raising a black canvas between poles, tried to rest. But rest was impossible in the heat, and with one or two exceptions, the group sat quietly, eyes closed, waiting for the afternoon to pass so that they could move on. They traveled far into the night before they set up camp, had their evening meal and slept for a few hours.

Christy didn't complain of the heat. She knew that Hassan tried to make the trip as easy for her as he could. During the day, although he rode at the front of the column beside Ameen, he often came to the back of the line to check on her. At night when they rested he pulled her close, but he made no attempt to make love to her.

On the fifth day of their journey they reached an oasis.

"We will rest here," Ameen told his people. "We are only a day's ride from Al Mahbas. We must think how we will approach the town and begin to plan how we will free the Chambers man." He turned to look at the men around him. "I do not think it will be easy; thus we must go cautiously."

"I could go into Al Mahbas first," Christy said from her place beside Zohra and Zahira. "I could find out whether or not it really is Matt and if he's all right. I—"

"You will do nothing!" Ameen scowled threateningly.

"But he's my brother. I—"

"Be silent, woman!"

"I won't be silent. I appreciate everything you've done for us, and I'll be grateful to you for the rest of my life for trying to help Matt, but he's my brother, Ameen al-Shaibi. I want to help."

"You can help by staying in the background as any decent woman should," Ameen said. "Besides, one has only to look at you to know you are not one of us. Your skin is too fair. Your hair is too light. Once we near the town, you are to stay out of the way. I do not want you seen."

Christy glared down at him. But before she could speak Hassan took her arm. "Please forgive my wife," he said to Ameen. "It is her concern for her brother that makes her speak out."

"But—" Christy started to say.

Hassan's hand tightened. "I will see that she stays out of the way," he said.

Christy yanked out of his grasp. "I wouldn't have to if I looked like Zohra and Zahira."

"Probably not," Hassan said. His face was tight with anger. "But you don't look like them, Christy, so leave it alone."

"But I *could* look like them. I could darken my skin and wear a veil. Zohra could help me." Christy looked at Hassan, her green eyes wide with appeal. "Please, Hassan, don't make me stay behind. I want to be a part of this."

"It would be possible to darken her skin," Zohra said.

Ameen froze. He turned to where his wife sat. "I did not ask for your comment," he said.

"But it is true," she said stubbornly. "Zahira and I can make a paste that will stain Mrs. Christy's skin. We can bind her hair, and if she wears a veil she will pass for one of us."

Ameen got to his feet. Hands on his hips, he looked at his wife. "Since when do you meddle in the affairs of men?" he asked.

"Christy has told us that a woman has rights, that she no longer is a man's chattel. In Rabat and Casablanca and Marrakesh women hold jobs. They make their own decisions and don't have to ask their husbands what they can or cannot do." Zohra took a deep breath. "I am your wife, Ameen al-Shaibi, but I am a person, too. From now on when I have something to say, I will say it."

Ameen looked at this woman he'd been married to for twenty-nine years. The others were silent, waiting, wondering what he would do. "I should beat you," he said at last.

The trace of a smile tugged at Zohra's lips. "You never have before, my husband. I doubt that you will now."

He moved a step closer, but Zohra didn't retreat. With a sigh Ameen shook his head. "The day may yet come," he said softly.

The next day, after Zohra and Zahira had mixed mud from the pool with some of the ointments they carried with them, they took Christy into one of the tents.

"You must never wear these ugly trousers again," Zahira said when Christy handed them to her.

Zahira was an unattractive woman of indeterminate age, her body all awkward bends and angles. Her features were sharp. She had a nose like a gull's beak, small black eyes and a permanently pursed mouth. In all the time that Christy had been at the nomad camp Zahira had had little to say to her. It had been obvious to Christy that because she was a foreigner Zahira wanted nothing to do with her.

Perhaps it was the challenge of making Christy into a desert woman that appealed to Zahira. Whatever it was, she tackled the job with zeal. When Christy was clad only in her panties and bra the two women began applying the brown mud paste to her body.

"It is like a stain," Zohra told her. "It will wear off in time."

"In time?" Christy swallowed as she looked at her darkening skin. "How much time?"

"A month or two, perhaps," Zahira said.

Christy groaned inwardly, then stood patiently as the two women continued their work. Just when she thought they were finished, Zohra said, "Now the henna."

"But I don't think—" Christy started to say.

"Zfft," Zahira said, "if you are to look like one of us, we must henna the palms of your hands and the bottom of your feet. Now sit."

When they were done they bound Christy's hair in a cloth that came to the middle of her forehead and wrapped around her neck to the point of her chin.

"Now the veil," Zohra said.

It tickled Christy's nose, and she experimented with small puffs of breath as she tried to blow it away from her face. She'd never felt so swathed in clothing. She didn't know how she looked, but she felt like a mummy.

Zohra and Zahira stood back to admire their handi-work. "I would not know she was not of our tribe if I met her as a stranger," Zohra said.

"May I have a mirror?" Christy asked nervously.

Zahira nodded. She turned to search through a pile of her belongings and with a triumphant "Aha!" handed Christy a jeweled hand mirror.

Christy raised the veil. The face staring back at her was that of a stranger.

"You are one of us now," Zohra said in a soft voice.

It was dark by the time the three women emerged from the tent. They prepared the evening meal, fixed their own plates, then went to sit together under a group of date palms. Several times Hassan glanced over at them. He hadn't been able to get a close look at Christy when she'd served the meal, and now it was almost too dark to see.

"We will leave at dawn," Ameen told the men. "By late afternoon we will near Al Mahbas, then we will decide what we will do. Let us sleep now, because tomorrow will be a busy day."

When Hassan got to his feet he looked over at Christy and motioned her to follow him to their tent. Quickly he built a small fire, and when it began to crackle and glow he said, "It is a beautiful night. Let's sit here for a while."

Christy nodded and sat across the fire from him. She stared down at her hennaed hands. Hassan hadn't really seen her, and she wasn't sure she wanted him to, afraid of what his reaction would be.

She looked across the fire at him. His dark eyes wid-ened, then narrowed, as his gaze lingered on her face and traveled down her body. He saw her hennaed hands and feet and drew his breath in.

"Is it really you?" he asked.

"Yes, Hassan." Christy lowered her gaze.

"You look . . ." He tried to smile, but a strange excitement had begun to build. A flame crept through his body into his loins and his heart raced with the need to touch her. Not knowing why he did it, he reached into the bowl of dates next to them and said. "Will you have a date?"

Her green eyes widened. In a husky voice she said, "Yes, please."

His eyes never leaving her face, Hassan took a date and held it to her lips. When his fingers lingered on her lips, she caught the tips of them in her mouth and quickly ran her tongue across them. She saw his eyes widen and heard the sharp intake of his breath.

Christy lowered her gaze. She knew that soon Hassan would get to his feet. He would offer his hand and she would take it.

Hassan drew her close and lifted her face to his. With a sigh he kissed her, and with his lips still close to hers, he whispered, "Come with me now." Then he picked her up and carried her into their tent.

And Christy knew her dream had became a reality.

Chapter 14

Hassan knew by the way her arms came up around his neck and by the softness of her body that tonight Christy would be totally his. He laid her gently down on the Persian carpet, mesmerized by the expression in her green eyes. For days she had been cool and withdrawn. Now her face was soft with love.

Her hennaed hands were cool against his face. "Hassan," she whispered. "My love, my love."

His breath caught in his throat. "Let me undress you," he said.

Without a word Christy sat up and raised her arms so that he could pull the robe over her head. Hassan gasped at the darkness of her skin, then touched one bare shoulder, rubbing it to see if the color would come off. Before he could speak, Christy took his hand. "For as long as my skin is this color, I will be yours, Hassan," she said.

"Christy...?"

She reached up to unwind the scarf that covered her head and release the sun-gold hair.

For a moment Hassan only looked at her. He knew that never before had a woman stirred his senses as she did. He wasn't sure what miracle had brought about this change, and he didn't understand what she meant by saying that as long as her skin was brown she was his. He only thanked Allah that tonight Christy belonged to him.

Hassan drew her into his arms. "I love you," he said, and knew that it was true. Her darkened skin was warm against his. He could feel the softness of her breasts pressing against his chest. He held her away from him and looked into her eyes. Again he said, "I love you, Christy, whatever the color of your skin. There will never be anyone else for me. You are mine. I will never let you go."

Hassan pulled his burnoose over his head and took her in his arms, sighing with pleasure when he felt her nakedness against his own.

"Christy," he said. He breathed in the scent of her hair. He kissed her closed eyes, her nose, her cheeks and finally her lips.

Pliant in his arms, warm and soft and yielding, Christy whispered Hassan's name as her hands tightened around his shoulders. Her fingers traced the smooth line of his back, marveling at the texture of his skin, the play of fine muscles under her fingertips. She turned her face into his shoulder, kissed him, tasted him and felt the kindling of flame in her body turn to a raging fire.

Hassan lifted her face and kissed her. His tongue sought hers, and she answered in a teasing, silken duel that made him moan with pleasure. When he let her go he urged her back against the rug. With a smile he said, "You look as if you are wearing a white bathing suit." He touched her bare breasts, then ran his hand down her stomach to the apex of her legs.

His dark eyes grew warm with desire. He took her hands, as he had done once before and raised them over her head. "Your breasts are like small pomegranates," he said in wonder. "Firm and ripe, waiting to be tasted." He brushed his lips across her breasts, and when she gasped in pleasure he captured one rose-colored peak between his teeth and flicked it with his tongue.

"Hassan..." Christy's voice trembled with desire. "Oh, Hassan." She arched her body and yielded herself to the mouth that so sweetly caressed her, to the teeth that scraped and gently tugged. When it became too much and she tried to move away, his hand tightened on her wrists and he began to kiss her other breast.

Through half-blind eyes Christy looked up at the dark canvas top of the tent. She smelled the desert air, heard the rustle of the palms and her own voice whispering his name. "Let me go," she pleaded incoherently. "Hassan, please, I have to touch you."

When he did, she wrapped her arms around his neck, murmuring, and her fingers tightened in the thickness of his hair, holding him close as he rubbed his beard against her breasts.

Christy was beyond thought now, lost in her dream, a woman of a different century giving herself to her desert lover. Soon he will raise his body over mine, she thought. I will be his, held by his strength, by his arms, by his love.

His tongue was like velvet against her skin, and Christy forgot everything except the terrible urgency of her body. Trembling in need, she whispered, "It's too much, Hassan. I can't bear it. Darling, please..."

Her voice trailed off into a fevered gasp as his lips began a torturous path down her body, tasting her, nipping her tender skin with small love bites that left her shivering with pleasure. "So good," he murmured against her skin. "Ah, Christy, you taste so good."

Hassan wanted her with a hunger that was almost past bearing. But oh, how he loved to kiss her this way, to feel her body tremble with need, to hear her soft cries and the sound of his name on her lips. He caressed her with his hands and his tongue, and when he parted her legs to touch her, his body swelled in a frenzy of need.

With an anguished cry Hassan brought himself over her, into her, filling her.

Christy was lost in the arms that held her, in the body that covered and consumed her. She gave herself completely, reveling in him, raising her body to his as she undulated against him, meeting each movement, each thrust, with cries of gladness. This was Hassan, the man she would love forever. Tonight and for all the desert nights they would share, she belonged to him. When they left the desert ... Christy's arms tightened around him. With a hunger that bordered on starvation she lifted her body to his.

Hassan sought her mouth, their bodies merging as he carried her higher and higher on a crest of passion so intense that she forgot where she was or who she was. All that mattered was Hassan and this shattering moment of shared paradise.

He collapsed over her, his heart thudding against her breasts. "Christy, Christy," he said over and over again. "What do you do to me?" His fingers threaded through her hair as he buried his face in the warmth of her neck.

Finally, when their hearts had slowed, Hassan rose so that he could look at her. "I will never let you go, Christy," he said. "I love you."

Her breathing stilled. "And I love you, Hassan." She pulled his head down to her breast and held him there, soothing his dark hair, caressing his shoulders. You'll let me go, my love, she thought, because I can never be the kind of a woman you want me to be. Tonight was a dream, Hassan, as all these nights on the desert are. In my robe and my veil, with my skin as dark as the women you have known before, I can pretend to be someone I'm not. but the dream will fade with my skin, and then it will be time to leave you.

With the thought of that, with the knowledge that the day would come when she would say goodbye, Christy held him closer. "Hassan," she whispered against his hair, "Oh, Hassan, I do love you."

The caravan prepared to start out before the first pale streaks of color lightened the desert sky. When Christy emerged from the tent, dressed in her robe, her hair and most of her face covered, the other men looked at her approvingly. Even Ameen, who had never smiled at her, said, "Aha! Now you are one of us."

Christy lowered her head in a bow as she had seen the other women do.

They rode almost all of that day, stopping only for a brief lunch and to rest the camels. When they came to a small oasis, Ameen raised his arm to stop. "We will camp here. The women will wear their veils, because we are only a few miles from the town and we may see riders. Tomorrow we will ride into Al Mahbas."

"I want to be with you when you go into the town," Christy told Hassan when he helped her off Clyde.

Hassan's hand tightened on hers, and with a smile he said, "What has happened to the obedient Moroccan woman I held in my arms last night?" Surreptitiously, so the others wouldn't see, his hand crept up her arm under the robe down to the rise of her breast. Quickly he brushed his fingers against it and then removed his hand. "I don't know how I can wait for the darkness," he said in a low voice. Then, stepping away from her, he said, "I know how anxious you are about your brother, Christy. But Ameen is in charge. He has brought us this far; now we must follow his lead."

Christy sighed. It was hard, after all these months, to be this close to Matt and not be able to rush to his side. Let him be all right, she prayed. Don't let anything happen to him now.

That evening when the men gathered around the campfire to talk, the three women went to the far side of the pond to bathe. "But you must not scrub your skin," Zahira warned Christy. "Only soap it lightly, so that the color does not fade." Her small eyes narrowed in concentration as she studied Christy. "If it were not for your hair and the color of your eyes, you could be one of us."

"I have seen eyes that color among our people," Zohra put in. "You forget that we Moors ruled Spain for eight hundred years. Our blood runs in their veins, and their blood runs in ours. If anyone gets close enough to see her eyes, they will think she has Spanish blood." She grinned at Christy. "You look nice with your skin this color. Very pretty. You should keep it like this all the time."

Zahira nodded. "If it begins to fade, we will darken it again for you. What does your husband say now that your skin is like ours? Does he like it, or does he prefer that you look sickly pale?"

"Zahira!" Zohra admonished. "Watch your tongue."

Zahira shrugged her bony shoulders. "But what is attractive about skin the color of milk? I think—"

"Well, don't think!" To Christy, Zohra said, "You must forgive Zahira; she is too outspoken. But she is right, you know; you do look pretty. Your skin is the color of sand that has been kissed by the sun. It becomes you." She hesitated, then put her hand on Christy's arm and said, "I hope that we will find your brother tomorrow. Ameen al-Shaibi is a strong man and a good leader. He will know what to do."

"I wish I could go into Al Mahbas with the men tomorrow," Christy said.

"That is impossible," Zahira said. "Ameen is our leader. We must do as he tells us, because he is a man and we are only women."

"Only women!" Christy sputtered. She stared at Zahira in disbelief. This was the twentieth century. Wasn't Zahira aware that women no longer depended on men for every breath they took? She'd been surprised the other day when Zohra had spoken up to Ameen, and she'd seen Ameen look at his wife with surprised speculation and even admiration. There was hope for Zohra, but a woman like Zahira would never change. She would go on living as her mother and grandmother and all of the women before her had lived. Nothing Christy said would every change that.

The three women, dressed in their robes, returned to the camp.

Christy wanted desperately to ask what plan had been made to rescue her brother. But she knew she dared not. The men would make a decision, and when it was made Hassan would tell her. With a sigh she went into the tent that had been erected under a stand of palm trees. She knelt on the sand and spread the rug. Then she took off her robe and the rest of her clothes and, covering herself with the robe, lay down to wait for Hassan.

The men talked far into the night. From her tent Christy could see the light of the fire and hear the low hum of voices. She was tired, but she couldn't sleep. She had to wait for Hassan; she had to learn how they were going to rescue Matt.

When at last he came, he opened the tent flap and, looking down at her, whispered, "Christy? Are you asleep?"

She sat up. "No, Hassan, I was waiting for you." She pulled the white robe closer around her body against the chill of the desert night. "Are we going into Al Mahbas tomorrow?"

He closed the tent flap. Then he pulled the robe over his head and came down to the rug next to her. "Ameen and I are going."

"But—"

Hassan put a finger against her lips. "We want to see the layout of the town and talk to some of the men. We shall find out where the jail is and where your brother is being held. It may take several days to learn anything, so try to be patient." He drew Christy into his arms. "I know this is difficult for you, my dear, but you must trust me."

"I do trust you, Hassan. It's just that I've been trying to find Matt for such a long time. Now that I know where he is, I want to storm the jail single-handed."

"I know." Hassan urged her back down to the rug with him and put his arms around her. "We must go carefully," he told her. "There are only eleven of us. We need to know how big the jail is, how many men guard it and exactly where in the jail your brother is." His arms tightened around her. "But we will get him out, Christy. I promise you that."

It was two hours after daylight when Hassan and Ameen rode into Al Mahbas. Old turbaned men sat together near the ancient gates of the city, soaking up the sun's early rays and exchanging news. They stared at the two strangers with curious eyes and murmured among themselves.

"I have heard that a dozen years ago the town gates were bolted each night from eight until dawn," Ameen said. "And that if you walked the streets at night you had to carry a lantern." He glanced around him. "It doesn't seem that much has changed, does it?"

Hassan looked around him. He had seen desert towns like this when he was growing up. It had seemed then that these towns were exciting and wonderful places. Now, as a man, he was appalled as he looked around him by the meanness of the place and the narrow houses that opened out onto the filthy cobblestone streets.

"Let's find a place where we can have coffee," Ameen said, and led the way toward the center of town.

Everywhere men stopped and stared at them. Once they passed three women who, though they were veiled, turned their faces away. When they found a coffee shop they went in and sat down. The owner, a skinny man with a dirty turban and a spot-stained apron, looked at them suspiciously before he shuffled over to their table.

"We would like two coffees," Hassan said.

The man grunted in acknowledgment. When he returned with two cups and a battered silver pot he said, "From where do you come?"

"The desert near Der'a." Ameen sipped his coffee. "We are nomads, and soon we will move on to another place."

"Why have you come to Al Mahbas?" The man scratched his stomach.

"We are on our way to Bir Lahlou to buy horses," Ameen said.

The other men in the coffee shop grew silent, listening to the conversation. Then one of them said, "The horses of Bir Lahlou are the best one can find in Morocco."

"So we have heard." Hassan nodded at the man. "But of course we would appreciate any advice we can get about where to buy in Bir Lahlou."

"I have a brother there," another man said. "He could advise you."

"That would be a great help to us. Please—" Ameen motioned to the man to join them "—allow me to offer you another coffee."

In a short time all of the men in the shop were gathered at the table, offering advice on how to select horses, arguing about the merits of one breed over another and the current going price.

"I have heard that the horses from Texas in the United States are known for their strength and that the horses from a place called Kentucky run faster than any in the world," Hassan said.

The men from Al Mahbas looked at him in surprise. "The United States?" a man with a gray beard said. "What do they know about horseflesh there?"

Hassan motioned to the shop owner for more coffee. "I asked an American about their horses once, and he told me they raised fine animals. You should speak to one of them sometime if you have an opportunity." He took a sip of his coffee. "But then I suppose you would never get an American in a town like Al Mahbas."

One of the men laughed and poked the man sitting beside him. "What would this desert man think if we told him we had an American here right now?"

Ameen stared at the man, disbelief written all over his face. "An American?" he scoffed. "What would an

American be doing in a dung heap like this? You have had too much sun, my friend."

"Have I?" The man bristled. "I could take you to him right now. You could look through the bars of his cell and see for yourself."

"Shut up, Raji," one of the other men said. "You talk too much."

"And dream too much," Hassan said with a laugh. "An American in your jail? I would have to see him to believe it."

The man's chair scraped as he jumped to his feet. "My brother is the jailer," he said angrily. "Come along with me, and I will prove we have an American here."

Ameen shrugged. With a wink at Hassan he said, "We might as well have a look. If it is an American," he said with a laugh, "we can ask him about Kentucky horses."

The town jail was in an old seventeenth-century fortress. The eight-foot stone walls were guarded by one man who paced up and down the parapets and by another man who sat cross-legged at the entrance with a rifle across his knees. He raised the rifle when he saw the men, then lowered it when they came closer and he recognized his brother and the other men. *"Marhaban,"* he said. "What are you loafers doing?"

"Good morning, Abdeslem," Raji said. "We have come to show these desert nomads that we have an American in our town, even if he is in jail."

Raji's brother looked at Ameen and Hassan. "We have one," he said.

"What is his crime?" Hassan asked.

Abdeslem shrugged. "Who knows? Over six months ago two men brought him to Al Mahbas. They paid our mayor a lot of money and said that the American was to be locked up in our jail."

"Did they say for how long?" Ameen rubbed his hand across his beard. "Have these men returned? And what if they don't? Will you keep this poor American here forever?"

"It makes no difference to me how long we hold him," Abdeslem said. "Money comes every month, and as long as it continues to come, we will continue to hold him. That is what the man named Driss told us to do."

"Driss?" Hassan couldn't keep the shock out of his voice. When the others turned to look at him, he said, "I have heard of a man called Mustafa Ben Driss. He is a shady character. I wonder if it is the same man."

"Who knows? Now, do you want to see our American guest or not?"

"Lead the way," Ameen said. "It has been a long time since I have seen an infidel dog. I think I am going to enjoy this."

Abdeslem led them through a crooked stone passage, then down a flight of steps to another passage with empty cells. The jailer passed them, and when he came to the end of the corridor he turned right and said, "Here he is." He motioned them forward. "Hey, American," he called out in Arabic, "you have some visitors."

The light in the cell was so dim that Hassan could barely see. He edged closer. A tattered, threadbare rug partially covered the rough stone floor. There was a three-legged stool in one corner, a bucket in another.

A man sat on the stool reading a newspaper. He turned, then got slowly to his feet. "What do you want, Abdeslem?" he asked.

"To show you off, American." The jailer turned to Hassan and Ameen as he pointed to the man behind the rusted bars. "See?" he said. "What did I tell you? He's an American, all right."

"How do we know that?" Hassan said scornfully. "All infidels look alike." He motioned toward the prisoner. "Come closer," he ordered. "Let me have a look at you."

The man stepped forward and Hassan's eyes widened with shock. The hair was redder than Christy's, but the eyes were the same sea green. He was taller than she was, and older, but the features were similar. There was no doubt in Hassan's mind; this was Christy's brother.

"He looks like a Frenchman to me," Ameen said.

"French!" Abdeslen said. "I told you, he is American."

"Say something in English," Ameen ordered the prisoner.

Matt Chambers's eyes flashed in anger. "Go to hell," he said.

"Do you understand him?" Hassan asked.

The men shook their heads. "Do you?" the jailer asked.

"I have a few words of English. I'm not sure what he said. Let me ask him to say it again." Hassan took hold of the bars. "Hey, American," he snarled, "don't change your expression. Don't show any emotion. I am a friend of your sister's. I am going to get you out of here."

The color went out of Matt's face. His nostrils flared, but other than that his face was passive. "Go to hell," he said again.

"What did he say to you?" the man called Raji asked.

Hassan laughed. "He told me to go to hell. I told him he had better behave himself or I personally would stake him out on an ant hill."

The others laughed. "Let's get out of here," Ameen said. "This place smells." Without a backward look at the prisoner, the men turned and walked away.

Matt Chambers stared after him. His hands gripped the bars of his cell. My God, he thought, what kind of an insane joke is this? The man was an Arab. How could he know Christy?

Christy. Matt closed his eyes and thought of home. For the first time in a long time he felt a flare of hope.

Chapter 15

Matthew Chambers was thirty-six years old. Before his capture he had tipped the scales at 195 pounds. Today he estimated his weight to be no more than 150. He'd existed for over six months on a diet of rice, with occasional pieces of lamb thrown in, coffee and bread. His jailers were not unkind to him; for the most part they ignored him. Occasionally one of them gave him a newspaper, and from time to time another jailer gave him a couple of oranges with his evening meal. Until a month ago there had been two other prisoners in this corner of the jail. One of them had died; the other had been set free. Since then the loneliness had all but closed in on him.

During the first week that Matt had been here in the Al Mahbas jail he had repeatedly asked to see a lawyer or a judge. "What am I charged with?" he'd demanded to know. "What is my crime? Why am I being kept here?" No one ever answered his questions, and little by little the horrible suspicion that his uncle was behind his imprisonment crept into his mind.

During the past year Matt had become increasingly worried about the company and the way his uncle was running it. Decisions were made that Matt had no part in. Funds set aside for one project were suddenly channeled into another project, usually in the Middle East or Morocco. Matt had begun investigating on his own, and late one night at the office he'd stumbled on a secret file in Uncle Albert's office. He had been in his office when the phone in his uncle's office rang. When the ringing persisted he hurried in, but the ringing stopped just as he picked the phone up. With a muttered, "Damn," Matt put the phone down, so eager to get back to his own desk that he accidentally dropped the phone. When he picked it up he saw the key taped to the bottom of it.

For a minute or two Matt only looked at the key, wondering why his uncle found it necessary to be so secretive. He closed the key in his fist and tried to tell himself Uncle Albert's business was his own. But not when it concerns the company, he thought. He looked at the key again, then he tried to fit it into the middle drawer of the desk. It didn't fit there, nor did it fit any of the other drawers. Next Matt tried the file cabinets, and finally, in the last drawer he opened, behind a file marked, "Middle East," he found a folder marked "Mg:s/k."

A puzzled frown creased Matt's forehead. Mg was the symbol for magnesium, but what in the hell was "s/k"? He drew the file out, took it over to his uncle's desk and opened it. Now, over six months later, Matt still remembered the sickness that rose in his throat as he leafed through his uncle's file and realized that for almost two years, without his knowledge, Chambers Mining had secretly been dealing with an enemy Middle Eastern country. The undercover transactions had taken place in Morocco.

The next day Matt told Albert Chambers that he'd decided to make a quick trip to Morocco. His uncle's face went white and perspiration beaded his forehead. "Why?" he'd asked. "You're needed here. Things are going smoothly in Morocco. There's no need for you to go."

"I know things are going smoothly there," Matt said, trying to sound casual. "I just thought I'd take a look. Remember, I was born in Morocco. I love the country and the people. I'll only be gone for a couple of weeks, time to combine a little business with pleasure."

Albert Chambers did his damnedest to prevent his nephew from going, but Matt persisted. He flew into Casablanca, and from there he rented a car and drove to Marrakesh. According to the file he'd found, Bir Lahlou was the place to start his investigation. Because he'd been away from Morocco for eight years, Matt made a couple of inquiries at his hotel in Marrakesh about taking a caravan into the desert. On his second day there he was approached by a man named Mustafa Ben Driss.

"I was born and raised in the Sahara," Driss told him. "I have taken caravans to Bir Lahlou many times. I am an experienced desert man, Mr. Chambers, and I have the credentials to prove it."

The credentials checked out, and Matt hired Driss to take him to Bir Lahlou. By the third day out on the desert he knew he'd made a mistake. It wasn't that Driss didn't know the desert, because he did. But there was something sneaky about the fellow. On the fifth day they came to Al Mahbas. "We can rest here and replenish our supplies," Driss told him. "There's a hotel in town. You'll be comfortable enough there."

That night when Matt went to bed he lay for a long time
staring up at the ceiling. He felt an uneasiness he couldn't
explain. He didn't like the town, and he didn't like Driss.
He had half a mind to pay the man off and go the rest
of the way on his own. Finally he'd fallen into a restless sleep. He'd awakened abruptly when a floorboard
squeaked.

"Who is it?" Matt asked. "What—?" Something hit
him then. The next thing he remembered was being
thrown onto a hard stone floor. He lost consciousness
again. When he awoke in the morning he realized that he
was in a cell. He banged on the rusty bars until a jailer
came.

"What's going on?" Matt demanded to know. "Why
am I here? Where's Driss?"

"Driss? I know of no man named Driss." The jailer
shoved a tin tray of food through a slot at the bottom of
the bars, and before Matt could ask anything else he disappeared.

That was over six months ago. Matt had never seen or
heard from Driss again. The only men he saw were the
jailers who brought his food.

For the first few days Matt had tried to tell himself it
was just a terrible mistake. He told his jailers that he was
an American citizen and demanded that the United States
Embassy be told where he was. When that didn't work he
tried to bribe his way out by promising that money would
be sent to him as soon as he was released and that then he
would pay his "fine." But nothing he said or did had any
effect on his jailers; they had no interest in Matthew
Chambers or why he was there. They had been told to
lock him up, and that's what they had done.

Matt had tried to tell himself that both his uncle and
Christy knew that he was in Morocco. If they didn't hear

from him within a month his uncle would contact the embassy and begin a search for him. Then one day, like a light bulb going off over his head, the realization hit him that his uncle was behind his imprisonment. He tried to tell himself that he was crazy, that because he was locked up he was trying to blame somebody. His uncle was a rich and powerful man. It was true that he could be unscrupulous, but he was Matt's own flesh and blood; surely he couldn't be behind this.

But as the months passed, Matt became convinced that Uncle Albert was behind the plot to keep him here and that he'd been right about everything else, too.

Matt determined to hang on. He made himself eat everything he was given. He did both physical and mental exercises to keep his sanity. And he clung to the hope that someday he'd be freed.

There were times, like these past few days, when he'd almost given up. He'd been angry today when the jailer had brought some of the men of the town in to look at him. They'd done it before, and it had infuriated him. Today there'd been two strangers with the men. Matt had looked at them, hating their curiosity, hating their freedom.

Then one of the bearded man had spoken to him in English. He'd said that he was a friend of Christy's. And he'd said, "I'm going to get you out of here."

The shock had been so great that for a moment Matt had almost cried out. Something in the man's eyes had warned him, even calmed him. Then the man had turned away with the others and Matt was left alone again.

He leaned his face against the bars. Was it some kind of cruel joke? he wondered. How could Christy be in Al Mahbas? What did the bearded man have to do with her? For the first time in over six months Matt Chambers felt a flicker of hope. He would wait; he would be ready if the bearded man returned.

"I have seen your brother," Hassan said.

Christy stared at him. "Matt? You've seen Matt. He's alive? He..." She threw herself into Hassan's arms and began to weep. When at last she was in control of her voice, she said, "Can I see him?"

"No, Christy. That is impossible."

"But no one would know I'm an American. You said yourself that I look Moroccan now."

Hassan smiled down at her. "And so you do. But a Moroccan woman would never go into a jail." He tilted her chin up. "You forget, Christy, that this is a man's world. It is all right for men to spend their time in public places, in cafés and mosques, even in jails. But women stay at home behind the walls of their houses. Women stay with women; women talk to women. Only when a woman goes to market does she talk to a man outside of the family. Ameen's group has become our family these last few months. That is why you and Zohra and Zahira haven't had to wear veils in camp. But now we are close to Al Mahbas, and we have to be careful. It would be dangerous to your brother to do anything out of the ordinary now."

Christy looked up at Hassan. With a sigh she said, "You're right, of course. It's just that the thought of Matt's being so close and my not being able to see him is difficult." She squeezed his hand, knowing she couldn't kiss him because the others would see him. "Thank you for finding Matt," she said. "Oh, thank you, Hassan."

That night the men huddled around the campfire to make plans to rescue Matt Chambers.

"We have to take them by surprise," Ameen said. "There are only a few guards, but the place itself is a fortress. We could enter because they know us now, overpower the jailers and free Chambers. But all hell will break loose when we try to get him out of town."

"Not if we went in at night; we could be ten miles into the desert before the town knew what happened," Hassan said.

"But can you gain entrance to the jail at night?" Rahma asked.

"We would not ask for permission," Ameen said with a grin.

"We could take no more than two men with us," Hassan said.

"Two men are all we need." Ameen leaned forward, his face intense. "First we steal five horses. We get into the fortress, knock out the jailers, get the keys and free Chambers. Then we ride like the wind to where the rest of my tribe will be waiting and get as far into the desert as we can before daybreak."

Rahma and the other men nodded. "I want to go with you," Rahma said.

"Good." Ameen looked across the fire. "And you, Hadj, you are a good man with a knife."

The man he'd spoken to gave him an almost toothless smile. "As it is written," he murmured.

"It is settled, then," Ameen said. "Tomorrow night Hassan Ben Kadiri, Rahma, Hadj and I will go to Al Mahbas. The rest of you will be ready to travel fast." To Hassan he said, "You may tell your woman that soon her brother will be with her."

When he returned to their tent, Hassan waited until he had lowered the flaps. He turned to Christy and said, "We go after him tomorrow night."

She clutched the robe around her. It didn't seem real that after all these long months she'd found her brother. No, she thought, I haven't found him; Hassan has. She held her hand out to him, and when he sat down beside her she cupped his face and said, "There's no way I can ever thank you, Hassan."

"I can think of a dozen ways." He turned his head to capture her fingertips in his mouth. "You taste good," he said when he released them. He pulled the robe away from her body. "I wish we were alone. I wish that I could turn on a light and really look at you, because I want to make love to you in the sunlight, Christy. I want to be able to lay you down in a forest or on the desert floor or in any room of my home. I want to look at you with the sun shining on your body."

"Even now, when my skin is dark?"

"Light or dark, Christy. Because you are mine, and because when I look at you I am filled with hunger and with the need to touch you." Hassan pulled her down onto the rug beside him. For a long time he just held her close to him, luxuriating in the feel and the scent of her. These last few weeks in the desert with Christy had been the most important in Hassan's life. He had never thought he would love a woman the way he did Christy Chambers. Making love to her was the closest to heaven he ever expected to get. And just being with her, being able to reach out and touch her, gave him a feeling of satisfaction he had never before known.

Hassan's arms tightened around her. Tomorrow night he would bring Christy's brother back to her. There was a part of him that was afraid that bringing Matthew Chambers into their lives would make a difference. Christy had shared Hassan's tent for all of this time they had been in the desert, but he didn't know if she would continue to share it after her brother returned. Ameen's tribe thought that Christy was his wife; her brother would know that she wasn't. What would Chambers say when he knew that his sister was sleeping with him? Would this be the last night he and Christy would share?

He gave a low moan of need, and tightened his arms around her. I will not let you go, he thought. I cannot let you go. He kissed her, his mouth rough and urgent against hers in sudden hunger. He kissed the corners of her mouth; he took her lower lip between his teeth to suckle and bite. When she cried out in protest he thrust his tongue into her mouth. Oh, God, how I love you, he wanted to tell her as he pinned her beneath him, how I want you.

Even as a part of her wondered at this sudden urgency, Christy answered Hassan's kiss and her hands came up to caress his shoulders. Then, almost before she was ready, he entered her, moving deeply into her with such powerful thrusts that for a moment she was afraid. "Hassan!" she gasped. "I—"

His mouth covered hers with hard, thrilling kisses. His hands crept under her body to her buttocks as he urged her body closer to his.

Then, as suddenly as it had come, Christy's fear gave way. She raised her body to Hassan's and answered his kiss with a fire that matched his own. He gasped in pleasure. "I love you," he whispered hoarsely. "There will never be anyone but you, Christy. Never anyone."

Hassan was lost now, out of control, as he moved wildly against her. She whimpered his name in a litany of fear and need that set his blood on fire. He was a man, and this was his woman for as long as there was breath in his body.

Never had Christy experienced anything like this. Never had she felt so abandoned by her own body, so completely possessed by another. She had no will of her own; she was Hassan's. She belonged to him, and he could do, would do, whatever he chose. She followed his every movement. She grasped his shoulders and held on, knowing that if she didn't she would spin off into unreality. Without even realizing it, she whispered "Hassan!" again and again and told him how frightening this was, and how wonderful. Then suddenly she gasped and her body tightened in a frenzy of a desire that was past bearing.

"Yes!" Hassan said against her lips. "Yes, Christy!" He plunged against her and took her cry into his mouth while his own body convulsed in an agony of fulfillment.

He lay over her, too spent to move, feeling the terrible thump of his heart against his ribs. He buried his face in her hair and kissed her damp, sweet throat. When at last he could speak he said, "I am sorry. I don't know what happened to me. Did I hurt you?"

Christy shook her head. She kissed Hassan's shoulder and shuddered, because her whole body still felt as though live nerve ends were exposed.

Holding her, Hassan rolled so that she was on top of him. He smoothed the hair back from her face and kissed her. His hands caressed her back, and when she began to drowse against him he put his arms around her. "Don't move away from me," he said. "I like your body on mine this way." He kissed her eyelids closed. "Sleep, my Christy," he said. "Sleep, my love."

Chapter 16

Christy awoke slowly the next morning. With her eyes still closed, she reached out for Hassan. When she saw that he wasn't beside her she stretched, then smothered a groan. Her body ached; her mouth felt bruised. Then as she remembered, her face flushed and she turned her face into her pillow as a languorous smile tilted the corners of her mouth. She thought of the fierceness of Hassan's lovemaking the night before, of the almost desperate way he had driven himself into her and of her response.

There had been no holding back, because Hassan wouldn't let her hold back. Suddenly she'd been wild and free, soaring with him toward a release that had been almost too wondrous to bear, her body shuddering with need as she strained closer and cried his name.

The smile faded and inexplicable tears stung Christy's eyes, because she knew that what she felt for Hassan went beyond passion to a deep and abiding love, an impossible love.

Christy sat up and hugged her knees. Tonight Hassan was going to rescue Matt. She wanted to be a part of the rescue, but Hassan had said that was impossible, that this was a man's job. This time he was probably right. But what about the million other instances that come up in a marriage? How could a marriage exist when the man made every decision without asking the woman?

Slowly Christy got to her feet. Sunlight slanted in through the canvas, and she gazed down at her body. Except where she had been covered by her bra and panties, her skin was the color of warm sand. She looked like a Moroccan. But I'm not, she thought as she pulled the robe over her head. I'm an American. That's what I am, and I never want to be anything else. She brushed her hair back from her face, covered it with her scarf and, with her shoulders squared, stepped out into the sunshine.

Hassan, Ameen and some of the other men were cleaning their rifles. Without stopping to think about what she was going to say, Christy marched over to them.

"I want to help rescue my brother," she said to Ameen.

The nomad chieftain's eyes widened. His thick black brows drew together in a frown, but before he could speak Hassan said, "I have already told you that is impossible, Christy."

"Matt's my brother," she insisted. "Surely I can do something."

"You can do what I tell you." Hassan's voice was harsh and angry.

Christy glared at him. "Damn it, Hassan," she retorted, "I—"

"Go to your tent," he roared.

Too angry to speak, hands on her hips, Christy faced him. How dare he speak like this to her in front of the other men? She spun on her heel, but before she'd taken two steps, Ameen said, "Wait."

When Christy turned he said, "Perhaps you and the other women can be of help." Hassan started to speak, but Ameen held up his hand. "The three of you will go to the market in Al Mahbas this afternoon. It is just across from the fortress and a good vantage point to see if there is any kind of unusual activity going on there." Ameen rubbed a hand across his beard. "I would like to know whether or not they keep a guard posted up on the wall all night." He turned to Hassan. "It is something we need to know," he said.

"I don't like it." Hassan looked at Christy, his eyes dark with anger. "She is an American. She—"

"With her dark skin no one would know that," Ameen said. He turned to Christy. "Tell Zohra and Zahira that the three of you will go to the town this afternoon."

Christy nodded. Bowing her head, she said, "Thank you, Ameen al-Shaibi." She glanced quickly at Hassan, then away. She knew he was angry, and she was sorry, but this was something she had to do. Matt was her brother; it was important that she be a part of this.

The heat was stifling. Flies buzzed around the meager display of overripe bananas, oranges, pomegranates and a few vegetables. A whole skinned sheep, the carcass covered with flies, hung from a butcher's stall.

"*Zfft!*" Zahira said. "This place is a pigsty."

"But we must buy something," Zohra cautioned. "The oranges are all right. We will take them. And a few vegetables." She motioned to the man behind the stall.

Christy looked at the high, thick walls of the yellow stone fortress just across the way. Her throat tightened as she watched the guard pacing back and forth on the ramparts. Somewhere deep in that fortress her brother waited to be rescued. She closed her eyes. It won't be long now, Matt, she thought.

Moving to a stall where tired cabbages, bedraggled carrots and a few withered onions were sold, Christy frowned, as she had seen Zahira frown, and pointed to the carrots and the onions.

"You have Spanish eyes," said the man who owned the stall as he began to weigh her purchase. "Was your mother Spanish?"

Christy shook her head. Out of the corner of her eye she saw a movement. When she looked up, the guard on the ramparts of the fortress shifted his rifle and moved toward a flight of rough stone steps.

"I have heard there was a tribe of nomads near here," the man went on. "You are one of them, aren't you?"

Christy nodded. Taking a deep breath, trying to speak slowly and carefully, she said, "What is that place?"

"Our jail," he said proudly. "It has been there for five hundred years. It was built as a fortress to keep out invaders. There are dungeons below, where prisoners are kept." He shook his head. "Poor devils, once they are in the fortress, there is no escape."

"It is well guarded, I am sure," Christy said.

"The walls are so strong there is little need for guards."

"The man on the ramparts is leaving. Will another take his place?"

"There is no need." The man handed her the bag of vegetables. "Why do you ask?"

Christy shrugged. "I have never seen a jail before. Our men almost never allow us into a town. Today is an exception. I am curious, that's all." She looked down and fluttered her eyelashes.

The man added a dozen more carrots to her bag. "Perhaps you will come to the market again tomorrow," he said hopefully.

"Perhaps." Christy looked again at the fortress. "Are there many prisoners there now?" she asked.

"Only one. Some say he is an American." The man shrugged. "Abdeslem—he is the jailer—said that the prisoner causes no trouble. Abdeslem sleeps through the night with never a disturbance." The man lowered his voice to a whisper. "To tell you the truth, I think Abdur sleeps, too, even though it is his job to guard the entrance. He—"

"We must go now." Zahira frowned at the man, then at Christy. "Our men are waiting."

Christy nodded, and to the man she said, "*Shukran*, thank you."

"*Tusba al khair,*" he said. "Goodbye, little nomad. Remember that here the vegetables are always fresh."

"Fresh!" Zahira snorted. "They are older than you are!" She grabbed Christy's arm. "Come along. If we are not back by sunset, our husbands will be angry." Her bony fingers dug into Christy's arm. When they were out of earshot of the stall keeper, she said, "You should not have spoken to the man. A Moroccan woman doesn't—"

Christy jerked free. "I know what a Moroccan woman does or doesn't do," she said in a low voice. She looked at the fortress and saw the man with the rifle emerge. Two guards, she thought. There are only two guards now.

"You did well," Ameen said when Christy told him what she'd learned from the vegetable man. He nodded to the women, then, waving them away, he turned to his men. "Now this is what we are going to do. We..." He looked up. Zahira and Zohra had turned away, but

Christy was still there. "Do you want something?" he asked in an ironic tone.

Refusing to be intimidated, Christy nodded. "I would like to hear what your plan is," she said.

Ameen threw back his head and laughed. "I don't know what we are going to do with this woman of yours, my friend Hassan. She has a mind of her own, hasn't she?" Before Hassan could answer, Ameen said, "Very well, woman. You may stay if you will be quiet."

Christy nodded as Ameen turned to his men. She knew that Hassan was still angry with her for this morning and that he was even angrier with her now. But that couldn't be helped. Matt was her brother; she wanted to know what was going on.

The plan was a simple one. Under cover of darkness Ameen and Hassan would overpower the guard at the door. They would bind and gag him, then they would find Abdeslem, get his key and tie him up. "While we are doing that," Ameen said, "Rahma and Hadj will steal the horses. We will free Chambers and we will ride like hell."

Ameen looked at the other men. "I want you to break camp now. Go north in a straight line until we catch up to you."

"But what if something happens? What if something goes wrong?" one of his men asked.

"You are not to wait for us. You are to take the woman of Hassan Ben Kadriri to Tafarout."

Christy glanced at Hassan. All of her thoughts had been concentrated on Matt; she hadn't even stopped to think of the danger Hassan might be in. Suddenly she was afraid. She wanted Matt back, but if anything happened to Hassan...

The rest of the nomads began to break camp. Christy helped Zohra and Zahira pack the pots and pans and rugs, then went to get her own meager belongings together. The tents were already down and the men were loading the camels when she saw Hassan near the pool under a stand of date palms. She knew he was still angry with her, but that didn't matter. Nothing mattered except that he was walking into danger because of her.

"I want to talk to you for a moment," she said as she approached him.

"Yes?"

"I . . . I'm sorry you're angry, Hassan, but I had to be a part of this. I know I didn't really do anything, but—"

"You managed to find out there would be no guard on the rampart tonight, and that was helpful to us," Hassan conceded. He moved closer. "What am I to do with you?" he asked as he tilted her face to his.

"I don't know, darling." A smile trembled on her lips.

"You are stubborn and strong-willed, determined to have your own way. You are too independent, too . . . American. I don't know how to handle you."

Christy put her arms around him and, holding him close, said, "I love you, Hassan, but I don't think I can change. I'll never be the woman you want me to be." Her arms tightened around him. "This time, this *now*, here on the desert with you, has been the best of my life. But when it's over . . ." She buried her head in his chest, unable to go on.

Hassan gripped her arms. "What are you saying?" He shook her. "Damn it, Christy, what are you trying to tell me?"

"That it will never work between us." She looked up at him, and her eyes filled with tears. "You know it, Hassan, just as I know it."

"No!" He pulled her back into his arms. "I will not let you go," he said. "I will never let you go. How can you say these things after all the nights we've shared?"

"Hassan, please—"

"I have never experienced with a woman what I felt with you last night, Christy. And I know in my heart no other man will make you feel what you felt with me. You loved me, you clung to me, you soared with me. Now you tell me that when we leave the desert you will go back to your own people." His arms were like steel bands around her. "I will never let you go," he whispered against her hair.

"Mrs. Christy!" Zohra called. *"Yallah, yallah,* we are leaving."

"I don't want to go without you." She wept against his shoulder. "Let me go with you tonight. Let me—"

In spite of his anger and his desperation, Hassan laughed. "You are impossible," he told her. Then, not caring whether the others saw him or not, he kissed her. It was a hard and unrelenting kiss, a kiss of fire, that left Christy weak with longing. She stood on tiptoe, clinging to him, answering his kiss as her hands tightened on his shoulders.

When he let her go she said, "Please, Hassan, be careful. If anything happens to you I—"

"Nothing is going to happen to me." He kissed her again. "Now go," he said. "The others are waiting."

"Hassan . . ."

He shook his head. "Until tomorrow," he said, "when I bring your brother back to you."

It was easier than Hassan had thought it would be. There was no moon; the night was dark. He approached the guard at the gate in a casual manner, offered a cigarette and began to chat. The man took the cigarette. He was bored with the long hours of nothing to do and no one to talk to. He was a garrulous man and glad to have somebody to help him while away the lonely hours until dawn. He didn't hear Ameen moving stealthily through the shadows; he uttered only one hiss of protest when Ameen struck him.

Quickly Hassan and Ameen carried the man inside. They bound his hands and feet and gagged him so he couldn't cry out when he regained consciousness.

"Now to Abdeslem," Hassan whispered.

Ameen nodded and the two men moved quietly through the silent courtyard to the small room where Abdeslem had his office. He stirred when they entered. "Eh?" he said. "What's that? Who's there? What do you—?"

Hassan slapped his hand over the guard's mouth. "Quiet," he cautioned. "We don't want to hurt you."

"Gag him," Ameen said as he lighted an oil lamp. He moved to the old man on the cot, pulled his hands behind him and bound them. By this time Hassan had gagged the man and bound his legs.

The keys were on top of the desk. Ameen glanced at Hassan. "Let's go," he said.

With the lamp to guide them, they made their way through the dark, musty passages to the stairs. "Careful," Hassan warned. The stairs were treacherous, rough and crumbling with age.

They reached the bottom and made their way along the corridor. When the turned to the right Hassan called out, "Matthew! Matthew Chambers, are you there?"

For a moment there was no reply. Then Matt called out, "Yes! Yes, I'm here!"

Except for the circle of light from the lantern, the cell block was midnight dark. Ameen held the lantern higher.

"This cursed place," he muttered. "It smells of age and death."

Five hundred years of death, Hassan thought, and felt a shiver of cold run down his spine. "Where are you, Matt?" he called out. "Where...?" Then he saw Christy's brother, his hands gripping the bars, his face white against the light. "You came back," Matt breathed.

"Of course we came back." Ameen held the lamp close to the lock. "Hurry," he said to Hassan. "I don't want to spend any more time in this place than I have to."

Hassan tried five keys before the cell door finally swung open and Matt stepped out. He stood for a moment, then he clasped the hands of both men. *"Shukran,"* he said, "thank you."

"You're welcome," Ameen said. "Now let's get out of here."

Hassan led the way to the stairs. When they reached the top he said, "We'll wait behind the door for Rahma's signal." He turned to Matt. "Ameen's men are stealing five horses. They'll be here in—"

Suddenly a shot rang out. A man shouted and other men took up the cry. "Stop them! Thieves! They are stealing the horses!"

With that Rahma and Hadj galloped past. Damn! Hassan thought. He flattened himself against the wall as a group of men ran by.

"Were those your men?" Matt whispered.

"Yes," Ameen growled. He peered out into the street, then ducked back inside when he saw other riders approaching. "My men will head for the desert," he said. "They have no other choice now. We will have to make our way as best we can."

"Camels are tethered in the square," Hassan said. "We will have to use them and head in the opposite direction, at least for a while."

Ameen nodded. "That is all we can do now."

Cautiously the three men stepped out into the street toward the square.

"We must have water," Hassan said.

"There will be canteens in the stable if we're lucky." Ameen grinned, his strong teeth stark white against the darkness of his skin. "So pray to Allah that we're lucky."

They were. While Hassan and Ameen saddled three camels, Matt filled as many canteens as he could find. When they were ready they led the camels to the other end of town. Hassan glanced at Matt. He had no idea what kind of physical condition Christy's brother was in after all his months of imprisonment. But he knew that the next few days, until they caught up with the tribe, would be rough. He hoped to Allah that Matt would be able to keep up.

They rode a mile in the opposite direction before they began to angle back the way they wanted to go, trying to keep a distant but parallel course toward where they would rendezvous with their caravan. At sunup they dismounted, then surveyed the desert from a high dune.

"We have lost them," Hassan said. He studied his compass, then pointed a little to the right. "That's the way we want to go." He looked at Matt. "How are you doing?"

Matt grinned. "Ask me in a couple of hours," he said. "Right now all I know is how glad I am to be out of that cell. There's no way I can thank either one of you for what you've done. You've risked your lives for me, and I don't even know why."

"Hassan Ben Kadiri is my friend," Ameen said. "Your sister is his woman. He wanted to rescue you for her and I said I would help him. You see?"

Matt stared at Ameen, then his glance swung to Hassan. "Christy?" he said. "Christy is your..." He took a deep breath. "What are you talking about? My sister's in Montana. She—"

"Your sister is in Morocco," Hassan said. "She came here to find you. For the past month and a half we have been living with Ameen and his people."

Together? Matt Chambers stared at Hassan. Christy and this man, this bearded desert man with the strong, stern face and tall, powerful body.... "I don't understand," he said. "Are you and my sister married?"

Hassan glanced quickly at Ameen. With a nod he said, "We were married before we began to search for you." Then, before Matt could ask anything else, Hassan said, "We can discuss this later. Right now, if we have any sense, we will travel." Without waiting for an answer he strode down the dune to the waiting camels.

By midmorning the desert was an inferno. Hassan tore away part of his robe so that Matt could wrap it around his head. They drank sparingly from the canteens and tried not to think that they'd had nothing to eat since their noon meal the day before. Matt's face was white; the hands that held the reins were shaking. When he swayed in the saddle Ameen said, "We will stop for a while, there in the shade of that dune." He glanced at Hassan with a look that said, This man is too weak to travel. What are we to do with him?

When they dismounted Matt staggered to the shade of the dune and sank to his knees. Hassan held the canteen out to him. Matt took it, drank, then, handing it back, said, "Sorry, I guess I'm not as strong as I thought."

"There is no need to apologize," Hassan told him. "You have been locked up in a cage for a long time without even seeing the sun. Of course you're weak."

"I exercised. I moved around as much as I could, and I ate every damn bit of swill they gave me." Matt closed his eyes. "I'll be all right in a minute," he said.

The afternoon seemed to go on forever. The sun beat down with merciless persistence; the temperature climbed to over 135. The three men were silent, each lost in his own thoughts as the camels plodded on. Hassan thought of Christy. He remembered the first time they had been together, in the oasis after the sandstorm. He remembered how she had looked in the pool, how droplets of water had clung to her breasts and how cool her skin had felt against his hands. He whispered her name in his mind and kept going.

He looked at her brother, hunched low over the saddle, and knew what an effort it was for Matt to hang on. He is as stubborn as Christy, Hassan thought, smiling through his cracked lips.

At dusk they found a small oasis. The water was dank and covered with moss and scum; the palms were scrubby. But it was a haven. While Hassan helped Matt to the relative shelter of the trees, Ameen cleared the surface of the water. Then he soaked his head covering and handed it to Matt.

Matt took it without speaking and held it to his face. After a moment he was able to say, "Thanks, that helps."

"We will be all right here," Ameen told him. "There is water, such as it is, and some dates. By morning you will be able to travel again."

"Of course." Matt closed his eyes. "But I think I'll rest now."

Ameen looked at Hassan, then with a motion of his head indicated that Hassan was to follow him. "What do you think?" he asked. "Will he be able to travel tomorrow?"

"I'm not sure. It would be better if we could stay here another day and travel at night."

"By then the caravan will be three days ahead of us. We have no food but the dates, and Allah knows the water here is hardly fit to drink." Ameen glanced over at Matt. "But I think that if we travel tomorrow we will lose him." He sighed. "Do we lose him, or do we lose the caravan?"

Hassan looked at the man who had become his friend. "You go on," he said. "I'll stay with him until he's able to travel."

"*Zfft!*" Ameen grunted. "What kind of a man do you take me for? Now, shut up and let me get some rest."

Hassan lay back and closed his eyes. He thought of Christy and of how she would feel when Rahma and Hadj arrived at the caravan without them.

Christy, he thought. And then he slept.

Chapter 17

The caravan didn't find an oasis that night, so they camped against a rise of sand dunes. A lookout with a signal flag was posted to watch for five horsemen. A fire was built to serve as a beacon in the night. By dawn the five men hadn't appeared and the caravan continued on.

"They will catch up with us today," Zohra told Christy. "Don't look so worried; Ameen will find us before the day is done."

But Christy *was* worried. All that day she searched the horizon with anxious eyes. Where were they? she wondered. The caravan had been only half a day ahead of Ameen and Hassan. The men should have caught up with the caravan last night. Oh, God, what could have happened to them? Had Hassan and Ameen been captured when they tried to free Matt? What if they were imprisoned in the fortress, too?

The caravan found an oasis that afternoon. Again a guard was posted to watch for the missing men. By now

Zohra was as worried as Christy. "They should have caught up with us by midmorning," she fretted. "Ameen knows the desert better than any man alive. Maybe something happened. Maybe they couldn't get the horses."

"Maybe, maybe." Zahira scratched her long bony nose. "Don't worry so. Ameen will catch up with us—if not today, then tomorrow."

Dusk settled over the oasis and still there was no sign of the men. Christy paced back and forth and finally went to stand beside the lookout to scan the desert. Suddenly her gaze riveted on a distant cloud of dust.

"There!" She pointed to the east. "I see something!"

The lookout shaded his eyes, then turned and shouted to the others, "I see them! I see them!"

Zohra ran forward with the men. She gripped Christy's hand. "I told you my Ameen knew the desert," she said joyfully. "I have prayed to Allah to deliver him safely back to us." She smiled at Christy. "Soon you will see your brother again. I know how happy that..." Her voice trailed off, her eyes narrowing as the cloud of dust drew closer. "There are only two of them," she said in a strained voice.

Christy froze. She focused all of her attention on the riders, and as they came closer she knew that it was true; there were only two men.

The others gathered around them, talking excitedly as they strained to see who the riders were. Then someone said, "It is Rahma and Hadj."

For a moment Christy's world went dark. She clutched Zahira's arm for support, then with the others ran toward the two men.

"What happened? Where is Ameen? What happened to Hassan Ben Kadiri and the American?" The questions were shouted as the two men pulled their horses up and dismounted.

"Water," Rahma mumbled, and fell to his knees on the sand.

Quickly the other men helped Rahma and Hadj. They were given water, and after they had drank their fill the other men said, "Now, tell us what happened."

"There was trouble." Hadj doused his head with water, then, pushing his dripping hair back off his face, said, "We were discovered when we tried to steal the horses. We had already mounted and were leading the other three animals toward the fortress when all hell broke loose."

"Men began to shout," Rahma put in. "Somebody fired, then a whole mob of them took after us." He looked at Zohra, then away. "We had no choice," he said. "We had to run."

"But what about Ameen and Hassan?" a man named Brahim asked. "Where are they? What happened to them?"

Rahma and Hadj looked at each other. "We don't know," Rahma finally said.

For a moment there was silence, then everyone began to talk at once. "We should look for them," someone said. "No, we should go on to Tafarout," another said to Brahim. "Ameen said if anything happened we should take the American woman there."

Brahim hesitated. "Just so. That is what we will do."

"No!" Christy stood, feet apart, hands on her hips. "No," she said again. "We're going to wait."

"We can't," Brahim said. "Ameen told us we must take you to Tafarout. He's out leader; we cannot disobey him."

"Nor can you abandon him." Her voice was desperate as she faced the others. "Look, it wasn't Rahma or

Hadj's fault that they escaped without Ameen and Hassan. But that means that Hassan and Ameen had to find some other means to escape."

"There were camels tied in the square," Hadj said. "They could have fled on them."

"But the men of the town had horses," Rahma said. Shame and despair were written on his face. "If they gave chase, they would have overtaken the camels."

"The townspeople were too busy chasing us," Hadj said. "They didn't even know Ameen and Hassan were in town."

"Ameen could have ridden the other way," Rahma said. "Then later he could have circled around and headed in this direction."

"But if they had no water..." Brahim took a deep breath. "It has been three days," he said.

"Maybe they had water. Maybe they found an oasis." Christy turned to Brahim. "We've got to wait," she said. "And we've got to send out a search party."

"But that is impossible." Brahim scowled at her. "Ameen told us to—"

"I know what Ameen told you," Christy shouted. "But if he and Hassan and my brother are somewhere out there on the desert, they need help. We've got to—"

"It is not the place of a woman to tell men what to do." An elderly man stepped forward and shook his finger under Christy's nose. "Your tongue is sharp for a woman. You have no manners. Your husband should have beaten you and taught you how to behave." He pushed Christy aside and to Brahim said, "We must do as Ameen has told us. If he does not return, you are our leader and we will follow you. We should break camp now and travel by night. In—"

"No!" Christy's face was red with frustration and anger. "You can't do that. We've got to send a search party out."

"Be quiet." Brahim said. "The old one is right; it isn't your place to speak. Women do what men tell them to do. That's the way it has always been; that's the way it will always be." He turned to the others. "Prepare to break camp," he ordered.

"No." Zohra stepped forward. "I say that we do not break camp. I say that we wait until daybreak and that we send a search party out."

"Zohra!" Zahira's eyes widened in disbelief. "The men have decided what we must do."

"Then to hell with the men." Zohra's face was determined. "They can go if they like, but Mrs. Christy and I will stay and search for our men."

"Rahma and I will stay with you," Hadj said.

The other men were silent. They looked embarrassed and uncertain. "Very well," Brahim said. "We will stay, and tomorrow we will search. But only tomorrow. If we don't find them the next day, we move on."

Clyde swung his head and snapped at Christy's ankles. She took her hat off, swore at him and perfunctorily boxed his ears. After all these months together it had become a game they played, and Christy knew the camel would probably have died of fright if he ever had connected with her ankle.

Christy gazed around her at the endless expanse of desert and wiped her face with the sleeve of her shirt before she put the hat back on. It felt good to be wearing Western clothes again. At daybreak, when she'd emerged from her tent, the others had stared at her in disbelief.

"You are wearing pants!" Zahira's beady eyes widened. "Go at once and put your robe on."

Christy had ignored her. "Let's get started," she said to Brahim. "The sun will be up soon."

"But . . . but you . . . you are not going with us."

"Of course I am. Hassan and my brother are out there somewhere, and I'm going to find them." Without another word she turned and went to Clyde. She whacked him across his knees, and when he knelt she mounted him. Turning to the others, she said, "Well?"

There were five men and Christy. Brahim was in the lead. Using a compass, he headed back in the direction of Al Mahbas. Brahim spoke to her only when he had to. The other men didn't speak to her at all. But that didn't matter; all that mattered was that they continue this search.

They stopped in the shade of a dune at midday to eat a meager lunch and to drink from their canteens. When twenty minutes went by Christy said, "Let's go."

"We need to rest," Brahim said.

"We need to keep traveling." Christy glared at him.

With a sigh Brahim got to his feet. "You are a terrible woman. Your husband should divorce you." He nodded to the other men. "Let's get going," he growled.

The afternoon sun burned down, scorching their skin, drying their throats. "It is time we started back," Brahim said.

"Another hour," Christy pleaded. "We've got to keep going."

The desert floor seemed to dip and sway; the dunes shimmered in the sun. Keep going, Christy told herself. Hassan and Matt are somewhere, are here. We've got to find them. She closed her eyes against the sun's burning rays. How long could a man last out on the desert? she wondered. Hassan and Ameen were strong; they were survivors. But could they survive without water? And what about Matt? What kind of a condition was he in after all these months in prison? Would he be strong enough to survive a trip like this?

She opened her eyes, ashamed that she had closed them for even a moment. She had to look for Hassan; she had to find him.

They had finished the last of the water two hours ago. Hassan sucked hard on the date pit and tried to tell himself that he wasn't thirsty. He glanced at Ameen. The desert chieftain's lips were cracked and swollen, but he managed a grin. "We will make it, my friend Hassan," he said. "Any minute now we will find an oasis."

Will we? Hassan wondered. And if we do, will it be in time? He glanced at Matt's unconscious form hanging head down over the saddle. Christy's brother had been unconscious since a little past noon, and Hassan knew that if they didn't find water soon, Matt Chambers would perish.

I wanted to bring him back to you, Christy, Hassan thought. For a while I was sure he was going to make it, because he's like you. He is stubborn and has a lot of willpower; he hung on longer than I thought he would. But he was kept in that cage too long, Christy. He has had very little food and almost no exercise or fresh air. He is in terrible shape, but he still might make it if only we can find water.

Talking to her helped. So did thinking about her. Hassan remembered the first time she walked into his office. She had been wearing a green dress that was almost the exact color of her eyes. He had thought that she was one of the prettiest women he had ever seen. Her skin was flawless ivory. Her hair was the color of the sunset, and he had wanted to touch it. He had watched her mouth when she spoke, wondering how her soft lips would feel against his. She . . . Hassan felt himself sway and grabbed the reins.

That first night when he had taken her to dinner, then back to her hotel, they had walked in the garden. He had known then that she wasn't just pretty; she was beautiful, and he wanted her with a suddenness that surprised him. Allah forgive him, he had told her he would find her brother if she... Even now he felt ashamed of what he had said to her.

So Christy had found someone else to take her into the desert, and it had almost killed her.

As it was killing him.

The date pit was hard and dry in his mouth. Christy, he thought, if I could only see you once more.

That was what kept him going, the thought of Christy. Of her dear face, the way she felt in his arms, the way she whispered his name in the darkness of the night. Christy. She . . .

"Hassan!" Ameen's voice was harsh, jarring him out of his reverie. "There are riders!"

"What? Where?" Hassan sat straighter in the saddle and strained to see.

"There, to the left." Ameen whipped the covering off his head and waved it, standing high in the stirrups.

Hassan did the same thing. He tried to shout, but his voice was hoarse. "They see us!" he cried.

"Praise Allah." Ameen grinned at Hassan. "I don't know who they are or where they came from, but they are coming this way. Look, one of the riders is ahead of the others." He pointed to a slim figure waving a hat.

"A foreigner," Hassan said as he tried to pull the camel carrying Matt along. "He is wearing pants. He..." Hassan saw the red hair then. My God, it was Christy! He let go of the other camel's reins and spurred his own on. What was she doing out there on the desert? She should have been in Tafarout by now.

She was so close he could see her face now and hear her calling his name. She raced on, her red hair loose and streaming out behind her. When she drew nearer, she pulled back on the reins. He heard her yell at Clyde to kneel, and almost before the animal had she was off and running toward Hassan.

Hassan leaped from his camel and ran toward her. Then his arms were around her. He kissed her. He held her away from him so he could see her face, then hugged her to him.

"Christy," he said over and over again. "Christy."

She was crying now, crying and clinging to him. "I knew we'd find you," she said. "I knew that if we kept going we'd find you." She looked up at him. "Oh, Hassan, your face is burnt. Your poor lips..." She clutched his arms. "Are you all right? You're not hurt?"

"No, love." He managed a grin. "But I would certainly like a drink of water."

"Oh, God, I'm sorry." She looked back at Brahim and the other men. "Hurry!" she called. "Bring the canteens."

"It looks as though we have a new sultana," Ameen said as he rode up. His white teeth flashed in a smile. "I see you are wearing pants, Mrs. Christy. I don't approve of them, but they seem to fit you remarkably well." He handed the other camel's reins to Hassan.

Christy looked at Matt's limp body hanging over the saddle. "Matt!" she screamed. "Is he...?"

"No, Christy, but he is unconscious." Hassan motioned to Brahim and the other men as they rode up. "Help me get him off," he said.

The other men quickly dismounted and carefully lifted Matt from across the saddle. When they had laid him down on the sand, one of them held a canteen of water to Matt's lips. He didn't stir, and it dribbled off his lips. Hassan took the canteen and poured water on the head covering he'd taken off. Quickly he bathed Matt's face and wrists.

"How is he?" Ameen jumped off his camel and strode to Hassan.

"Still unconscious," Hassan said.

"Hold the wet cloth on top of his head. Perhaps that will help." Ameen held out his hand to Brahim. "I told you to go on to Tafarout," he said. "I am glad you disobeyed me, my friend, because I think you have saved our lives. Now let's see what we can do for the American."

Christy took the canteen and, kneeling beside Matt, said, "Let me try." She poured water onto her fingers and touched them to Matt's swollen lips. "Come on, Matt," she said.

He licked the water off her fingers, and with a glad cry she held the canteen to his mouth. His lips parted. He swallowed painfully and opened his eyes.

"Christy?" he croaked. "Christy, is that you?"

"Yes, Matt. Yes, darling." She kissed his cheek. "Oh, Matt," she said, "I've been looking for you for such a long time." She held the canteen to his lips again, and this time he drank more.

"The others?" he questioned. "Are they all right?"

"Yes, Matt." She looked up as Hassan tipped back another canteen and drank his fill.

When he closed the top of the canteen he bent down. "How are you doing?" he asked Matt.

"Better. All right now." Matt held out his hand. "Thanks to you and Ameen."

"You had better thank Brahim," Ameen said. "He had sense enough to disobey my orders to take your sister to Tafarout. Instead he came looking for us." He clapped Brahim on the back. "Thank you, my friend," he said.

Brahim flushed. He glanced at the other men, then at Christy. "It is not me you should thank, Ameen al-Shaibi; it is the woman. I wanted to leave the oasis we found last night and head to Tafarout. Mrs. Christy refused to go. She insisted we search for you, and when I didn't want to go, she said she would go alone." He looked at Hassan. "She is a difficult woman to control," he said. "But she has the heart of a lioness."

Without speaking, Hassan pulled Christy to her feet. He looked into her eyes. "I know," he said. "I know."

Chapter 18

They stayed at the oasis for a week, because Matt was unable to travel. The time he had spent in prison had weakened him; the three days in the desert had almost killed him.

For the first few days he drifted in and out of consciousness, and Christy spent every waking moment at his side. She was dressed like a desert woman again in her robe, her hair covered. Once when Matt awoke he said, "Christy? Where's Christy? I thought my sister was here."

"I am here, Matt," she said as she bathed his face.

He touched her. "But your skin is dark. And your robe... Why are you dressed like that, Christy?"

"I'll explain it all later, Matt." She kissed his forehead. "Rest now," she said.

Matt's face was thin; his cheeks were hollow and lined. Seven months ago he'd left home a young thirty-four;

now he looked ten years older. But he was alive, and that, Christy thought, was all that mattered.

At first he was able to eat only a small portion of rice, but little by little his appetite improved, and by the end of the week he was able to eat almost everything he was served. As his strength grew he was eager to talk. And Christy was eager to ask questions.

"What happened, Matt?" she said. "Why were you being held?"

"I don't know, Christy. I'm pretty sure it had something to do with the man I hired to take me to Bir Lahlou. He was a competent desert man, but I didn't like him and I knew I'd made a mistake in hiring him. I decided that when we got to Al Mahbas I'd pay him off and find somebody else to take me the rest of the way." Matt shook his head. "But I didn't have the chance. Somebody came into my hotel room that first night in Al Mahbas. They hit me over the head, and the next thing I knew I was in a cell. I never saw Driss again."

"Driss?" Christy's face paled. "Driss was the man you hired?"

Matt nodded. "Uncle Albert gave me his name before I left Montana."

Christy stared at him, unbelieving. Then she took a deep breath and said, "He gave me Driss's name, too."

"What?" Matt gripped her arms. "I don't understand. What are you talking about?"

"I was frantic with worry when we didn't hear from you, Matt. Uncle Albert contacted our embassy in Rabat and some officials with Moroccan government, but they couldn't find any trace of you. I decided to come to Morocco and look for you myself. Uncle Albert raised hell, but when he knew I was determined to make the trip, he gave me Driss's name. I went to Marrakesh and hired him to take me into the desert—to Bir Lahlou."

"You hired Driss to..." Matt's eyes widened in disbelief. "My God, Christy, the man's dangerous. He—"

"He's dead," she said.

"Dead?"

"I went to Tafarout with him. He hired two men there, and we started out from Tafarout. I felt the same way you did about him, Matt. I knew two hours after we started out that I'd made a mistake, but I didn't know what to do about it. I'd paid him half of what he asked before we left Tafarout, and I told him I'd give him the rest when we got to Bir Lahlou. He thought I had the money with me. We spent the first night at an oasis and the next morning..." Christy hesitated, remembering again how frightened she'd been that terrible morning. Her gaze met Matt's, and, beginning again, she said, "The next morning he and the other men tried to rape me. Then they were going to kill me. They would have if it hadn't been for Hassan."

Matt rubbed his hand through his brick-red hair. "I don't understand any of this, Christy," he said. "How does Hassan come into the picture?"

"I went to see him when I first came to Marrakesh. I wanted him to take me into the desert. He...we disagreed about something, and then I remembered Uncle Albert had given me Driss's name, so I went to see him. I'd already left Marrakesh by the time Hassan found out I'd hired Driss. He knew what kind of a man Driss was, so he came after me."

Matt's brows came together in a puzzled frown. "But how did you come to be with Ameen and his people?"

"There was a sandstorm," Christy told him. "We lost two of the camels, and a day or two later the camel drivers disappeared. Hassan and I were alone. We headed for

Bir Lahlou but ran out of food and water. We kept going and Ameen found us. We've been with him and his people for almost two months."

"The men—the day you found us—they said..." Matt looked at Christy. "They said you were Hassan's woman. Hassan said that you were his wife."

She'd known, of course, that this moment would come, yet she was unprepared for it.

"Is it true?" Matt asked. "Are you and Hassan ... ?"

"We're not married, Matt." She met his gaze with unfaltering eyes.

He stared at her. "But you share a tent. You're ... together?"

"Yes, Matt, we're together."

"But Christy..." Matt grasped her hand. "I know that Hassan's a fine man. He's protected you from God knows what and he saved my life. But he's a Moroccan, Christy, a Muslim. His beliefs, his customs, are different from yours. How can you even think of a permanent relationship with him? Can you see yourself going through life dressed as you are now? Continuing to darken your skin?"

"We had to darken my skin when we neared Al Mahbas," Christy said defensively. "The color will fade. I'll look like myself again by the time we get back to Marrakesh."

"But will you *be* yourself?"

Christy looked at him, then she dropped her gaze and said, "Yes, Matt, I will be. I've told Hassan that when this is over I'll leave him." She looked at her brother. "But for as long as we're here, Matt, I belong to Hassan. I want to belong to him."

For a long moment Matthew Chambers didn't speak. Then he said, "Do you love him, Christy?"

"Yes." Tears stung her eyes. "Oh, yes, Matt. I love him."

The desert night was clear and cool. A full yellow moon shone down on the rise and fall of dunes as Christy and Hassan walked a short distance from camp. Alone, away from the sound of other voices, it seemed to Christy that they were in a strange and uninhabited world of surrealistic moon craters, of sand and shadows and unbelievable quiet.

Hassan's arms encircled her waist, and she stood with her back to him as they looked out on the desert night. I'll never forget this night, Christy thought. I'll never forget the stillness or the moon or the feel of his body against mine. When it's over, when I have left him… She turned, and, taking his face between her hands, she kissed him.

Through the robe Christy's body felt delicate against his. She had lost weight this past month, and now Hassan could feel the fragility of her bones and was overwhelmed by how much he loved her. Never, as long as he lived, would he forget the way she had looked that day on the desert when she had raced toward him. Or the feel of her in his arms as he crushed her to him.

By her will and the strength of her love she had come out into the desert in search of him, urging the others on, Brahim had told him, refusing to give up when they wanted to turn back.

"She has the heart of a lioness," Bramin had said, and it was true. Christy was a woman of indomitable courage. Suddenly Hassan wanted to sweep her off her feet. He wanted to carry her farther away from the camp and lay her down and strip the clothes off her. He wanted to see the moonlight on her naked body and hear her whisper his name when he urged her close.

They hadn't been able to get enough of each other this past week that they had been back in the camp beside the oasis. Each night when Christy retired to their tent, Hassan had been forced, by custom, to linger around the campfire with the other men. But even as he had participated in the conversation, his body had been taut with impatience to get to her. When at last he broke away from the men, he found Christy awake and waiting for him, lifting her arms in eager welcome.

I will never get enough of her, Hassan thought now as he kissed her. I want her beside me until the day I die. I want to see her face when I close my eyes at night and again when I open them in the morning. He touched her breasts through her robe and felt her shiver against him.

"If we don't go back right now," he said as he held her away from him, "I am going to take you right here on the sand."

Christy's fingers curled in his beard. "I love you to want me," she whispered. She captured his lower lip between her teeth and ran her tongue over it. Then quickly she stepped away and began to run back toward the camp.

He caught her before she reached it and, turning her around, looked down into her laughing face. "You are a witch," he growled in mock anger. "It would serve you right if I took you here and now." He gripped her arms. "I ache with wanting you, Christy. I will never, if I live to be 110, get enough of you." He took her hand and brought it to his lips. "Tonight belongs to me," he said.

He put his arm around her and led her back to their tent, and when they were inside he kissed her with an urgency that left her weak with wanting. He nipped her lips and searched the moist recesses of her mouth before he trailed a line of fire down the white column of her throat,

around to her ears. He bit her earlobe, and when she protested his tongue darted into her ear.

"Darling," Christy whispered, "darling, please."

Never before had Hassan felt the need to so totally
possess a woman. He gazed down into her green eyes,
then slowly lowered her to the carpet-covered sand.

Gently he caressed her breasts with his lips and his
tongue.

With a shuddering sigh Christy touched his shoulders,
then ran her hands down the smooth plane of his back and
around his narrow hips. She touched him and heard the
sharp intake of his breath and knew he couldn't wait any
longer.

Together, joined in love, they moved in a slow, then a
quickened, cadence. They whispered each other's names,
clasping each other close, near the brink of completion,
trembling with anticipation, yet reluctant to end this perfect ecstasy. Again and again Hassan brought her to the
brink of fulfillment, only to retreat and soothe her and
begin again.

Finally, in a frenzy of desire, Christy whispered,
"Please, Hassan. Please, darling. I can't bear it any
longer. I can't..."

His arms tightened and he surged against her with all
the power and longing he'd held in check.

Christy cried out, burying her head against his shoulder to muffle her cries. Higher they climbed, and still
higher. Hassan found her lips. "I love you," he groaned
against them. "Oh, Christy, how I love you."

Too spent to speak, Christy cuddled against him while
he stroked her to calmness. How can I leave him? she
asked herself again and again. She touched his face, curl-
ing her fingers in his beard. When he gets back to civilization he'll shave off his beard, she thought. And when

the occasion calls for it he'll wear a suit. But he'll still be a desert man. He'll still think like an Arab, because he is an Arab. I'm not sure I can live with that.

Christy turned her head into his shoulder, and long after he slept she lay awake—wondering, wondering.

Two days later Matt and Christy and Hassan left the oasis and headed for Bir Lahlou.

"I have to go," Matt told them. "This whole thing, the trouble I suspected back in Montana, Uncle Albert, my imprisonment, Driss's treachery and his murder—they're all tied in together. I can't go home until I've found the answer to all my questions."

"We'll accompany you part of the way," Ameen said. "Then we head for Hawza to meet up with the rest of my tribe."

They broke camp the next morning, and on the third day out from the oasis, they came to another small fertile place, where they replenished their supply of water and rested for the night.

When it came time to leave, Matt said to Ameen, "I want to pay you for all you've done. You saved my life and my sister's life, and there's not enough money in the world to compensate for that. Everything was taken from me when I was captured, but as soon as I return home I'll send you whatever amount you ask."

"I want no money," Ameen said. "Hassan Ben Kadiri is my friend and my brother. I admire him and I admire his woman. She has great courage. I would be proud if she were a part of my tribe."

"Nevertheless," Matt said, "is there a place where you receive your mail?"

"Two or three times a year I am in Tafarout. A message can always be left for me there at the saddle shop of

Abdel Nasir. If I can be of service, that is where you can contact me."

Matt nodded. "You've been a good friend to me, Ameen al-Shaibi. I'll never forget you or the kindness of your people."

Then it was time for Christy to say goodbye, and that was more difficult than she would have imagined. Zohra and Zahira had become her friends, and she would miss them. It didn't seem to matter now that they were of a different world; they were women, sisters, and she had come to love them.

"Goodbye," Christy said, and took their hands. "Thank you for all your kindness. I'm going to miss you."

Zohra began to weep. She hugged Christy, kissed her on both cheeks, then turned away, too upset to speak. But Zahira didn't weep as she handed Christy a jar she had wrapped in an old piece of cloth.

"This is the dye for your skin," she said. "When you begin to pale, you can rub it on and look like a real woman again." She cackled and poked Christy in the ribs with a bony elbow.

Christy thanked Zahira with a straight face. She put the jar in her saddlebag, and when Hassan said, "It is time to leave," she nodded. Then for a moment she hesitated. She went to Ameen and bowed as she had seen the other women bow. "Thank you for all you have done for us, Ameen al-Shaibi," she said.

The nomad chieftain put a finger under her chin and raised her face. "You are a brave woman, Mrs. Christy. If you did not belong to my friend Hassan, I would keep you for my wife."

Christy smiled uncertainly. "You already have a wife," she pointed out.

"Ah, but in Morocco a man can have four wives." He laughed. "It is not often that a man meets a woman with the heart of a lioness. Now go before I forget that Hassan Ben Kadiri is my friend."

"Goodbye," she said again, hiding a secret smile as she turned away.

Hassan helped her onto Clyde, and with a last look and a wave to friends they had come to care about, she, Hassan and Matt turned toward Bir Lahlou.

Chapter 19

For over a week Christy had thought how wonderful it would be when they reached Bir Lahlou and a hotel with a bed and hot water. But there was no hotel in Bir Lahlou. There was nothing except for a few small shops, an outdoor marketplace and a scattering of houses.

"There are usually a few guest houses in a place like this, Christy," Hassan said. "Don't worry. We will find a place to stay." He looked at Matt. "Let's get Christy settled before we visit the mining office."

Hassan went into one of the shops, and when he came out he motioned for Matt and Christy to follow him. They tethered the camels in the square, then went to find the house the shopkeeper had told Hassan about. A woman, covered everywhere but the narrow slit for her eyes, greeted them. Yes, she said, she had two excellent rooms that she could give them. She looked questioningly at Christy.

"My wife and I will share one room," Hassan said. "Her brother will take the other."

Christy felt the hot color rush to her face. She glanced at Matt, saw his suddenly stiff and frozen expression and looked quickly away.

She hadn't slept in the same tent with Hassan since they had parted with Ameen and his people. It had been different when there was a large group of many tents and Ameen and his people had believed that Hassan was her husband. Even if she and Hassan hadn't wanted to, they would of necessity have had to share a tent. But when they left the group and there were only the three of them traveling together, it seemed awkward to Christy.

"Matt's my brother," she had told Hassan. "The three of us sleep close together at night. I'd . . . I'd feel uncomfortable if you and I . . ."

"I understand," he said with a frown.

But now they were in a guest house, and without asking her Hassan had said they would share a room.

"You will be all right here," Hassan said. "Matt and I will be back as soon as we can." He turned to the woman. "Can we take our meals?"

"Of course." She bowed and to Christy said, "Come, I will show you to your room."

"I'd like to go with you." Christy looked at her brother. "This concerns me, too."

Matt shook his head. "No, you stay here and rest. All we're going to do now is talk to the men in the mining office. I'll check with you as soon as we get back."

"All right," Christy said with a sigh. She looked up at Hassan. "Until later, then."

He took her hand. "Until later," he said.

Hassan was relieved that she hadn't put up more of an argument about going with them, because he did not want her along when he and Matt went to the mining company. Matt had told him about the undercover transactions his uncle was involved in. If Bir Lahlou was the place where the magnesium was smuggled from, then it might be dangerous, and Hassan did not want Christy involved.

"I can't believe Uncle Albert is involved in all this," Matt said when they left the boarding house. "We haven't always agreed on everything, but it's hard to imagine him dealing with an enemy country."

"When did you first suspect that he might be?"

"When I checked the books and realized that almost a million dollars couldn't be accounted for. I thought the accountant might have been skimming it off. It never occurred to me it was Uncle Albert until I found the file I told you about." Matt brushed the red hair back from his forehead. "He's my father's brother; it's hard to believe that he's a thief and a traitor. And in my book, anybody who deals with an enemy country *is* a traitor." He looked at Hassan. "This concerns your country, too, doesn't it?"

Just for a moment Hassan hesitated. Then he decided to tell Matt the truth. "I had a call from one of the top officials in Rabat before Christy and I left Tafarout." He grinned at Matt. "And before you give me hell for taking your sister into the Sahara, let me tell you that I had no choice. If I hadn't taken her, she would have rented a camel and followed me."

Matt laughed. "You're probably right. Once Christy makes up her mind to do something, she always does it. Dad sent her east to a boarding school when she was only seven. It was rough on her, but she learned early on to take care of herself. So I don't blame you for taking her with you. I know my sister, so I know you didn't have any choice."

Matt looked uncomfortable. "We haven't talked about money. I imagine Christy paid you something before you started this expedition. Whatever it was, I'm sure it didn't compensate for the months you've spent in the desert. As soon as we get back to civilization I'll—"

"I don't want your money," Hassan said in a cold voice. "Nor do I want Christy's money. I agreed to take her to Bir Lahlou because I knew if I didn't she would have found another character like Driss. I couldn't risk that." Hassan looked at Matt. "But there was another reason," he went on. "A couple of days before Christy and I were to leave Tafarout I had a phone call from an official of my government. He was as eager to find out whether or not magnesium was being shipped from here into the enemy country as you are, and he urged me to make the trip."

"Do you think now that we've finally reached Bir Lahlou it could be dangerous?" Matt asked.

"I don't know, but if it is, I don't want Christy involved."

"Neither do I," Matt said sharply. "But I'm her brother. I'll take care of her."

Hassan's eyes narrowed. "For as long as we are in the desert, Chambers, I am in charge, and both you and Christy will do what I say. I am just as anxious as you are to find out if your magnesium is being smuggled out of here, but we are going to do it my way, and Christy is going to stay out of it. It will be a different story when we get back to Marrakesh, but until we do, I am running things."

Matt faced Hassan. "And Christy?" he asked. "What happens to Christy when this is over?"

This was not something Hassan wanted to discuss now, but he knew that sooner or later he would have to talk bout it. "I love your sister," he said in an even voice. "When we get back to Marrakesh, I am going to do everything I can to convince her to marry me."

"I see." Matt took a deep breath, then he held out his hand to Hassan. "I don't know whether or not she'll agree to marry you, but if she does I won't interfere."

Hassan took the other man's hand. "Good," he said. "Now, let's get started."

The office of the Boukras Tfarity Mining Company was at the far end of town. Situated in a grove of palms, it was a long dun-colored, one-story building. When Matt and Hassan entered they were greeted by a robed man with glasses who said, "How may I help you?"

"My name is Matthew Chambers," Matt said. "I—"

"Chambers?" The man stiffened. "You are with Chambers Mining?"

"That's right."

"Ah." He looked at Hassan.

"My name is Hassan Ben Kadiri. I am accompanying Mr. Chambers."

"I see. Come with me, please." The man opened a door on his right. "If you will wait here, gentlemen, I will find someone to attend you." He ushered them into the room, indicated two chairs, and when they were seated he went out and closed the door. The lock snapped shut.

"What the hell?" Matt got to his feet. He yanked on the door, and when it didn't open he turned to Hassan and said, "We're locked in."

Hassan raised one black eyebrow. "It seems we were expected," he said.

"What are we going to do?" Matt threw his weight against the door. "Come on, help me," he said to Hassan.

But Hassan shook his head. "If we get out before we see whoever it is that wants us locked up, we will never find out what is going on, will we? Sit down, Matt. Take it easy."

"Take it easy!" Matt snorted in exasperation. "Damn it anyway," he muttered.

Five minutes later the door was unlocked and thrown open. Three men in uniform came in. One of them looked at Hassan. "You are Hassan Ben Kadiri?" he asked.

When Hassan nodded, the officer said, "I am Captain Mohammed Faruki." He bowed, then, and indicating Matt, asked, "Is this man Matthew Chambers?"

"That is right. He—"

"Arrest him," Faruki snapped at his men. "Put him in the cell next to the other infidel."

"Wait a minute," Matt protested. "You can't do this. I haven't done anything. I—"

"Not done anything!" Faruki said. "You call smuggling magnesium out of this country not anything? We've been waiting for you, Chambers. We learned what you were doing and that you were on your way here. It took you long enough, but we have been patient. You will stand trial for the crimes you and your company have committed against Morocco." Faruki jerked his head toward his men. "Take him away," he said.

"Just one moment." Hassan stepped forward. "I am here by the authority of my government."

"I know that, Mr. Kadiri. Almost two months ago we received a communication from Rabat that you were coming to Bir Lahlou to investigate a smuggling operation. The matter has been settled. We seized all of the culprits except Matthew Chambers. Now we have both him and his uncle."

"My uncle?" Matt said. "My uncle is here?"

"Resting most uncomfortably in our jail, Mr. Chambers."

"I want to see him," Matt said.

"Of course you will see him. You will be in the cell right next to him."

"Captain Faruki," Hassan said, "Mr. Chambers came to Bir Lahlou to get to the bottom of this smuggling operation. He suspected his uncle, and he wanted to find out for himself what was going on. He has been in jail in Al Mahbas. He was put there to keep him from coming to Bir Lahlou."

"In Al Mahbas?" Faruki looked doubtful. "Who put you in jail?" he asked Matt.

"Whoever didn't want me to come to here," Matt said. "A man by the name of Driss was involved. The jailers told me they were being paid to keep me there."

Faruki looked from Matt to Hassan. "The official that I communicated with in Rabat told me you were to be trusted, Hassan Ben Kadiri. If I have your word that this man was not involved in the smuggling and if you will assure me that he will not leave town until I question him further, then I will let him go."

"You have my word. Mr. Chambers is even more anxious to clear up this matter than you are. He feels a great responsibility to his company and to Morocco."

"Very well, Mr. Kadiri." Faruki looked at Matt. "Would you like to see your uncle, Mr. Chambers?"

"Yes, please. How long has he been incarcerated?"

"For a month." Faruki hesitated. "He is not well. I believe that he should have medical care, but we have no doctor in Bir Lahlou, only a traveling intern who visits these desert outposts every one or two months. Well, then, follow me. I will take you to him."

Hassan had no idea what Albert Chambers had looked like before his imprisonment, but he was unprepared for the disheveled, emaciated man lying on the straw mat in the cell.

Matt stiffened. "There's been a mistake," he said. "That's not my uncle." He took a step forward, trying to see through the gloom of the cell. Suddenly he gasped. "Uncle Albert?" he asked in English.

The man raised himself on one elbow. "Who is it?" he asked in a weak voice.

"Oh, my God." Matt gripped the cell bars. Trying to control his voice, he said, "It's Matt, Uncle Albert. I've come to help you."

Hassan left them alone. Whatever uncle and nephew had to say was not something that an outsider should hear. He went back to the guest house, and when the woman he'd spoken to earlier showed him to the room he and Christy would share, he knocked and said, "It is Hassan. May I come in?"

"Of course." Her voice was muffled, and he saw when he opened the door that she had been asleep. She sat up and said, "I couldn't resist the thought of a real bed. I only meant to rest for a few minutes, but I went to sleep the minute my head hit the pillow." She patted the place beside her. "Is everything all right? Where's Matt?"

Hassan hesitated. She had to know that her uncle was in jail, but he didn't relish telling her. "We went to the mining company," he said as he sat down and took her hand. "We talked to a Captain Faruki, and he told us that the smuggling operation has been broken."

"Thank goodness. I bet Matt was relieved. Where is he now?"

"He went over to the jail with Faruki."

"Oh?" She looked puzzled. "Did he want to question the men involved with smuggling the magnesium?"

Hassan nodded. "Christy..." He hesitated. "Christy, your uncle is here."

"Uncle Albert? He's in Bir Lahlou? Where is he?"

"He is in jail, Christy. He was arrested along with the other men."

"Uncle Albert?" She stared at him, her eyes wide with shock. "Uncle Albert's in jail?" She pushed Hassan aside and swung her legs out. "I've got to go see him."

"Matt is with him now, Christy. Why don't you wait until he comes back?" Hassan put his hands on her shoulders. "I don't think you could see him even if you wanted to. Faruki would never let a woman into the jail."

"But he's my uncle," she insisted. "He..." She looked at Hassan. "Why is he there? What was he charged with?"

"They think he was a part of the group smuggling magnesium."

"Uncle Albert? That's crazy."

"I will see Faruki after Matt has a chance to talk to your uncle. Maybe we can straighten it out." Hassan brushed the tangled hair back from her face. "I will try to get him released to my custody."

Christy bit her lip. There was nothing she could do now but wait for Matt to return.

It was after dark before he did. Hassan and Christy were drinking a glass of mint tea on the patio when Matt arrived looking pale and tired.

"Hassan told me that Uncle Albert is here," Christy said. "How...how is he?"

"He's sick, Christy. Very sick." He looked at Hassan. "We've got to get him out of there," he said.

Hassan nodded. "I will speak to Faruki in the morning." He stood up. "The two of you have things to discuss," he said. "I will leave you alone."

"No." Matt held up a restraining hand. "You're a part of this, Hassan. You might as well hear it." He looked at Christy. "About a year ago I began to suspect that someone was skimming money off the company profits," he told her. "I started checking, and one night I stayed late at the office. By accident I discovered a file in Uncle Albert's office that I knew nothing about." Matt took a deep breath. "Chambers Mining had become involved in an undercover smuggling ring that was sending magnesium to enemy nations."

"But Uncle Albert wouldn't do that," Christy protested.

"He would and he did." Matt began to pace up and down the small patio. "He'd taken money out of the company, Christy, money that he intended to put back. But the investments he thought were going to make him a fortune failed and he took a tremendous loss. He must have been in a desperate state of mind when the outlaw mining interests approached him."

"They probably knew he was in financial trouble," Hassan said.

Matt nodded. "I hadn't thought of that, but it's certainly possible. Anyway, he agreed to do business with them, but almost as soon as he did he had second thoughts. When he did they blackmailed him." He looked at Christy. "He panicked when I told him I was coming to Morocco."

Her face paled. "Did he... Was he responsible for having you thrown in prison?"

"No, Christy. The men he was working for knew they could only keep him in line for so long. He'd told them that he wasn't going to be a part of it anymore. That's just about the time I came to Morocco, so they grabbed me as a hostage and told Uncle Albert they'd kill me unless he continued supplying the magnesium." Matt ran his hand over his face as he sank down in a chair next to Hassan. "Then you decided to come to Morocco, Christy. When he found out you'd disappeared in the desert, he came to Morocco to try to find you."

Matt took both her hands in his. "Whatever he may have done, Christy, Uncle Albert didn't want anything to happen to us. He did his best to try to get me out of the jail in Al Mahbas and to find you. He got himself into a trap, and he didn't know how to get out of it. I hate what he's done, but I don't hate him. I hope you don't, either."

Christy thought of all the months that Matt had spent in Al Mahbas, locked in a cell. "I don't hate him," she said at last. "But I don't think I can ever forgive him for what he did to you."

"I can't tell you what to do, Christy. I can only tell you that Uncle Albert's very ill. If we don't get him out of that cell he's going to die."

"Die?" She swallowed. "Is he . . . is he that bad?"

"He's very bad," Matt said.

The three of them had a silent dinner that night in the dining room of the guest house. Though it had been weeks since Christy had had a really decent meal, she barely touched the couscous or the fresh-baked bread. Later she lay quietly in Hassan's arms, staring up at the slowly rotating ceiling fan. It seemed incredible that the uncle she'd found so cold and forbidding as a child had come to Morroco to find her.

He'd rarely had anything to say to Christy when she was a child, and he'd avoided her as much as he could. But once, when she was five and Aunt Margaret had spanked her for breaking a pot of African violets, Uncle Albert had said, "She's only a child, Margaret. Let her be." He'd dried Christy's tears and murmured, "There, there, that's enough of that," and he'd taken her out for a double chocolate soda.

He hadn't objected when Aunt Margaret and her father had decided that Christy should be sent to a boarding school, but once in a while he'd sent her a small check. "To buy a double chocolate soda," he would say in the note that came with the check.

What Uncle Albert had done could not be excused. Matt had suffered because of his dishonesty. If she and Hassan hadn't found him, Matt would still be in that awful cell in Al Mahbas.

Hassan pulled her closer. "Are you all right?" he asked.

Christy nodded against his shoulder. "Do you think you'll be able to get Uncle Albert released?"

"I am going to try, Christy. I am pretty sure Faruki will turn him over to me." But what Hassan didn't say was that Faruki was afraid that Albert Chambers was going to die and he didn't want him to die in the Bir Lahlou jail.

Instead Hassan said, "I shall have to take him back to Marrakesh. He will have to stand trial for what he's done." His arms tightened around her. "I am sorry. I know this is difficult for you."

Christy reached for his hand. She thought of her uncle alone in his cell and knew that she wouldn't turn her back on him. Tomorrow Hassan would bring him here, and she would take care of him.

Finally, safe in the comfort of Hassan's arms, she slept.

Chapter 20

The following afternoon Albert Chambers was released from his cell in the Bir Lahlou jail. Too weak to stand, he was brought to the guest house on a stretcher and taken to a room that had been provided for him.

Christy, who had been anxiously waiting for him since morning, could barely hide her dismay when Matt and Hassan carried the stretcher into the house.

"Uncle Albert..." Her throat constricted and she tried again. "You're going to be all right now," she said as she took his hand. "We're going to take care of you."

"Christy..." She had to lean close to hear him. "I thought you were lost. I...I came after you." He tried to sit up. "I didn't want anything to happen to you."

"I know. Please don't worry. We're all together now."

"We had better get him into bed," Hassan said. "You can see him after he is rested."

Christy nodded as she followed the stretcher down the corridor to the room that had been provided for her uncle. A few minutes later Hassan came to their room.

"Matt is bathing him," he said. "I thought it best to leave the two of them alone."

"He looks so ill. He's got to have a doctor."

"Bir Lahlou doesn't have a doctor, Christy. There is only an intern that visits every month or two. Captain Faruki says that he could arrive at any time."

"At any time!" Christy jumped to her feet and began to pace the room. "My God, Hassan, Uncle Albert could die if he doesn't get medical attention. Isn't there something we can do?"

Hassan took her hands. "We can make him comfortable. Perhaps with proper food and rest he will feel better in a few days."

But Hassan didn't think that Albert Chambers would ever feel better. He had seen this look of death before, and he knew that Chambers was a dying man.

During the next few days both Christy and Matt spent almost all of their time with their uncle. Again and again the older man pleaded with his nephew for forgiveness.

"The money I took went into a gold mine in southern Peru," Albert said. "I expected to make a fortune, Matthew, and who knows, perhaps I would have if the men I dealt with had been honest. But they weren't. I doubt that any of the money I gave them ever went into trying to get the gold out."

"We'll go to Peru after we get back to the States," Matt said. "If there's gold in that mine we'll find it."

Albert managed a smile. "There's gold there, my boy. I can feel it in my bones."

He talked then of how he'd been approached by Middle Eastern powers, of their friendliness at first when he

had begun to do business with them, then the veiled threat
of blackmail when he wanted out. Finally came the ulti-
matum: do what we ask, or we tell your nephew and the
authorities that you're a thief.

"I was so ashamed, Matthew. You and Christy were my
brother's children, and I had stolen from you. I panicked
when you told me you were going to Morocco, because I
was afraid you'd find out what I'd been doing. When I
heard that you were missing I almost killed myself, because I knew that I was responsible. Then word came that
you were being held and that unless I continued to ship the
magnesium you'd be killed."

His hand, so thin and white it looked transparent,
reached for Matt's. "Then Christy came to Morocco and
I knew finally that I had to do something. I tried to find
her, and when I couldn't I came here to Bir Lahlou and
told Captain Faruki everything. The smuggling ring was
broken, the men I'd dealt with were punished, and I . . . I
was imprisoned."

He closed his eyes. "It's over now," he whispered.
"You and Christy are safe. That's all that matters."

That night Albert Chambers died in his sleep.

Three days later Christy, Hassan and Matt set out on
the journey to Marrakesh. Captain Faruki provided them
with two pack camels and men to drive them.

At dawn of the day they were to leave Bir Lahlou,
Christy went to the small cemetery on the edge of town.
As she knelt to put a bouquet of desert flowers on her
uncle's grave she thought of how, as a child, she'd been
afraid of him. Except for the one time he'd defended her
against Aunt Margaret, he'd rarely spoken to her. But
he'd given her a home, and in his own way he'd done the
best that he could for her and for Matt.

She laid the flowers on his grave and, touching the warm earth with her fingers, said, "Goodbye, Uncle Albert. God bless you."

Hassan and her brother were waiting for her when she returned. Hassan had been up before Christy, so he hadn't been in the room when she dressed in her jeans and a long-sleeved shirt. For a moment he stared at her. Then his dark brows had come together in a gesture she knew so well.

"You are wearing pants," he said in an accusing voice.

"They're more comfortable to ride in."

"I will never be able to make a proper Moroccan woman out of you, will I?"

"Probably not." She grinned. "But once in a while I enjoy having you try."

Hassan glared at her. "When we near a town," he said between clenched teeth, "you will wear a robe and a veil." Then, turning to her brother, he said, "One of these days I am going to take this sister of yours over my knee and paddle the contrariness out of her."

"You'd better have your battle armor on when you do," Matt said. "I tried it once when I was twelve. It took a week for my bruises to heal." He put his arm around Christy. "I think you look terrific, kiddo. But Hassan's right. As soon as we get near any kind of a settlement, you'd better wear the robe."

"Agreed," Christy said. "Now, let's get going. It's three hundred miles back to Tafarout."

The days passed slowly. It was summer now, and the heat on the desert was so intense it hurt to breathe. The travelers covered their heads and faces with cloth, trying to protect themselves from the sun. They started each day's journey at three in the morning and rode until they could no longer bear the heat. Then they rested, at an oasis if they were lucky, under a canvas cover if they weren't.

At night they didn't bother putting up the tents; they simply rolled up in blankets and slept close to the fire.

Each night after Christy fell into an exhausted sleep, Hassan and Matt talked. Matt had a lot of friends, men he'd met in college and later in his work, but he'd never felt closer to a man than he did to Hassan. He'd seen Hassan's strength; he admired his courage and his honesty. At first when Matt learned about Christy's relationship to the Moroccan he'd been shocked and angry. But the more he came to know and like Hassan, the more he began to see a certain rightness to their being together.

There was no doubt in Matt's mind that Hassan loved his sister or that Christy loved him. But Matt didn't think it would work, because he was sure Christy couldn't live the kind of a life Hassan would expect her to live if she married him. She'd been independent since she was seven years old. How could she live with a man who, as much through love as custom, supervised her every waking moment? He wanted it to work out for them, but he didn't think it could.

Twenty-two days after they left Bir Lahlou they arrived in Tafarout, and Christy said goodbye to Clyde. "I'm going to miss you, beasty," she told the camel. "You're cranky and ill-tempered, but you got me through the desert and I'll never forget you." She gave him a light swat across his ears and said, "That's to remember me by."

They checked into a hotel for one night, and the next morning Hassan ordered a car to drive them to Agadir.

"What the three of us need is a few days' recuperation by the sea," Hassan told Christy and Matt. "All I could think about this last week was being in an ocean-front room right on the Atlantic. If it is all right with the two of you—if you are not in a hurry to get back to Marrakesh—I would like to go to Agadir."

Christy looked at Matt and with a smile said, "It sounds wonderful to me."

"To me, too," Matt agreed. "Do you suppose there's such a thing as a gin and tonic in Agadir?"

Hassan laughed. "You can bank on it," he said.

It took them three hours to make the sixty-mile trip. As they neared the coast Christy closed her eyes and said, "I can smell the sea." When they came up over a rise of mountains, she gasped. Below lay endless miles of sandy beach and clear blue water.

"It's like another world," Matt said. "I'm glad you suggested it, Hassan."

"Agadir is as nice as any resort along the Costa del Sol in Spain or even your Palm Beach," Hassan said. "I have booked us into a hotel right on the beach."

"Room service, ice water and air-conditioning." Christy sighed. "It's good to be back in civilization, gentlemen."

As soon as they checked in, Christy showered and washed her hair. Then she put on a short cotton robe that had been in the baggage she'd left in Tafarout and went to stand out on her balcony overlooking the beach. For months she'd seen nothing but sand; now here was the sea, endless miles of it. She closed her eyes and felt the ocean breeze riffle through her hair. Then for a moment her eyes stung with tears. There'd been times these past months when she didn't think they'd make it out of the desert alive. Yet here they were, the three of them, she and Hassan and Matt.

"A dirham for your thoughts," Hassan said from his adjoining balcony.

Christy opened her eyes and looked at him. With a gasp she said, "What have you done? What...?" She hesitated, studying his face. "My God, Hassan, you've shaved off your beard."

"I feel naked," he said sheepishly as he ran a hand across his chin. "I guess I had gotten used to it."

"So had I." She reached through the wrought-iron grillwork that separated them and touched his chin. "Smooth," she said in an attempt at lightness.

Hassan captured her hand and brought it to her lips. "I've missed you," he said.

"And I've missed you, but I...I wouldn't have felt right—out on the desert with Matt along, I mean."

"I understand." But they hadn't been on the desert last night. He had been tempted to come to her room, but at the last minute he had hesitated. Whatever happened now had to be Christy's decision; he wouldn't push her.

Hassan let go of her hand, because touching her, yet not touching her the way he wanted to, was torture. "I know a great restaurant," he said. "Why don't we get Matt and go out to dinner?"

"I'd love to, but I don't think Matt has anything to wear except the clothes we found him in."

"I'll take care of that." Hassan glanced at his watch. "You get dressed, and we'll meet you downstairs in an hour."

Christy nodded, and when she went back into her room she dressed in a light blue summer dress and white high-heeled sandals. She brushed her hair back from her face, but rather than pinning it up, she let it flow loose around her shoulders. She looked into the mirror to touch eyeshadow to her eyes, then stopped and really looked at herself.

The dye that Zahira and Zohra had applied had faded. Her skin was slightly tanned, but the tan would fade as the color had. The blue dress she wore now seemed strange, because it was so different from either the robe or the safari shirt she'd worn for such a long time. The neckline, which she hadn't thought low when she had bought the dress, now seemed too revealing. The high heels made her legs look grand, but she felt unsteady on them.

"Who are you, Christy?" she whispered to her reflection. "Will you ever be you again, or have you been indelibly marked by the desert and by the man you shared it with?"

Hassan and Matt were waiting for her when she went downstairs. Matt was dressed in a pair of light gray trousers and a sport shirt. "This was the best we could do on short notice," he told Christy. "I've ordered some other things, and they'll be ready in a couple of days. After tonight all I'm going to need is a pair of swimming trunks." He put his arm through hers. "Ready for dinner?"

"I've been ready for dinner for a long, long time," she said with a laugh.

Las Arcades, on the Avenue Allal Ben Abdallah, served French as well as Moroccan cooking. Over three tall, cool gin and tonics they looked at the menu and decided on fish for the first course, steak, a native ragout and stuffed savory pastries.

"Either this is the best food I've ever eaten or I've been hungry for so long I don't know the difference," Matt said when he finally pushed his plate away. He looked across the table at Hassan. "Thanks for bringing us to Agadir. It was a great idea." His face grew serious. "I know I've thanked you before, Hassan. Money could never compensate for what you've done for Christy and me. I'd still be in that hell hole in Al Mahbas if it hadn't been for you."

"And that indomitable persistence of Christy's," Hassan said. "Don't forget that."

"I never will." Matt looked at Christy. "I've thought of you as my little sister almost all my life," he said. "Now I have to start thinking of you as a woman." He took a deep breath, summoning up the courage for what he wanted to say.

"I know that you and Hassan are in love, Christy, and I know you've stayed apart these past few weeks because of me. I don't want you to do that now, not if you want to be together."

"Matt..." Christy felt the hot color rush to her cheeks. "I...I don't know what to say."

Hassan took Matt's hand. "You are quite a man, Matt Chambers," he said. "Thank you for what you have said." He didn't look at Christy.

They walked back to the hotel, then down to the beach. In a little while Matt yawned and said, "I'm afraid I've had it. I've got to get to bed." He kissed Christy's cheek and, with a nod to Hassan, turned and went back to the hotel.

For the first time since she'd known Hassan, Christy felt awkward with him. She looked out at the sea, then quickly slipped out of her sandals and ran down to the shore. When a wave washed over her ankles she turned and called, "The water's wonderful. I wish we could go for a swim."

"Tomorrow, Christy. We will have plenty of time for a swim tomorrow." Hassan held out his hand to her. "Come back," he said.

She looked at him, caught for a moment in a shaft of moonlight reflected on the water. He stood waiting, a tall figure dressed in a white linen suit, his hand extended to her. She could feel the beat of pulse in her throat, a curl of flame deep in her body. A wave washed over her bare feet, but she stood, unheeding, then with a sigh she went back to Hassan.

"Here I am," she said as he took her in his arms.

It had been such a long time. Christy's hands trembled as she slipped Hassan's jacket off his shoulders and began to unbutton his shirt. "It's so strange to see you in a suit," she said as her fingers caressed his bare chest. "I like you this way." She pulled the shirt loose from his trousers. "But I like you in a djellaba, too." Her hands tightened around his back. "Oh, Hassan," she whispered. "Hassan."

He carried her to the bed and quickly stripped her clothes away, then his. "It has been too long," he said hoarsely. "I thought I would die with wanting you." He pulled her on top of him and, clasping her to him, kissed her with all the urgency and the passion he'd held in check for these past weeks they'd traveled with Matt.

Then there was no time for talking, only for touching and fevered kisses. When that was not enough, Hassan rolled Christy beneath him and joined her body to his. He gasped with pleasure, then sought her mouth as he moved against her. His hands crept under her back to her buttocks to urge her closer, and when she lifted her body to his he whispered her name against her lips and told her in Arabic how much he loved her.

Her hands caressed his back. She turned her head into his shoulder, uttering small cries of a passion that she couldn't control. Suddenly it was too much. "Hassan," she cried in a frantic voice. His arms tightened around her.

"Yes," he said. "Yes, now, love. Now."

Christy lay in his arms, watching the gentle movement of the curtains that covered the open balcony door. She could smell the sea and hear the roll of waves against the shore. Reaching up, she touched Hassan's cheek. "I miss your beard," she told him.

He kissed her fingertips. "Then I will grow it again."

"No, I like you this way, too." She snuggled against him. "I like you any way at all, Hassan Ben Kadiri, any way at all."

Chapter 21

The week they spent in Agadir restored and refreshed Christy, Hassan and Matt. They swam in the sea, lolled in the shade, drank glass after glass of orange juice and luxuriated in just being lazy.

"I shouldn't be doing this," Matt said one evening after a dinner of tasty *tajine*, lamb cooked with olives and fresh hearts of artichoke. He leaned back in his chair looking healthy and content. "I've got to get back home and begin straightening things out."

"Uncle Albert turned a lot of things over to Dan Roycroft after you left," Christy said.

"Dan's a good man. I'll call him as soon as we get back to Marrakesh. There are some things I'll have to straighten out with the government in Rabat before I can leave." Matt looked at Hassan. "I may need your help."

"No problem. We will go to Rabat together. We can decide when we're in Marrakesh." Hassan glanced at Christy. "I would like you both to stay with me," he said.

When Christy opened her mouth to object, he said, "Please, I insist."

This past week here in Agadir with Christy had been one of the happiest in Hassan's life. They had shared wonderful times in the desert, even though there were times when they hadn't known what the next day might bring. Now that they were safe, they could take time with each other and know that no new danger awaited when they awoke.

Christy was Hassan's constant joy. She came to him without reserve, offering herself in gladness and anticipation, as hungry for him as he was for her. But at times there was a feeling of desperation in her response that worried him.

One night Hassan awoke to find her crying, and when he asked, "What is it, love?" she turned her face into his shoulder and said, "It's nothing, darling. Just a bad dream."

Hassan drew her closer and turned her face to his to kiss away her tears. Christy sought his mouth, kissing him with an abandon that demanded an instant response, and before he could move she came up over him. Hassan's eyes widened with surprise as she lowered herself on him. "Christy?" he whispered. "Oh, Christy."

She began slowly at first, then quickened her pace, murmuring his name over and over again as her fingers dug into his shoulders. She was abandoned, out of control, her head thrown back as she murmured in a frenzy of ecstasy.

Hassan gripped her waist, as wild as she was as they neared the brink of passion and spun together through the world into whirling kaleidoscopic space.

"Christy," he said when he could breathe again. "Christy..."

"No." She lay, collapsed over his body. "No, don't talk. Don't say anything."

Hassan's heart, which had been beating so hard, stilled. There was a note of almost unbearable sadness in Christy's voice. He thought of her tears, of the explosion of her passion and now of the sadness, and suddenly he felt a chill of fear. He knew with certainty that Christy had begun to say goodbye to him.

At the end of the week the three of them flew from Agadir to Marrakesh. Again, as she had on her first trip to that city, Christy looked out of the window as the plane began its descent. The red city of Marrakesh, she thought, this where it began, this is where it will end.

She had told Hassan that when their trip was over she would leave him. She didn't think that he had believed her then, but she knew that he believed her now. Last night they had walked down to the beach together. He'd drawn her into his arms, but before he could kiss her Christy said, "I'll be going home soon, Hassan."

He tensed. "Your home is with me," he said.

Christy drew in a deep breath. "My heart is with you, but my home is in Montana." Before he could speak she put her finger against his lips. "We knew it had to end, Hassan. Let's not make it any more difficult than it already is."

"I will not let you go," he said in a desperate voice.

"Darling..." Christy looked up at him through her tears. "I love you—I'll never love anyone but you—but I can't marry you." She tried to smile. "Whatever would you do with a wife who runs around in blue jeans and a T-shirt instead of a veil and a robe? Who wears mascara and lipstick instead of henna? And who would never be properly silent when you entertained but would always, no matter how she tried to restrain herself, have to express her opinion on everything from the way vegetables should be cooked to the way the world should be run?" She looked up into his dark desert eyes. "I can't be the wife you want me to be, Hassan. I'm sorry. I wish I could be, but I can't."

"It would not have to be the way you think," he said quietly. "You would not have to wear a robe and a veil, not all of the time. And you could express whatever opinion you chose to express when we were alone—"

"But not when we were with your friends." Christy shook her head. "It's impossible, Hassan. We could never make it work between us."

"Rashid and Katherine have made it work," he said. "You saw for yourself how happy they are."

"I met them only once," Christy protested. "They seemed happy, but—"

"They are happy," Hassan said. "They love each other, and they have a good marriage."

"Then perhaps Katherine is a better woman than I am." Christy leaned her head against his chest. "We'd make each other miserable, Hassan," she said. "Please don't make this any harder than it already is."

Hassan stepped away from her. "Harder than it is?" His voice was cold. "You are making a mistake, Christy," he said. "But I cannot force you to become my wife; the decision has to be yours. Shall we go back to the hotel now?"

He walked her to her door. "The plane leaves at ten," he said. "Please be in the lobby by eight-thirty." Before Christy could answer he turned and went into his own room.

* * *

Matt and Christy saw little of Hassan during the first few days they were in Marrakesh, because he spent all his time in the office he had in the city. Matt telephoned Dan Roycroft and was told that everything was running smoothly.

"I'm sorry to hear about your uncle's death," Roycroft said. "But I know you'll keep things going, Mr. Chambers. How soon can we expect you back?"

"It'll be another two weeks at least," Matt told him. "I've got to go to Rabat and straighten some things out with the government there. I'll call you before I leave, but meantime, if anything comes up you can't handle, you can call me here in Marrakesh."

It was decided that the three of them would fly to Rabat on Monday morning. Matt and Hassan had scheduled appointments with government officials there, and after the business had been taken care of, Matt and Christy would fly home from Casablanca.

"You're sure that you want to leave?" Matt asked Christy a few days before they were to leave Marrakesh.

"Yes, Matt, I'm sure."

"Christy..." He hesitated. "Look, I know that marriage between you and Hassan might be difficult, but if you love each other—"

"Please, Matt," she interrupted. "I don't want to talk about it. I'm going back to the States when you go."

But Sunday morning when Christy awoke she was unable to speak, because her throat was sore and she had such a headache she couldn't lift her head off the pillow. She took two aspirins and went back to sleep, sure that she would feel better when she woke again. But she didn't. By afternoon she had an earache and a temperature of 102.

"I have to fly to Rabat tomorrow," she croaked to the doctor who came to see her.

"You're not flying anywhere for at least two weeks," the doctor said. "You've got a strep throat, and your ears are infected. You're to stay in bed for a week, then we'll talk about when you can fly."

Christy glared at him helplessly as he turned her over and gave her an injection of penicillin.

She was still mad when Matt came into her room. He sat beside her and, taking her hand, said, "I'm sorry, kiddo. I hate to leave you, but Hassan and I have got too many appointments in Rabat to cancel out now. Hassan's hired a nurse, and the doctor will be in to check on you every day."

"But I want to go with you," she said, and began to cry. "I want to go home."

"You will, Christy, just as soon as you're better." Matt patted her shoulder. "Now, stop crying. It isn't good for you."

Oh, damn, she thought. Damn, damn, damn!

She was asleep that night when Hassan came in to tell her goodbye. The bedside lamp was on, and he stood for a moment looking down at her. Her hair was spread out on the white satin pillow, and one hand was tucked under her flushed face. With a sigh he touched her shoulder and said, "Wake up, Christy. You have to take a pill."

She opened her eyes and tried to focus on his face.

"How do you feel?"

"Awful," she croaked.

"I hate to leave you, but the appointments have been made, and Matt is anxious to get back to the States." He helped her sit up so that he could give her one of the pills the doctor had left. "A nurse will be here in the morning, and Dr. Cuervo will see you in the afternoon. The nurse has instructions to call me in Rabat if you feel worse.''

"I *couldn't* feel worse," Christy grumbled.

Hassan repressed a smile. "I will be back in a week," he told her. "Behave yourself."

"What choice do I have?"

"None." He kissed her forehead and turned out the light. He waited there in the dark until he was sure she was asleep, then he took off his clothes and stretched out on the chaise so that he could be close by if Christy needed him.

Hassan was sorry that she was ill, but he wasn't sorry that she was unable to leave Marrakesh. For as long as she was here he had a chance.

Hassan and Matt phoned every day. Christy grumbled that Dr. Cuervo was a grouch and that the nurse, a Miss Sefiana Masadi, was a martinet. By the end of the week her voice was better and her head had stopped hurting. Dr. Cuervo said that she could get up and sit in the garden, and Nurse Masadi finally gave her something decent to eat. Katherine Hasir called and sent flowers, and Christy invited her to lunch at the end of the week.

"I'm flying home on Saturday," Matt said the last time he called. "I'll phone from there next week. Let me know when you're coming, Christy, and I'll pick you up in Billings. Hang on a minute. Hassan wants to speak to you."

"I have been trying to talk Matt into staying longer," Hassan said when he came on the phone. "But he insists he must get home." He hesitated. "Are you all right?"

"Yes, Hassan, thanks. I'm fine. Katherine Hasir is coming for lunch tomorrow. When . . . when will you be home?"

"Tuesday afternoon. I thought I would be able to make it back this weekend, but I've got an important appointment on Monday." He took a deep breath. "I am glad you are going to be there when I get home, Christy."

She closed her eyes, unable to answer when Hassan said, "Goodbye, my love."

Katherine arrived the next day at noon, looking elegant and beautiful in a short white linen dress. Her wheat-blond hair had been drawn back from her face, but instead of the chignon she'd worn the night Christy had met her, her hair was done in a French braid interwoven with a dark blue ribbon that matched the blue beads she wore with the dress.

"I've brought you a few books," she told Christy. "They're hard to get here in Marrakesh, so I always pick up a supply whenever Rashid and I are in Paris. I've finished with these, so don't bother returning them."

"Thanks a lot," Christy said. "Hassan has a few books in English, but they're not exactly what I'd like to read. I won't be here much longer, but I know I'll enjoy them while I'm here."

"You're going home?" Katherine asked. "I assumed you'd be staying in Marrakesh. I thought that you and Hassan . . . well, I suppose I thought there was something serious between the two of you, especially after all the months you spent together in the desert." She touched Christy's hand. "I don't mean to pry, but Hassan's a fine man, and I thought the night I saw you together that you made a wonderful-looking couple. Rashid says that I'm an incurable matchmaker, and I guess that's true. I have a happy marriage, so I want everyone else to have one, too."

Katherine smiled. "Would I be terribly out of line if I asked you how you felt about Hassan?"

"I love him," Christy said.

Katherine looked puzzled. "Hasn't he asked you to marry him?"

"Yes, he's asked me." She looked at Katherine. "But I don't think it would work. I'm an American. I'm too independent to ever live the kind of a life Hassan would expect me to live. He's an Arab. He..." She bit her lip. "Oh, dear," she said. "I'm sorry. I didn't think—about you and Rashid, I mean."

"That's all right," Katherine said with a smile. "For a while I had the same doubts you have. But Rashid and I worked our problems out. I think two people can if they really love each other."

"I love Hassan," Christy said, "but I can't be the kind of a wife you are." Then, changing the subject, she said, "I thought we'd have lunch outside in the garden if that's all right with you."

"Yes, that would be lovely." Katherine looked at her questioningly, but she didn't say anything as Christy led her to where a table had been set up under the trees. When they were seated Katherine said, "I'm sorry you were ill. How are you feeling?"

"Much better, thank you. I'd planned to fly back to Rabat last week with Hassan and my brother, then on to the States with Matt. But the strep throat knocked me out." Christy made a face. "All those months on the desert and I was as healthy as a horse. But the minute I got back to Marrakesh I got sick. I guess the shock of civilization was just too much for me." Christy motioned to one of the servants. To Katherine she said, "Would you like a gin and tonic, or do you prefer iced tea?"

"Gin and tonic, please," Katherine told her. When the servant left she said, "I didn't know what had happened to you until Hassan called Rashid from Agadir. I couldn't

believe that you'd gone through almost the same thing
that I had three years ago."

Christy looked at her curiously. "Hassan told me that
you and Rashid had been lost in the desert, Katherine.
Were you on a caravan, too?"

"No." Katherine paused. "Did Hassan tell you anything about Rashid and me?"

"Only that you were lost and missing for months."
Christy waited, and when the other woman didn't say
anything she said, "I can't help being curious. If you
weren't on a caravan, what in the world were you doing in
the desert?"

Katherine looked up as the servant placed a drink in
front of her, and when he had gone she said, "I was running away from Rashid."

"You were...?" Christy's eyes widened in disbelief.
"I'm sorry. I don't understand."

"I've never told anyone else," Katherine said. "But I'd
like you to know the way it was." She took a sip of her
drink. "I met Rashid at a Princeton reunion when I was
twenty. He had a younger brother, Jamal. When Jamal
and I became engaged, Rashid came to Princeton to have
a look at me and break it up."

"And did he? Break the two of you up, I mean,"
Christy said.

Katherine nodded. "He sent Jamal back to Morocco.
I didn't see either of them for seven years. By that time I'd
graduated from Princeton and had joined the State Department. After a couple of years with the department, I
was assigned to the embassy in Rabat. I saw Rashid there,
and later I saw Jamal and somehow—I'm not even sure
how now—Jamal and I got engaged again. And again
Rashid tried to break us up."

"Because he loved you?"

Katherine shook his head. "I don't think he loved me then, Christy. If he did, he wouldn't admit it to himself. He sent Jamal out of town, and after a few weeks he told me that Jamal was going to Marrakesh and that he, Rashid, would fly me there so that I could see Jamal." Katherine ran a slim finger up and down her frosted glass. "Instead he took me to his home in the desert, Christy. He told me that he was going to keep me there until I agreed not to marry Jamal."

"He kidnapped you!" Christy said in a horrified voice. "My God, weren't you terrified?"

"Terrified, bewildered..." Katherine shook her head. "I was a lot of things, Christy, and so I ran away. I stole a Jeep and I headed to the nearest town. But a storm came up and the Jeep stalled. I thought I was on the road and that I'd be all right if I just sat it out. But when daylight came I found myself stranded in the desert." A thin film of perspiration beaded Katherine's brow. She rubbed her fingers against the frosted glass and touched them to her forehead. "By a miracle I found an oasis that first day. The next day Rashid found me. He was so angry, Christy, and so relieved to find me that he could barely speak. He pulled me into his arms. He kissed me and...he made love to me."

Katherine bowed her head. "We were in the desert for two months and every day and night for those two months Rashid and I made love."

Christy looked at this beautiful, graceful woman, unable to believe that the man she married, the man she loved, had kidnapped her.

"When you were rescued...is that when you were married?"

Katherine shook her head. "No, we separated. But then I went back to see Rashid at his desert home, because there was something I had to tell him. I'd planned to stay only for a day or two, but when I saw him again I knew that I loved him, that I'd loved him since I was twenty."

"But he'd . . . he'd done some terrible things to you," Christy protested.

"Only because he wouldn't admit to himself that he loved me. You see, he was afraid, Christy, just as you are, to make the commitment of marriage, because we came from different backgrounds. I resisted, too, because I didn't think I could be the kind of a woman I thought Rashid wanted me to be." A gentle smile touched her lips. "We've compromised," she said. "When we're alone I dress as I please, and in what I know pleases him. When he entertains friends and I make an appearance, I wear a robe and a veil." A flush of color rose in Katherine's cheeks. "Afterward, when his friends have gone, he comes to our room and removes both the veil and the robe."

She reached for Christy's hand. "I love Rashid more than I ever thought it possible to love anyone. When we have to be separated for a day or two, it's like a part of me is missing. And if once in a while I have to pretend to be something I'm not, it's all right, because of what I receive in return, his total love and devotion. I wouldn't want any other kind of life. I love Rashid, and I love being married to him."

"You're an exceptional woman," Christy said.

"I'm not any different from you." Katherine's golden eyes were filled with compassion. "True love is so rare, Christy. Don't be afraid of it." She smiled gently. "There can be joy in surrender if it's to the right man."

Joy in surrender? Christy looked at her new friend over her drink. Then, because she didn't know what else to say, she said, "Shall we have lunch now?"

Chapter 22

On Saturday morning, accompanied by one of Hassan's servants, Christy went to the Djemaa El Fna. The giant souk was as crowded as it had been the last time Christy had been there. She'd been frightened then by the mass of people that day and by the prospect of finding the man Driss. But today, with someone to push the sellers back, she was able to enjoy all the sights and sounds of the souk.

She stopped to watch the monkey trainers and the trick cyclists, even the flame eater, who held a blazing torch over his head, then with a cry thrust it into his mouth. She applauded the jugglers and the acrobats, but skirted around the crowd gathered in front of the snake charmer.

With Hassan's servant leading the way, Christy visited the shops that sold caftans. She found it difficult to choose what she wanted, because the minute she paused in front of a shop someone rushed out to usher her in, and before she could speak a dozen or so garments were thrust on the counter for her approval. Not allowing her time to gather her wits, the shopkeeper and his helper bombarded her with, "This one, lady? Or this? Feel the fabric, lady. Is it not beautiful? The finest silk in all of the Orient went into making this garment, madam."

Christy retreated from the first two shops, too confused to make a decision. Then, steeling herself, she entered the third store. The man in charge immediately began shouting that he had the finest caftans in all of Morocco. Christy let him place a dozen or so on the counter, then she held up her hand and, in much the same tone she'd used to bring the recalcitrant Clyde under control, said, "Stop! I cannot make any kind of a decision unless you are silent."

The man stood back and gaped at her. Two of his helpers, who had also rushed forward the moment Christy entered, fell back as though stunned.

Slowly and carefully Christy looked at the caftans. She picked several of them up, holding them against her as she looked in the full-length mirror hanging on one wall. They were made of brocade, chiffon or silk. Some were simple, some ornately decorated with simulated jewels or with silver and gold braid. At last, while the shopkeeper wrung his hands in frustration over having to keep silent, Christy selected a caftan crafted of pale green-blue silk chiffon run through with silver threads. Gossamer-light and almost transparent, it was the loveliest, most feminine garment that Christy had ever seen.

"I'll take it," she told the shopkeeper, who almost wept in relief as he thanked her, bowing half a dozen times. He wouldn't permit her to leave until she drank a glass of hot mint tea.

Next she found a pair of jeweled green slippers and the other items that suited her.

Tuesday morning dawned bright and clear. Christy was awakened early by the Muslim call to prayer. She didn't get up but lay listening as the call echoed over the silent city, and with a sigh she closed her eyes and went back to sleep.

When she awakened the second time she took a leisurely bath. The bathroom adjoining her room had been outfitted with scented oils and imported soaps, and although she was more accustomed to quick showers, this morning Christy filled the tub with scented bubbles. She eased herself into the tub and lay back in the foamy water, completely relaxed and more at ease with herself than she'd been in a long time.

When she got out of the tub she washed her red-gold hair and, before she went out on the balcony to dry it in the sun, phoned down and asked if she might have breakfast in her room. This was her morning, a special morning, and she was going to be completely, voluptuously lazy.

Hassan hadn't told her what time he would arrive, but she expected it to be late afternoon or early evening. At the thought of him a shiver of anticipation ran down her spine. Hassan, she said to herself, Hassan.

Christy still remembered the very first time she had seen him, standing behind the desk in his office. She had thought that he was very tall, well built, handsome and forbidding. Then she had looked into his eyes, and for a moment she'd been unable to speak. She'd had, even then, a certain awareness, almost a sense of recognition, and a knowledge that this man was different from any man she'd ever known.

It was a little after seven that night when Christy heard the crunch of tires on the graveled driveway. Dressed in blue jeans and a T-shirt, she went out to her balcony just as Hassan got out of the chauffeur-driven car.

"Hello," she called down to him. "*Marhaban*, welcome."

He looked up and saw her. "*Shukran*, Christy. How are you?"

"I'm fine now, Hassan."

Have you had dinner?"

"No, I was waiting for you."

"I would like to shower and change, if you don't mind waiting a bit. Shall we say in an hour?"

"An hour will be fine." Christy took a deep breath; it would take her that long to get ready.

She took another bath in the scented oil. Then she got out the jar of dye that Zahira had given her and, standing naked in front of a full-length mirror, began to tint her skin. When she had finished she looked at herself and smiled.

The only makeup Christy applied was to her eyes. She outlined them carefully, then applied pale green eye shadow, and finally mascara. When that was done she put on the green-blue caftan that she had bought on Saturday. The neckline, trimmed with silver threads, was cut to a V to show just a portion of the curve of her breasts.

She brushed her hair and let it fall in shimmering waves down her back. She put perfume behind her ears and in the hollow of her throat, then stepped into the green jeweled Moroccan slippers. She was almost ready.

But first... She took a tissue-wrapped package from the dresser and opened it. For a moment she looked at the veil, then with a slow smile she put it on.

Hassan waited for her in the patio. "I thought we would have something cool to drink before we..." He stopped, staring at her, a shocked expression on his face.

"Good evening, Hassan. Isn't it a lovely night? How was your trip?" She touched his arm. "You look tired. Please sit down while I tell someone to bring our drinks. I asked the cook to prepare couscous and a pastilla. I hope that pleases you."

"Christy—" Hassan took a deep breath "—your skin... You've tinted your skin."

She nodded. "I wanted to remind us of our days on the desert, of the camp, of Ameen and Zohra and Zahira. I wouldn't want to go back, Hassan, but I won't forget any of it."

"Nor will I." Hassan looked at her. Christy had never been more beautiful or exciting than she was tonight. Her eyes behind the veil were luminous; her body, faintly outlined through the gossamer caftan, was sweetly curved. He longed to take her in his arms but he didn't.

He took the drink she offered and sat in the striped lounge chair across from her. This was Christy's game; he would let her make the first move.

She chatted in a pleasantly modulated voice; when they went in to dinner she insisted on serving him. She ate little, taking small bites under the veil. After the meal she poured his coffee and said, "Katherine Hasir came for a visit last week. We're invited for dinner on Thursday, if that's all right with you."

Hassan's throat went dry. "Thursday will be fine," he said.

"They're coming here for brunch on Sunday."

"That means..." He was afraid to ask, but he had to be sure. "Does that mean you are going to stay, Christy?"

"Yes, Hassan. If you still want me."

"If I want you!" He got to his feet and drew her into his arms. "You will marry me," he said, and it was a statement, not a question.

"Whenever you say." Christy rested her face against his, so filled with love that she could barely speak.

Hassan held her away from him and said, "Why did you wear a robe and veil tonight?"

Christy looked into his eyes. "I wanted show you that I will to dress this way for you, to please you. But sometimes, to please me, I'll wear jeans."

He smiled down into her eyes. "I will never really tame you, will I?"

"Probably not. But there will be nights, like tonight, Hassan, when I'll be anything you want me to be."

His hands closed on her shoulders. "My love," he said in a voice choked with emotion. Then he swept her off her feet and carried her across the dining room to the stairs leading up to the bedrooms.

With the utmost care Hassan removed the veil from Christy's face so that he could kiss her with all the hunger and the passion he'd held in check for so long. He threaded his fingers through her glorious hair to urge her closer, shaking with need at the feel of her body against his. He slipped the green-blue caftan over her head and laid her down on his bed.

"It doesn't matter whether your skin is light or dark or whether you are dressed in a robe or blue jeans. I love you, Christy."

Christy looked up into his dark, desert eyes. "As I love you, Hassan," she said. And opened her arms to receive him in joyful surrender.

ATTRACTIVE, SPACE SAVING BOOK RACK

Display your most prized novels on this handsome and sturdy book rack. The hand-rubbed walnut finish will blend into your library decor with quiet elegance, providing a practical organizer for your favorite hard-or soft-covered books.

Only $9.95

Approximately 16" x 8" when assembled

Assembles in seconds!

To order, rush your name, address and zip code, along with a check or money order for $10.70* ($9.95 plus 75¢ postage and handling) payable to *Silhouette Books*.

Silhouette Books
Book Rack Offer
901 Fuhrmann Blvd.
P.O. Box 1325
Buffalo, NY 14269-1325

Offer not available in Canada.

*New York residents add appropriate sales tax.

BKR-2R